I Guess

Love

~

DENI ROGERS

This book is dedicated to another Denise.
If you're out there, thanks for all the fun. This book wouldn't have been written without our brief friendship and the adventures we had.

Cover art is 'Girl looking at a star filled sky' by the very talented Nataliia Moroz

Edition 2: Previously released as "Girlfriend or Groupie"

Copyright © DENI ROGERS 2016

All rights reserved

No part of this publication may be reproduced in any other binding, stored or transmitted in any form or by any means without the prior permission in writing of the author.

All characters in this publication other than those clearly in the public domain are fictitious and any resemblance to real persons, living or dead is purely coincidental.

CONTENTS

DELILAH SPRING 95
ONE — Page 6
TWO — Page 20
THREE — Page 38

SCARECROW JUNE 95
FOUR — Page 57
FIVE — Page 77
SIX — Page 98
SEVEN — Page 124
EIGHT — Page 143

FRANCE SUMMER 95
NINE — Page 163
TEN — Page 188
ELEVEN — Page 212
TWELVE — Page 230

ENGLAND AUTUMN 95
THIRTEEN — Page 249
FOURTEEN — Page 270

VINCE EARLY 98
FIFTEEN — Page 281

FATE SUMMER 2000
SIXTEEN — Page 300
SEVENTEEN — Page 313
EIGHTEEN — Page 336

FRANCE SUMMER 2005
NINETEEN — Page 364

AUTHOR'S NOTE
ABOUT THE AUTHOR

DELILAH SPRING 95

~

ONE
~

At twenty-five Delilah Grace had never been in love. Like most little girls she had grown up reading fairy stories, where the beautiful heroine meets an enigmatic, handsome man, falls in love and lives happily ever after. She'd dreamt of being Cinderella, dancing into the night with the Prince, who then vows to find her again no matter what after her dramatic exit. And when not looking for fairies in the garden, she spent hours staring at the frogs in the pond, brooding about the princess who kissed one who miraculously turned into her true love. Unfortunately, fairy stories aren't real and as she grew up Delilah realised that the prince she'd spent the night dancing with, who says he'll call, doesn't and the frogs she kissed turned out to be, just frogs. It hadn't stopped her dreaming of her own happily ever after though, the idyllic country church, the magical gown and the love of her life waiting at the altar. So how much pixie dust had she inhaled, when despite not being in love with him, she had agreed to marry a frog?

It was nearly midnight on the first Friday in May and some months earlier she had arranged her dream wedding for the fast approaching new day.

The weather forecast for tomorrow sounded like it would exceed expectations for the time of year, adding the final perfect touch to the arrangements. Her parents, Bryn and Alice Grace had found their own happy ever after, when they had married three months after a whirlwind romance thirty years ago and were still together. Tonight though they stood shivering in the kitchen of their ramshackle home, listening to the inexplicably loud minute hand of the kitchen clock as it inched on towards their cherished daughter's wedding day. Spellbound by the lonely ethereal figure with the inscrutable face in the garden, her parents knew what turmoil lurked beneath the surface and it scared them. So just as she had always done since the very first day they'd met, a worried Alice reached anxiously for her husband's hand and in return he squeezed it, offering her what he hoped was a reassuring smile.

Illuminated in the moonlight Delilah stood motionless, her much admired sapphire blue eyes as cold and hard as the stone staring blankly up at the sky. Unseen above her head the moon raced across the ink black sky pulling a million twinkling stars behind it, but the splendour of the universe was unnoticed. Her full mouth was resolutely set and her slender arms were wrapped so tightly against her body that her knuckles were starting to blanch. A passing acquaintance might have thought it pre wedding jitters, but to her concerned parents watching unseen, it signalled something else entirely. Then with a sigh and a final glance towards the heavens she walked back indoors with a heavy heart, barely acknowledging her parents as she passed. Older and wiser they already suspected that if anyone was going to be wounded on this momentous day, it was going to be their impetuous only child.

Despite an infuriating lack of sleep, Delilah woke early the next morning and stretched her tense muscles languidly as she slipped out of bed and started the preparations for the big day. Pulling open the curtains the cloudless crystal blue sky that the forecasters had promised greeted her and forcing a smile she knew that it was going to be a beautiful day, perfect for a wedding. Everything had been planned meticulously and she carried the arrangements off with a cold military precision. She had begun with a simple breakfast followed by a bath bursting with extravagant moisturising bubbles, which left her drenched in the scent of flowers after a rainstorm.

At precisely ten o'clock she arrived at her local beautician for a manicure and pedicure, where trying to contain the uneasiness within she sipped herbal tea and talked about trivialities. Then she'd walked the short distance to her hairdresser, where the previous day she'd had the hated long straight hair she had grown with great reluctance to please Nick, dramatically cut to just above her shoulders. At this length it popped back into an inherited natural curl and after her hairdresser had coloured it back to its natural rich chestnut, Delilah was pleased at how dramatically different it made her look. Pleasing Nick stopped today, from now on life would be on her terms and this new radiant Delilah began the change.

The dress that her mother had carefully laid out on the bed was not the slinky white look at me number she had originally chosen for today in the shop, but she had decided it was much more her and very suitable. A fifties Dior inspired dress of creamy silk, embellished with little yellow daisies that she'd found in a charity shop in West London, it emphasized her narrow waist and was exquisitely made. She ran newly French manicured fingertips over the delicate embroidery and sighed with pleasure. She teamed it with soft yellow pumps and the look was complete, sheer sophistication...Nick would hate it.

With a deepening satisfaction she stood back and looked at the mouth-wateringly desirable finished article in the mirror and gave her reflection a satisfied smile before slowly gliding elegantly down the stairs to where her parents waited at the bottom. Her father, who was glowing with pride whistled softly in appreciation and her mother wiped away a tear. Then arm in arm with her smiling dad she walked up the garden path to the waiting car and began to psyche herself up for what was to come. Today would be the start of a whole new life and at the end of it Delilah Grace would be someone else.

The classic car drove up the narrow country lane and stopped outside the pretty little church nestled into the bosom of the South Downs. Garlands of scented flowers intertwined with pale satin ribbon were strung along the short path and the local bees filled the air with their happy droning as they worked their way among the fragrant blooms. Delilah stepped out of the car, swallowed her nerves, forced her full mouth into a sunny smile and carefully walked to the heavy oak door, which stood open awaiting the arrival of the bride.

Stepping inside the cool interior she walked carefully over the uneven patchwork tiles to the end of the aisle, it was adorned as she had asked with cream roses and daisies in small posies on the end of each pew and a large arrangement including lilies either side of the altar. There was a sudden hush followed by the rustling of a myriad of materials as the people packed into the tiny church turned to look at her. There were one or two sharp intakes of breath and quite a few shocked whispers. Motionless she stood and drank in the moment where all eyes were focused just on her. At the end of the aisle Nick dressed in the grey lounge suit that she had carefully chosen, fidgeted nervously as he waited for his bride. He'd slicked back his mousey hair and had shaved his rugged outdoor face clean of its usual four-day stubble and as he turned, scowled and muttered something to his best man, his expression was priceless. Delilah grew tired of the performance and gave her audience a deep mocking bow, her long slender arms outstretched like a swan about to fly. Somebody in the front rows of the pews clapped, she was pretty certain it was Nick's dad.

Well that's how she had spent the last few months imagining her revenge. Instead she had snuck in to the church nestled in the middle of a large group, unrecognised and had tried to make herself invisible as she slid quietly into the far corner of the last pew. Yes, today should have been Delilah Grace's wedding day and everything was just as she had happily arranged it earlier down to the last detail except one. Nick, the man she was supposed to have married was waiting at the altar for another woman.

It would be someone else who would walk down the aisle in a virginal dress to the wedding march, she would listen to the choir as they sang Ave Maria during the signing of the register and she would walk back out into the sunshine as Mrs Nick Jones where Delilah's carefully chosen photographer would be waiting with his camera to capture the perfect moment. Later she would stand beside Nick at the swanky hotel down the road to greet their guests and it would be her sitting at the top table enjoying Delilah's thoughtfully chosen and delicious menu. Far worse than all that was the fact that Delilah and her parents had paid for it all and they were yet to see their hard saved money returned. Music signalled the arrival of the bride and everybody rose to their feet except Delilah who pressed herself tightly against the whitewashed stone wall and fought and failed to stop the salty wetness slipping between her lashes and falling unchecked down her flushed cheeks.

Livy, Olivia Woods until recently Delilah's best friend, her closest ally and her deepest confidant since childhood made a beautiful bride. Glowing with happiness like any new bride, her long honey blonde hair twisted elegantly on top of her head and a self-satisfied smile on her lips, she swept into the aisle beside her father. She hadn't been smiling five months ago when Delilah had surprised Nick at the cottage he'd been renovating and found her best friend naked on all fours on the lounge floor with her fiancé grunting behind her. Unseen by the oblivious couple, Delilah had calmly walked to the kitchen filled a jug with iced water and taken it quietly back throwing it over them just as you would have done a dog who was unwelcomely mating a bitch. It had unquestionably cooled their ardour and Delilah had wiped any remaining smugness off Livy's face when she had landed a solid right hook, which had left her once best friend in a crumpled pile on the floor. When Nick had tried to intervene, she'd kneed him hard in the groin dropping him moaning to his knees. It had taken her what seemed like hours, but was probably no more than ten minutes to throw her few possessions that she kept there into a bag and walk out the front door for good.

Now she watched as Livy walked slowly down to meet Nick at the altar and the Reverend who'd been a friend of her family for years stepped forward to begin the service. When he got to the bit about "anyone here present..." He stared past the happy couple and his eyes seemed to be fixed firmly on Delilah. Surely he didn't think she would say anything, it had taken every last ounce of her courage to crawl into this corner. Uninterrupted by dissent the service droned on and with annoyance growing inside, Delilah tried to work out why she had agreed to marry the man in the first place.

Before he had proposed to her she'd been trying to end it, had already done so once and so she'd known then that she didn't love Nick Jones. OK, so he was terribly attractive with the whole dishevelled look, the outdoor perma-tan and the body of a god, but when she'd thought about it there wasn't a lot going on up top and most of his brains seemed to have been centred between those heavily muscled thighs. And now she thought about it the sex had been pretty lacklustre too, although Nick she recalled had been very fond of his own performance.

The consequences of their parting had been devastating, friends had become unwanted enemies taking sides against each other. Terry, who was standing beside Nick as his best man had not been his original choice. Bob his closest friend and first choice had quickly chosen to keep his loyalty to Delilah whom he worked with. She had tried to explain to him that Nick was his friend and so there wasn't a problem, but in reality he thought with Nick out of the way he could try it on with her. Pathetic man with his ulterior motives.

Molly her other old school friend had instantly taken Livy's side, but then Molly who idolised Livy had always done that. Delilah could see her sitting up the front of the church her scrawny body, the result of constant dieting lost in the awful baby pink dress she had chosen to wear. By her side sat her seemingly permanently angry husband, whose hand she clutched as though he'd somehow up and disappear and how Delilah pitied her despite her best efforts not to.

Following the whole debacle Delilah had shut herself away feeling worthless and wracked with self-pity. She'd been so lost in her own wretched, bottomless little dungeon that it had never occurred to her to cancel the wedding and her parents who'd been desperately worried about her hadn't thought about it either. So it stayed booked and perfectly arranged like a monument to her own folly. Slowly with the help of her parents and some very surprising supporters Delilah had regained her previous inner strength and shutting the past away where it belonged she had finally walked toward the beckoning light beyond her prison cell.

By the time she'd recovered her wits enough, a desperate Nick capitalising on her error, had already pleaded with her parents to allow him to keep the wedding plans for his impending nuptials with Livy. Everything had been paid for and he'd promised that he'd pay them back, except he hadn't.

So hurt and angry beyond words Delilah hatched what might have been today's disastrous plan.

The ceremony finally over, Delilah watched stony faced from her corner as the newly married couple walked out past the smiling congregation. Livy, several months pregnant was already showing and the material of her plain white strapless dress though pretty and probably hideously expensive was a bit tight across her abdomen. This had been the desperate reason for using Delilah's arrangements rather than make their own, although Delilah had been a little slow on the uptake. It hadn't surprised her that she'd wanted Delilah's wedding, because as her dearest friend she'd been in the thick of the arrangements and it certainly hadn't been the first time Livy had taken ownership of her ideas. Delilah was the organised one, the sensible one, but Livy was the one everyone saw as the perfect shining light, the woman everyone wanted to be, even now she thought sadly.

The happy couple didn't notice their silent witness as they walked past, although they both briefly glanced blankly in her direction. Ultimately breathing a sigh of relief she realised that they hadn't recognised her with her newly cut and coloured hair. Other people glanced at her as they left the church and just like the happy couple they didn't make the connection either. Nick's mother frowned, as if she was trying to work out where she knew her from and muttered something to her partner about gate crashers. His Dad, long divorced from his mother and already a bit tipsy leant over the pew, put a kindly hand on her arm and winked, no fooling him. She'd always liked his dad. Livy's parents walked past just a little too quickly, her mother slipped slightly on the smooth stones and was only held upright by her husband's firm grip on her arm. Delilah thought that he looked pained, even a little guilty and he stared straight ahead pretending not to see her, although he most certainly had.

'Are you alright Delilah?' It was the Vicar. 'I'm glad you didn't go through with that little show you'd planned; it was a bad idea.' He sat down heavily beside her 'did it help or hurt coming anyway?' His hand was on hers.

'Dad told you eh? I thought I needed some kind of closure, some final answers...But really I already had them. So it was a pointless exercise. They didn't see me anyway so nobody was hurt.'

'Glad you're finally moving on with life and revenge; well I can't condone that you know.'

'Oh I think in truth I moved on past revenge months ago, but I still needed to get my feelings for Nick straight in my mind. It would have been the biggest mistake of my life if I'd married him. I never loved him, I just sort of drifted along with the tide. I really do hope they'll be happy, but I know Livy and she'll get bored and next time it could be Nick coming home at the wrong time.' She shrugged her shoulders. 'I'm sure God will understand and forgive my original motives, we don't always see things the same way, although I think we have an understanding.' She flashed her pleasant vicar a wicked smile. 'I don't bother him and he ignores me.'

He rose stiffly rubbing his back. 'I'm sure he does nothing of the sort and forgiveness is one of his big things. Well I must get back to my wandering flock, say hello to your parents and tell your dad he owes me a fishing trip.' He offered her a gentle smile and pointed to the side door. 'You know your way out.' She watched him with concern as he shuffled out. He was looking tired, so she would have to chivvy her dad about that fishing trip. Before anyone else worked out she that was there she tiptoed silently up the aisle and out of the sacristy door.

Looking around the corner of the church she saw the happy couple having their photos taken at the front. Oh well she thought, no way around them I'll have to climb over the wall and hitching up her skirt did just that, scrambling inelegantly down the bank the other side. Checking her dress and brushing herself down she crept unobtrusively down the lane past the front of the church, glancing at the wedding party as she passed. They were all milling around the photographer as he tried to arrange them into groups, she could hear Livy whining that he was doing it all wrong and that she wanted it like this or like that. Then for just a moment Nick turned and their eyes met, he looked terrified. Delilah just smiled, looked straight ahead and skipped off down the road like a happy child to where her father was leaning nonchalantly against his old car.

'Well how did it go Lola sweetheart, pleased you came or a complete clanger?' Only her father ever called her Lola. She smiled as she remembered her mum chiding him and reminding him that if he'd wanted to call her Lola they should have christened her that.

'It had to be done Dad that was supposed to be my wedding. They needed to be reminded of that, but in the end I didn't go through with it, crept in like a cuckoo hidden within another family group.'

'Hmm, good girl. Bastard needs reminding to pay us our money back though, I know that.' He smiled fondly and ruffled her curls 'I much prefer your hair like this, you look just like your mother when I first met her.'

'What stoned and grooving to The Kinks or someone.' She did a cheeky imitation of her mother waving her hands above her head in abject wonder. 'Ooh groovy man, really cool.'

'What kind of monster have we created...Perhaps Delilah suited you better after all?' He directed to the heavens as he sighed and fell dramatically into the driver's seat.

She slid in beside him and drew in a long breath. She loved the aroma of her father's car it smelt of polished leather, the sandalwood in his cologne and the faintest trace of fragrant pipe tobacco. It was the only place he still smoked and she smiled at the memory of him sitting in the car with pale smoke curling around his ecstatic face. It always made her chuckle that when he'd finished lovingly smoking one of his rare pipes, he got the leather polish out and gave the car a good clean. They drove home in relative silence, her lost in unexpectedly troubled thoughts and him humming along to an old Stones number on the radio.

Within a few minutes of getting home she had hung her pretty dress up, made a mental note to take it to be cleaned and tucked the yellow pumps into the shoe rack in her wardrobe. She'd stripped her face of makeup and changed into an old pair of joggers and a baggy t-shirt and by the time the newly married couple were tucking into their expensive banquet Delilah was sitting at the table with her parents eating her Mum's delicious Irish stew with dumplings and home grown cabbage.

TWO
~

Quite out of the blue Livy's father arrived at the Grace's door a few days after the wedding.

'Hello Reg, what can we do for you? Come on in, would you like a cup of tea?' Delilah heard her father greet his old friend warmly in his soft lyrical welsh accent.

'I didn't think I'd be welcome Bryn.' Reg Woods always sounded a bit breathless.

'Wasn't you was it eh? No hard feelings and all that.' Delilah glanced down the stairs at her father, he had a firm hand on Reg's shoulder and was guiding him gently into the lounge. 'Put the kettle on Alice we've got a guest.' Delilah watched her dad's back as he disappeared through the door and tried to weigh up whether she should be there as well or would that embarrass the man that she had always affectionately known as Uncle Reg. Deciding that the visit was as much her business as her parents she ambled nonchalantly down stairs and went to help her mum with the tea.

'Oh good Delilah you're here, can you grab some mugs please, the nice ones.' Delilah opened the cupboard with the decent china with a quiet smile playing on her lips. Normally they used the ragtag mugs with the assortment of slogans, the tea stained ceramic and the odd chip here and there. Her mum was a surprisingly proud woman at times and whenever a guest arrived out would come the nice china, the ones that all matched and as she expected there was a tray with a sugar bowl, a small jug of milk and a teapot. Guests in this house did not just get a teabag shoved in a mug, they got the full treatment. Putting four mugs on the tray Delilah reached for a small plate, matching the mugs of course and filled it with chocolate digestives. 'Oh well done dear I'd forgotten we had those, when did we get them?'

'I got them last week, because I fancied something chocolaty, only I put them away and the craving passed.'

'At least it wasn't me having a senior moment.' Like she was that old Delilah thought appraising her mum. Her figure was fuller than it used to be, but her hair was still the same rich chestnut although there were the odd strands of grey now and her skin was beautiful, something to do with her distant Irish genes, she guessed. She touched her own face feeling the same cut glass cheekbones and the inherited silky complexion, if I age like her I'll be happy she thought. 'Grab the biscuits love and let's go and see what Reg Woods wants, shall we?'

Delilah glided innocently into the lounge behind her mum with the plate of biscuits in her hand. Livy's father's big florid face was redder than usual and his pinstripe suit a little creased after a long day's work. He was seated on what they classified as the good chair, the one basically that their old ginger tabby cat didn't like so it was free of cat fluff. A workaholic with a household of high maintenance women, his wife had never worked and his three daughters had pretty much always had whatever they wanted. The two families had known each other for years as Reg and Delilah's father Bryn had started at the same company at the same time.

Reg Woods had been an ambitious man and had climbed the ranks quickly and was now Deputy CEO of another firm. Bryn Grace on the other hand enjoyed his minor finance roll and preferred not to have the continuous stress of the top flight. The difference was obvious Delilah thought, the two men both the same age looked years apart. Her dad ever the hippy with his greying hair pulled back into a pony tail was lithe from walking and cycling, his only vice the odd pipe and Reg was as round as he was tall and a crisis away from being an alcoholic. She offered him a biscuit while her mother poured the tea and he nibbled on it nervously.

'So Reg, what's the problem, you're not peeved with our Lola for turning up at church? After all it was supposed to be her wedding day.' Bryn Grace asked in an even tone.

'No, don't blame her at all, would've done the same in her shoes.' He stared at the mug in his hands as if he was trying to frame the words in his mind before he spoke. 'Shame, my friend has brought me here this evening, shame and humiliation. I've come to apologise.' He looked hesitantly at the three noncommittal faces watching him intently and took a sip of his tea. 'I decided to take my future son-in-law aside the night before the wedding to tell him a few home truths. I'll be honest with you I don't like the boy, never have, always thought you were far too good for him Delilah and thought you could do better. So you can imagine my horror when Olivia came home and told me they were a couple.'

He let out a long breath. 'She told me that Nick had tired of you and was madly in love with her. Then she gave me some cock and bull story about Nick telling you it was over and that you were causing trouble for them by refusing to let go. I didn't believe her, you were always the pragmatic one and I couldn't ever imagine you desperately hanging on to a man's shirt tails.' He smiled softly at Delilah, but she found that she couldn't quite meet his eyes because hadn't she fallen apart at the time. 'Anyway thought I'd have this chat over a few beers and Nick it would seem was carrying a whole load of guilt and the more he drank the more he unloaded. He told me a completely different story to Olivia about what happened that day, actually admitted that he was rather enjoying bedding two women at the same time. Told me that you'd slapped Olivia...'

'I landed a right hook on her chin, sorry...Just while we're apologising.' Delilah shrugged.

'That would explain the bruise then, she said she and Nick were messing around and she fell over a rug.' He chuckled before regaining a serious face. 'When Olivia told us about the baby and that they were getting married, she told us that they would be using the previously made arrangements because Nick had already paid for it all. I even offered to give him some money towards it, but he said no. Then that evening he dropped the bombshell, told me it was a pack of lies and that in reality you'd paid for it as a family and his outlay amounted to nothing. Seems he was trying to work out how with a baby on the way and an unfinished house that he owed huge amounts of money on, he was going to get out of repaying you at all. Told me you'd written to him about possible legal action and that scared him, that's why he sold the house. The boy's a proper little toe rag.'

'He's sold the house?' Delilah sounded more than a little surprised.

'Didn't you know? He had re-mortgaged it at least twice and in the end he had no more money left to spend on it. Sold it a couple of months ago to some city chap and his wife who wanted to retire down here, got a bit of profit, which he wasn't expecting in the current market, but has had to put that down on another place. He and Olivia have bought one of those new places on the harbour.'

'So how much did you put in?' Bryn Grace's voice was kind but there was a hard glint in his eye.

'Not as much as you might think Bryn and if I'd had my way I wouldn't have given them a penny, but the wife insisted.' Delilah looked at her dad, his face was set. 'Well to get down to the reason I'm here...' He reached into his briefcase and pulled out a large envelope and handed it to Bryn who opened it and held out the large wad of notes inside, a look of total disbelief flooding his face.

'Bloody hell Reg.' Bryn exclaimed and gave the heaving envelope to Delilah.

'It's all there, plus an extra thousand for Delilah for her inconvenience. For you to go and spend it on something special, something that gives you pleasure.' He stood up abruptly. 'My wife didn't want me to do this, thought it was up to you to get it back. As you know my wife is a very silly woman.' His round face took on a pained expression. 'I hope you'll all be able to forgive me, if I'd known about it before, you would have had it back months ago.' Delilah watched as her parents ushered him out and sat staring stupidly at the money in her hands.

'I think I need a walk. Do you mind?' She handed the money to her dad and not waiting for an answer rushed for the door. Just down from their house was a gate into the fields that led to the back of Nick's place, or what had been his. Delilah walked across the bone dry surface treading cautiously around the deep ruts left by the cattle after the last rain and if she took a deep breath she could still smell their passing. The last time she had taken this short walk she had discovered Nick's treachery and even now she still wondered what would have happened if she had driven up there that day. Would they have heard the car crunching up the gravel lane and been sitting innocently together with the kettle on or would they not have noticed anyway? What's more why was she still giving the thought space in her mind, after all it was done and finished with?

Climbing over the rickety stile she could see the sold board in the rubble strewn front garden. She walked up the drive and the pea shingle that Nick had shovelled over the mud made a satisfying crunching sound, before peering in the downstairs windows. As Reg had told them Nick had done very little with the place since she had last been there. She was still standing deep in thought staring vacantly at the nearby hills when a large black four-wheel drive pulled up and Delilah decided that she was probably trespassing and should make a move. 'Sorry, my ex's place', she blurted out as she raised a hand in appeasement and rushed out the gate. She was over the stile and back home in less than ten minutes.

Her mum was bustling around the kitchen with pots and plates 'Dinner's nearly ready go and wash your hands.' Like she was still ten years old, thought Delilah. When she came back down the most delicious aroma filled her nose, ginger, garlic, coriander and cardamom, her mum's signature curry. She quickly set the table her mouth watering in anticipation. Her dad set a large pitcher of water on the table and a small plate with still warm homemade chapattis and then the steaming fragrant plates of deliciousness were ready to be eaten. Delilah tucked in filling her chapatti with curry and tried to fill her mouth before it oozed out of the bottom. She was halfway through the meal when her dad spoke.

'Lola we've had a little chat your mum and me.' She eyed him suspiciously. 'When did you start working love?'

'When I was thirteen I delivered papers six days a week, summer season at the Priory when I was fifteen.' Delilah thought for a moment. 'Twelve hour days if I remember right and then there was weekends in the kitchens at Luigi's.' She looked from one to the other, 'then I finished school on the Friday and started work on the Monday in the bank, not forgetting the shifts down the pub on top of that. Why?'

'Because you haven't stopped, you give me too much keep and you've never had any proper fun time.' Her mum said quietly, a tinge of sadness in her voice. Delilah looked at her parents, they knew why she worked, she needed to. Ever since her mum's accident when she'd had to give up her job as a nurse, money had been tight. She had always believed it was important that she paid her way.

'I go riding twice a week. That's fun. I go out sometimes at the weekend, if I'm not too tired.'

'But you are tired and we both know you've hated your job. And riding dear is an escape and not the sort of fun I was thinking of. Your dad and I think it's time you took some time for you. This money is going to allow you to do that.' She patted the envelope of cash on the side of the table. 'Things are better now, I get my disability pension from the clinic, your dad earns more than he ever did and his inheritance paid off the mortgage. We're ok. So we think you should go off and have a summer of fun. Take your redundancy money, which will give you a nice little buffer and sign up for that trip you've been mooning over.' Her mum smiled, the one she used when there was to be no argument. 'They're shutting the branch in a couple of weeks so you'd be finishing in time. That nice Lena phoned while you were out, she wanted to know if you were still interested.'

Delilah wrapped another chapatti around another spoonful of curry and took a deeply warming mouthful. 'It would be an amazing opportunity why don't you give her a call, she sounded really nice.' She narrowed her eyes at her parents it was a conspiracy, this wasn't something they'd just dreamed up. Her favourite curry, they'd been planning this long before Reg Woods paid that money back.

'You've just out manoeuvred me, haven't you?' She said in as much of an accusing tone as she could muster. 'Well actually I've already agreed to take the redundancy and I suppose I could ring Lena, I've still got all the details she sent me and I hope that your only child becoming a groupie will make you proud.' And with that she set about finishing off her food with gusto.

Lying on her bed up in her room later Delilah considered her options. Outside she could hear the blackbirds saying goodnight to the world as dusk fell and she knew if she watched carefully out of her window she would see bats swooping about the garden catching insects. She closed her eyes and focused on the birdsong letting her breathing slow, clearing her mind. After about twenty minutes the birds had gone to their roosts and she had made her decision. She pulled the large envelope down from her 'to do' pile and pulled out the paperwork.

'Scarecrow' her favourite group when she'd been in her teens. She'd had posters all over her wall like any normal teenager and like a lot of girls at the time it had been the handsome lead singer Teddy with his pale blue eyes and platinum blonde hair who she had sat in her room daydreaming about. She had even got to see a gig at Dingwalls in Camden Lock eighteen months before they split. She remembered how excited she'd been, going up to London by herself to her first ever music gig, she'd had to find her way over to Dingwalls and she smiled at the terror she'd felt when she'd got lost, her sense of direction had always been atrocious. The smoky atmosphere and the reek of spilt alcohol, yes she could still call that to mind.

She had taken a seat next to a girl who looked much the same age as her, Lena and they had chatted briefly before it all started giggling excitedly at the thought of seeing their idols in the flesh. Afterwards they'd grabbed a burger in Wimpey's and discovered that they shared the same taste in music and the same love of the old films like "Now Voyager". A proper pair of romantics they'd been, sharing their fantasies and their ambitions.

She looked down at the pile of papers in front of her. On the letter at the top Lena's face peered back at her with a sultry gaze. Delilah remembered the pretty fresh faced girl from Suffolk with the short mousy hair, glasses, braces on her teeth and the kind of delicate frame overshadowed by large breasts that had made even the athletic Delilah feel like a carthorse next to her. The siren on the invitation letter had long silken blonde locks, heavily made up smoky eyes and pouting red lips, little Lena was long gone she guessed.

Back then she and Lena had swopped addresses and phone numbers and had kept in touch for a couple of years. Lena had snuck backstage at a show just before Scarecrow had split, met Teddy and had a brief fling with him. He had treated her abysmally and Delilah had tried to make her friend see sense, but Lena had accused her of being jealous and so ultimately they had drifted apart and lost touch. Poor Lena though had clung on to her handsome singer and her brief brush with fame to the bitter end, never quite getting over him.

But it seemed Lena hadn't lost her details and had obviously thought about her old chum when the group had recently got back together. She had put together a kind of music expedition, which would follow the last part of the group's European tour in June during which, they would go to gigs and get to go backstage and meet the group. Lena had been sponsored by one of the big gossipy music magazines to write a piece and in her letter she stated proudly that this was going to seal her place in the world of music journalism. Delilah doubted that, she guessed it was more Lena needing an excuse to get close to Teddy again now that his marriage was history and he was single again.

Delilah picked up her bedroom phone and dialled the number, 'Hi Lena, its Delilah, how are ya doing?'

'Delilah,' Lena trilled 'are you going to come, it's going to be brilliant, please say you're coming,'

'I'm coming, I don't know why, but hell why not eh?'

'It'll be amazing, you can share with me and we can catch up and everything.' She sounded genuinely pleased. 'You've got all the details, are you alright with the deposit? I'll get the rest just before we go. The guys are really excited to be having "Rent a fan's" with them. Gosh Delilah, how did we ever lose touch with each other?' Delilah rolled her eyes, they'd stopped speaking because Lena was far too caught up in the whole famous boyfriend thing, if that's what he'd been and Delilah really hadn't given two hoots about the celebrity world. 'You'll like the others I think they are a proper mixed bag, I know several of them from the old days and they're great fun.'

'I'll look forward to it. And Lena, it will be really great to catch up. Well I guess I'll see you in a couple of weeks. Thanks again for thinking of me.'

'You were always first on my list. See you soon.' She blew several kisses down the phone and was gone.

I must be bloody mad thought Delilah, chasing around Europe like a rabid groupie after a bunch of guys desperate for a second shot of fame.

She knew that she was being a little harsh as she'd seen a TV interview on the BBC with Teddy and Seb a few months ago when they'd released the comeback album. The two of them had laughed and made the intimation that both had recently been divorced and needed some cash to pay their very expensive ex-wives. They also told the interviewer that the other two members of the band, the two main song writers Vincent and Louis had been less than keen on the idea and had taken a lot of persuading.

Should be interesting she thought, two that are worried about the money and two that really don't want to be there and how keen she wondered would they really be to have a rag-tag bunch of fans getting under their feet. Still Reg said do something extraordinary and wasn't this exactly that. It would be a chance to travel a little, see some sights and meet new people. It would also give her space to think, work out what to do next with her life.

She sifted through the papers and found an original photo of the group from ten years ago. They were a handsome bunch she thought holding it up, Teddy had been downright pretty for a bloke back then and the others, well they'd all had their own charm. Vincent Angel who played lead guitar and who on stage threw himself into every performance like some kind of demented lunatic had a slightly dangerous air and with his naughty wide boy smirk resembled a young Terrence Stamp. Louis Rolland the groups classically trained French keyboard player was very Gallic with his mahogany hair and dark eyes, but always looked melancholic. Then there was Sebastian Cole or Seb as he was known, the bands replacement drummer and serial womaniser with his loud voice and constant smile, always far too full of himself she'd thought. When she'd watched the recent interview she'd been surprised at how little Teddy and Seb had changed, a little older perhaps, but the looks were still there.

She unfortunately was also older and had to admit that she hadn't listened to any of her Scarecrow albums for years though she still had them all, and the twelve inch singles, the previously well played vinyl all carefully stored in plastic dust covers. Perhaps a good starting point would be to dig them out from the box under her bed and reacquaint herself with the music. She probably ought to listen to the new album as well and she made a mental note to buy the CD tomorrow.

Dragging her old Record player out of a cupboard and carefully removing the fluff from the stylus she hoped the thing would still work as she hadn't used it for ages. Later as she lay there letting the familiar mix of electric pop and rock with its edge of protest wash over her she realised that the music had aged incredibly well and probably had more relevance now than it had when it was new. Favourite tracks came and went and she sang along as though she'd never stopped listening. Putting on the third album that she'd not really taken to and had been her least listened to of the five she was surprised to find that her tastes must have changed as she found it weirdly provocative. It contained one of her favourite singles "Lonely". She had never really listened to the original album version properly before and so she hadn't noticed Vincent's soft smoky vocals taking the lead, Teddy had sung on the single release.

What a haunting voice he has she thought, giving the track all sorts of hidden depths and meanings. Even now his wistful vocals seemed to reach down into the depths of her soul and embrace the sadness hidden there and an involuntary shiver ran through her like some sort of weird premonition. He had also taken the lead on a very haunting cover of the old Country classic "He stopped loving her today", which she hadn't even realised was on there. She listened to the two evocative tracks again and again finding something new each time she listened, eventually the heart breaking lyrics brought on the tears that had been threatening to fall for months.

Along with the albums she had found a book written by Hilly Bob the band's original drummer, which she vaguely remembered buying but not reading. So having put her old stereo back in the cupboard and her albums carefully back in their sleeves she settled down to read her discovery. Hilly bless him had ended up overindulging in just about everything, girls, drugs and booze. He'd spent money like water and had finished up broke and on life support in his local ITU. With Hilly unable to continue the group took on several transient drummers before they found Seb. It had taken her a few days but by the time she'd finished she had some sort of insight into the groups various characters.

Vince, Louis and Hilly had started the group at college with Vince taking the vocals. Originally they had called themselves "Anglo French Relations", not exactly a title that skipped off the tongue, but they had a certain following. Their influences had been varied from Country to Punk to the electronica of the early eighties and groups like Duran-Duran and Ultravox. They'd met Teddy in a bar and he'd offered himself as a singer/guitarist joining them after a successful trial. The change of name had been his idea based on the whole "Dr Syn the Scarecrow" legend, which came from his home town of Dymchurch. They'd all agreed and Scarecrow where born. Roscoe Martin their manager had seen them in action one night performing their own material and had been impressed by the group and the adoring fans that seemed to shadow them. He'd taken a chance and it had paid him handsomely as the group had been an instant success.

What wasn't to like, they wrote all their own material, played a wide variety of instruments, were personable characters and were handsome to boot. They had lived the high life and poor old Hilly had paid for it. Although Vince and Louis had made certain that he continued to have his share of the royalties. What came out of the book was that these were just nice ordinary guys made good, they'd made mistakes and paid for them to various extents.

Perhaps it would be ok this trip she thought, the group obviously weren't monsters and they were older, more mature now and hopefully a bit more settled. She wasn't sure about the whole summer of fun that her parents wanted her to have, but one decision was made and Delilah had already started to see the possibility of a life away from the local bank that had been her life since the Monday after leaving school.

~

THREE

~

At Victoria coach station Delilah had found a seat near the front of the surprisingly comfortable large minibus that she knew they'd be spending an awful lot of time in over the next couple of weeks. Most people were in pairs and Lena had immediately bagged herself the front seat next to the driver so Delilah was able to relax in a sort of peaceful solitude. On the ferry she had grabbed a bit of breakfast with Lena and had been surprised at how much her old friend had changed. She remembered Lena as being really star struck, but now a little older and more mature she appeared jaded with the celebrity scene. She told Delilah that she had been working as a junior reporter on her local rag for several years after stints working for virtually nothing at various music companies, TV and radio stations. Now though she wanted to branch out and leave behind the weddings and council meetings that had dominated her recent working life.

She'd sent a brief portfolio including a recent interview with Teddy to one of the big scandal magazines and had included her idea for this current endeavour. They had printed the piece about Teddy and had sponsored her on this trip providing that they had the exclusive at the end of it. Lena with a job dangling on the end of a stick instead of the virtual carrot launched herself into the project with gusto. It had of course thrown her back into contact with Teddy now that he was free, but from the way she spoke Delilah felt that Lena was now working on the basis that she would never really be anything but a convenience to him. Having suffered from a dark melancholy several times in the past Delilah recognised someone who wouldn't need much of a push to send them tumbling down into the depths and so she hoped that this trip went the way it should for Lena's sake.

Back on the bus she swatted lazily at an irritating little black fly that had found its way on board and Nick slid unbidden back into her head. Just like the fly, he was an irritation she couldn't quite rid herself of. She'd moaned about it to her riding instructor Bunty on her last ride before coming away and had been rewarded with one of the older woman's resigned and slightly pained expressions. 'Dear one...' She had said in that gloriously plummy voice. 'I've been married three times, all total bastards and without fail I've not been able to get them out of my mind until a suitable new distraction came along. Well apart from the last one and he wasn't worth wasting time on.' She'd leant over from her old mare and patted Delilah's thigh. 'Find someone new, you're a gorgeous creature, have some fun on your trip, go screw a handsome pop star and you'll find that the boorish Nick will just disappear...poof.' She smiled at the memory and in a fit of pique she squashed the unfortunate insect against the glass, wishing she could have dealt with him in a similar fashion. Regrettably every time she thought she'd put it out of her mind the whole grubby saga kept opening up like a festering wound and poisoned her life.

She rested her head back onto the small travel pillow that she'd brought and closed her eyes shutting out the blurring countryside outside the windows. She'd been reasonably happy living her easy going small town single life before he came in and tore it all to shreds along with her confidence and self-esteem. It hadn't been a wildly exciting life, she'd spent happy evenings out with friends and there had been other men, nothing serious, just fun. Well apart from a year spent with Tony who she'd met at a party down at the local rugby club, a tree of a man with the soul of a poet and a lively sense of humour. In hindsight it had been a purely sexual connection, which in time had run its course and they had parted company as friends. There had been others but she had wanted her freedom again and none of them had made her feel any different about that choice.

Then she had been introduced to Nick. Tall, athletic and rugged with a permanent bronze tan from his work as a tree surgeon she had found him attractive, but then who wouldn't? Right from the start Delilah had found him dull and not terribly bright although some women probably wouldn't have been quite as bothered because his looks far overshadowed his lack of personality. He though had been persistent in his pursuit of her and was obviously not used to being turned down or so she'd guessed at the time. So in a moment of weakness she had given in and gone out with him for all of two months and she'd been bored out of her box by him. He didn't even have Tony's prowess in the bedroom, lounge, kitchen, as her mind slipped easily into the always pleasant memory of Tony. So she'd sat Nick down and told him it was never going to work.

He hadn't taken it well and for weeks afterwards he had bombarded her with flowers and messages telling her how much he loved her, that he couldn't live without her, total bollocks of course. Eventually between his endless chasing, her parents telling her what a nice boy he was and her friends telling her she was mad to let him go she had given in and tried again. Having fallen in love with the old cottage he was restoring she had pushed her unease to the back of her mind and threw herself into the project at his side with gusto. He had caught her off guard when he had proposed, as she yet again had been working up the courage to tell him to take a permanent hike. So why the hell had she said yes she wondered staring out again at the endless Belgium fields? Why indeed? She hadn't even thought about it, she'd just stood there like a rabbit caught in the headlights of an oncoming car and agreed to marry him.

Then she'd panicked because it was going to be a huge mistake, but when her parents got all caught up in the idea the same rabbit went off and started to make the arrangements after dating him for what was it six, seven agonising months. She was an intelligent, independent woman in her mid-twenties, but she'd just been barrelled along and if there had been doubts it had all been arranged hadn't it? Crazy, idiotic she realised that now.

Then she'd walked in on them. Of course now she could see it all clearly, Livy was always there flirting with him, which she had thought harmless and then there was the way they'd looked at each other sometimes like they had a secret only they knew. Well they had one didn't they? So why had he proposed, money for the house? Beforehand he had often asked her for money as he knew she had some saved and she had always turned him down because she had seen no future in the relationship. That had slowly slipped into her mind after Livy's dad had come to their house, that Nick had not only shamelessly chased her the first time she'd dumped him, but had proposed with the sole intention of getting his hands on her very meagre savings. Why she wondered would anyone do that?

    But the biggest question of all was why had it caused her so much distress? Finding them together had been her way out, the perfect escape and the answer to that was simple. Nick wasn't the issue as she wasn't bothered about losing him. No it was the loss of the woman she considered her closest friend that had hurt so badly. Livy's betrayal hung there like a huge roadside hoarding at every road junction with her smug face in caricature on it peering down at the pathetic little rabbit with Delilah's face lying flattened like road kill at her feet. Their friendship had obviously been totally worthless to the selfish Livy, only gathering any substance when she had needed something. All those years had meant nothing and that had been the final crack in Delilah's already stressed and tired mind, sending her sliding down into that dark spiral of despair and indifference.

'Penny for them?' One of the two Goth's had swung lightly into the seat next to her 'you looked so sad I had a horrible feeling you were going to cry and I wondered if I could help. I'm Mia by the way'

'Delilah hi. That's really sweet, thank you. I think I need some sort of distraction otherwise I'll just continue to wallow in self-pity.'

'Not something you want to talk about then.'

'No, I seem to have talked and thought about nothing else for months and I'm getting really bored with it, but I just don't seem to be able to put it away, preferably in the file marked shit.'

'I know where you're coming from, I have much the same problem, but mine's not a man.'

'It might have been a woman...' Delilah chuckled 'and it could be something else entirely.'

'Nope definitely a man, I saw you checking that guy with the cute arse out on the boat and to be honest only a bloke could cause that kind of upset, another woman would have been kinder.'

'Font of all knowledge then are you.'

'Bloody know it all you mean, yep that's me or so I'm told. He...' She pointed to the other Goth 'my twin brother Tom is always telling me that. Delilah, so does that ever get shortened?'

'My dad calls me Lola, it's about the only form of shortening I tolerate. I've heard them all, I was "Deli belly" at school and my most recent boss called me "Lilah" and I hated him with a vengeance so that's off the table.'

'I like Delilah it's kind of dramatic, although I think you're really a Lola. I changed mine to Mia from ordinary old Maria by deed poll when I was eighteen. My dad understood, but my mum who's Italian insists on Maria and I've learnt to compromise, you wouldn't believe the arguments we had when I was younger.' Delilah took stock of her companion as she stretched her slender arms out and briefly inspected her dark purple nails. She was she guessed a few years younger than her with naturally black hair, which shone slightly blue like a magpie's plumage as the sun caught it through the glass. She was petite and perfect and her big eyes were the softest grey. Very pretty, though she doubted that Mia would be impressed if she said so.

'So what keeps you awake at night Mia?'

'Failed my second year at uni, the folks aren't very impressed. The course was just not my thing, I knew at the end of the first year that I was bored to tears by Sociology and I'm afraid I didn't put enough in this year. I wanted to do art and clothes design, but the folks weren't having it and they were paying.' She shrugged. 'Our older brother Matt treated us to this trip because he thought it'd be cool, wanted to come himself. We come from Dymchurch, you know down in Kent and so we were always surrounded by the whole "Dr Syn the Scarecrow" legend and he was always into Scarecrow. You know the group came up with the name because Teddy comes from the village, he wanted them to be called Dr Syn, but I think he lost out. Anyhow we started to get interested and when this trip came up he signed us up even though he couldn't make it. He's a trader in the city, very handsome...'

'I'm kind of done with the whole handsome thing I think.'

'I can always give you his phone number, you're definitely his type.'

'Thanks I think.'

'You're welcome. Oh goody a toilet break, absolutely dying for a pee' and with that she was gone. Delilah chuckled, she felt an immediate connection with Mia even though she was easily distracted and didn't appear to have an off switch. Perhaps she would be a new friend, perhaps just for once things were looking up.

The hotel Lena had booked was located in a sort of no man's land, not the best part of Brussels and probably not the worst. It was one of those bland cheap modern places with zero character both outside and in and staffed by bored individuals who seemed to wish they were somewhere else. Lena allocated the rooms and as the first gig wasn't until the next evening Lena had arranged a get-to-know you meeting in the hotel that evening, armed with the details the group then mooched wearily off with their luggage. The room Delilah was to share with Lena had a certain warmth to it and was surprisingly comfortable. She kicked off her shoes and collapsed back onto the bed her arms spread wide 'well a lump free bed is a good start.'

'My uncle recommended the place, he'd been to a conference here said it was alright.' She sounded a little uncertain of something.

'Are you ok Lena?'

'Oh, yes, long journey.' Delilah fixed her with a suspicious stare. Lena flopped down on the bed beside her 'I've just realised who two of our group are and I think they'll cause problems.' She sighed loudly 'I think I might need to hit the mini bar before this evening.'

'Who are you talking about?'

'I might be wrong Delilah, wait and see eh...You joining me in something?'

'I'd rather have a cup of tea to be honest, you go ahead though.'

'Do you think they'll have decent tea?'

'Nope, that's why I packed my own, how sad is that? My family have spent enough time in Europe to know they just don't do tea. Do you want one?' she said trying to distract Lena from drowning her sorrows.

'Why not, probably more sensible. I wish I was as sensible and solid as you Delilah.' And with that she was off into the bathroom leaving Delilah scowling after her departing back.

'Great, I'm sensible and solid.' She muttered to herself through gritted teeth.

The evening get together was held in one of the hotels small private function rooms, Lena had laid on drinks and a small buffet. Delilah was pleasantly surprised, the room was bright and set out with comfortable chairs and small tables. The buffet actually looked quite delicious and Lena had made sure that there was a good selection of drinks available. Her slightly ditsy exterior detracted from hidden depths and Delilah was pleased that her old friend had excelled herself, well tonight at least. Wandering around the room she found herself standing next to a full length antique mirror, which was totally out of keeping with the rest of the room and she idly wondered why it had been put there.

She wasn't vain, but like most women stood next to a mirror she couldn't help appraise the image before her and the reflection suggested a woman comfortable in her own skin, which was sometimes a long way short of the truth. She was taller than average with what her mother called an evenly distributed body, which was mostly a size ten. She considered it to be athletic although her well defined shoulders from years of horse riding were evened out in her hips, same reason and in between her waist was trim. She liked her breasts, which were pert enough to go braless, but still carried just enough fullness for a cleavage. The fluid black silk jersey trousers and unfitted sleeveless cream top finished with a simple pair of pearl stud earrings suggested a casual elegance when in fact the outfit had been chosen more for comfort than style. Her often unruly chestnut curls were smoothed out and she had opted for a slick of mascara to emphasize her dark eyes and a touch of rosy lip gloss on her mouth. Yeah, you're ok Delilah she thought.

Gazing around at her fellow travellers twelve in all including Lena and herself, she wondered what tonight would reveal about them if anything. Out of the corner of her eye she saw Lena do a quick headcount and deciding that everyone had arrived she stood in the middle of the room and banged a glass with a spoon.

'Hi everyone. I hope your rooms are all ok and that there are no problems.' She waited as if expecting someone to moan. 'Anyhow I'd like to thank everyone for coming, this is a big thing for me. I've organised events before but this is something else. We're all here because we're Scarecrow fans so I'm sure we're all going to be great pals.' She looked around at the group, flashing everyone there her best and most engaging smile. 'I thought we'd have a round robin introduction session to break the ice and then we can just mingle. I'll go first shall I?' There was a faint ripple of embarrassed applause. 'I'm Lena and I'm twenty-five, I come from a small village in Suffolk and until recently I worked for the local newspaper. I've now moved into London and have a junior job at a celebrity weekly, this trip is my chance at moving into one of the big music magazines.' She gave a small satisfied smile before moving on. 'Hopefully you'll have lots of chances to socialise with the boys in the band when we get to go backstage, although it won't be at every show. But...' She held a beautifully manicured hand up for effect and said in a slightly breathy tone. 'But we'll be staying at the same hotels as the boys once we get to

Switzerland, won't that be brill?' She waited for a response, nothing. 'Ok who's next...Delilah?'

Great she thought drop me in it why don't you. 'Hi, I'm Delilah and I'm the same age as Lena. We met at a Scarecrow gig many years ago and have more or less been pals ever since. I come from the south coast and up until recently worked for one of the big four banks. I was made redundant when they closed my branch, too many people at my grade.' She shrugged 'so here I am, sensible and solid and really quite boring.' That was all they were going to get. She watched as Mia her new pal from the coach came forward. She really was extremely pretty without her favoured Goth make-up and clothes. Tonight she'd opted for a naked face with her long raven hair pulled back in a loose plait and jeans with a loose black shirt. She beamed at the group and gestured to her brother to join her. Like his sister Tom had jet black hair and big soft grey eyes. He had a shy smile and seemed uncomfortable out in front of the group.

'Hi, I'm Mia and this is my twin brother Tom, although I expect you've all guessed that.' She giggled 'both of us are at university and we come from the same Kent village as Teddy Rose although we have never met him. Tom doesn't say much, probably because I'm the noisy one and he's a little bit shy. Once you get to know him though you'll discover he can be the heart and soul of any party. We're into anything Goth and I'd really love to get a job in the fashion world although Tom's going to be a brilliant engineer.' Tom smiled at the group and was quick to make a retreat behind his sister. Delilah smiled, she rather liked them and she could sympathise with Tom because she'd been a painfully shy teenager too.

The next pair to come forward were chalk and cheese, she and Mia had christened them the grammar school girls during their extensive chat on the coach. Carrie was a stocky short haired brunette with limpid brown eyes and her friend Sarah was tall and slim with ginger hair, freckle filled face and hazel eyes. They said they hadn't done anything like this before so were feeling a little anxious. They both had cautious smiles and had opted for short skirts, which Sarah was obviously feeling self-conscious in as she kept fidgeting with it trying to smooth it down. They had met at uni and were both trainee teachers. Easing back to their seats Delilah noticed that Sarah's pale face was now the colour of a beetroot and she had immediately taken quite a large mouthful of her wine. Teaching she thought was probably a very interesting choice of career for someone who found standing in front of a group of strangers so daunting.

Then it was the turn of Lena's two old school friends Fran and Neil. Fran was as round as she was tall with laughing eyes and rosy cheeks and she spoke in a quiet, but forceful voice while telling them that she was Lena's oldest friend. Hmm thought Delilah, she didn't want to bunk with you, did she? She had been frugal with her description of herself, but it was clear from the way she looked at tall and bespectacled Neil that she had feelings for him. Delilah guessed from the naked devotion on his face that Neil on the other hand was actually a lot more concerned with Lena and that he probably put up with all her little foibles because he loved her, whether Lena returned that affection was another matter entirely.

The next four to introduce themselves had kept their distance from the rest of them all day. They had sat together on the back seat of the minibus and had disappeared on the boat. Delilah had already guessed that they were probably a little older than the majority of the group and she half wondered if that explained their rather distant and reproachful attitude, although what difference a few years made she didn't know. They obviously weren't very impressed with Lena's get together and the first pair to introduce themselves did so with sardonic disinterest. Rob and Nicki who were both thirtyish had been long term fans from the beginning. They gave nothing else away as Delilah expected although Nicki made it very clear that they were just friends who'd often travelled to gigs together and Rob's face fell a little at that comment. The final two were another matter entirely and came to the front like a pair of queen bees.

Tash was a peculiar looking woman. She was bean pole thin with a pair of large probably surgically enhanced breasts perched on top of her ribcage and short legs. A huge moon shaped face with small piggy eyes sat on a non-existent neck and her bobbed hair had been over worked and over dyed and was a strange mixture of bleached blonde, ginger and pink with dark roots in it. Her voice was high and whiny and carried an air of haughtiness when she spoke. 'I'm Tash and I control the Scarecrow fan club. Roscoe...' She used the group's manager's name as though he was a long term friend. 'Roscoe trusts me entirely and I've known all the group for years. Vincent is an especially close "friend".'

'Smug bitch.' Mia muttered to Delilah 'I can't imagine any of them being interested in her, she probably has a very robust imagination.' Mia rolled her eyes dramatically.

'Either that or she's very accommodating...Some men just aren't very fussy.'

Delilah replied probably a little too loudly with a sceptical shake of her head. Tash threw them a vicious glance, which was repaid with two totally nonchalant expressions although Delilah wondered if they'd just made a very dangerous enemy.

The final member of the group was a tall willowy woman very badly dressed in head to toe designer labels. Her dark hair was thinning from too many extensions, she had dark bags beneath unfriendly eyes and a thin mouth, which finished a cruel face. 'I'm Jane and I'm a media journalist for "Music Today". I was the one who broke the story that Scarecrow were re-forming and I have unlimited access to the group during this trip. Those of you who have any sense will stick with me as I can offer you far more than she can...' She pointed rudely at Lena. That was all she was prepared to offer about herself, but it was obviously enough. Delilah could already see two camps forming as she watched Carrie sidle surreptitiously over to join Jane's group. Her friend Sarah seemed torn between Carrie and these women that offered so much and an obvious attraction to the handsome and very shy Tom.

The evening had not been the overwhelming success that Lena had craved, but her side of the room probably had the most fun. They had also decided to go sightseeing the following day although when the day dawned wet and miserable most had decided to forgo the outing. So it had been just Delilah, Mia and Sarah who had braved the miserable Belgium weather trooping to points of interest in their guidebooks before soggy and cold they too gave up and headed back.

Delilah taking some time to herself took advantage of the hotel gym and pool and did her best to shrug off the advances of one or two of the more persistent hotel guests. Why did men see a woman as an easy target the minute she puts on a swimsuit she wondered? It wasn't as though she'd been prancing about in a virtually non-existent bikini was it? She'd had a work out, a sauna and a quick swim and they'd been fluttering around her like moths to a flame. Behind the indignant exterior though she was quietly flattered that strangers found her attractive and her confidence going in to the evening was sky high.

Waiting outside the theatre that had been pretty much knocked out of her as Jane again covered in designer brands had delivered a stinging rebuke about her choice of jeans and a silky top. "A shame she hadn't made much of an effort, and didn't she know what make-up was". Lena had told her to ignore it as she'd been told that she "looked like a prostitute looking for a pickup" and Mia that she'd "look more at home in a cemetery." But it didn't take much to knock Delilah's fragile confidence and she had entered the small theatre head down and a bit battered. The concert had lifted her spirits, Teddy had been in good form and he had belted out the old standards and the new material to rapturous applause. Vincent had given Teddy a break taking Invisibility one of their newer tracks and had broken hearts in the process with his husky haunting vocals. The rest of the group had thrown themselves into the performance and at the end of the show Delilah felt quite elated although she wasn't sure that she was looking forward to what came next. Unlike Lena she had never done anything as daring as going backstage and she felt the inevitable butterflies starting in her stomach.

~

SCARECROW
JUNE 95

~

FOUR
~

Delilah watched with amusement as the group of rent-a fans gathered around their chosen leader. She watched Jane as she held court and felt really sorry for Lena who for the moment at least still held the majority. Her mouth was starting to wobble as if she wasn't far from tears and Delilah walked over and laid a hand gently on her shoulder whilst giving her what she hoped was an encouraging smile. She didn't know whether that buoyed her up, but Lena was back in charge and trundled them off back stage.

Delilah stayed towards the back of the entourage and waited, a quiet smile creeping onto her mouth as they all rushed after Lena, worried that they might be left behind. The Backstage area surprised her as it was dingy and more than a little unloved, its peeling walls yellow from years of cigarette smoke. Woodworm riddled tables were set up in what appeared to be the central area filled with various forms of alcohol, soft drinks and an unexciting buffet including what looked to Delilah suspiciously like spam rolls so feeing thirsty she grabbed a beer.

There were a colourful selection of people milling about and the boys from Scarecrow were mingling, a word here and a photo there. Delilah was quickly dragged off to meet Teddy by Lena. At just past thirty he'd retained his boyish prettiness with his trademark spiked up platinum hair, but Delilah thought that his ice blue eyes had a hardness in them that hadn't been there when he was younger. He was very magnanimous and was happy to chat for a few minutes and pose for a photo with her. She then returned the favour and took a very cosy photo of Lena wrapped in his arms. It surprised her how genuinely fond Teddy actually was of this enigmatic young woman and after a few minutes of listening to them thought that it possibly wouldn't take much to reignite their previous association. Not wishing to be in the way she left them to chat, but when she looked again Jane and her sycophants had muscled in on the situation and Jane was once again lording it over Lena.

Seb the groups drummer was standing in the middle of the room holding court, telling the assembled group of fans the bawdy story of how he'd been cautioned last night for streaking back to his room from the pool after going skinny dipping. 'It was after midnight there was nobody around so who did it hurt?' He asked with a chuckle. Although Delilah wanted to warm to the man there was something very insincere about him and she couldn't. He was actively flirting with any woman within his immediate vicinity and most of the girls seemed captivated by his obvious charms. That was no surprise as he was a very striking creature, his strong masculine Caribbean features, the tightly cropped coal black hair and those big puppy dog brown eyes. It crossed her mind that he was going to cause some trouble amongst the girls although she felt immune and then it came to her, there was something of Nick about him.

Looking about her she saw French keyboard wizard Louis sitting all by himself in a small alcove, he looked lost and out of place she thought. She stopped and studied him for a while, if her Grandmother Hazel was here she would have said that he wasn't meant to be in this world. She'd never quite understood the comment, but she did now. There was a shaft of moonlight shining through a crack in the heavy blinds and it seemed to envelope him in an angelic golden glow. His hair was a similar colour to hers, perhaps slightly redder and it curled over one eye increasing the impression of sadness, his features were soft and his eyes were the most intense blue. He was nursing a glass of what looked like brandy, but could have been anything and was watching the proceedings going on around him with a kind of serene indifference. She wandered over hoping that he wouldn't mind being bothered.

'Hi Louis, am I disturbing you?'

'You can disturb me anytime Chéri, you have me at a disadvantage though.'

'I'm Delilah.'

'Très joli, sit down. Named for the song or is it a biblical reference I wonder, the beautiful Delilah robbing Samson of his legendary strength, eh? Sit down and make yourself comfortable.' He patted the space beside him and she lowered herself down sinking into the old leather couch. He slipped what was nothing more than a friendly arm across the back of the sofa and offered her a soft smile increasing the whole angelic look. 'Did you enjoy the show?'

'Very much, the new material is stunning live. I loved your piano solo in "Into Darkness" so poignant, I wish I could play as well.'

'Merci, you play too, childhood lessons perhaps?'

'My gran was very accomplished, she taught me. I'll only ever be average I'm afraid, not enough practicing.' She smiled shyly. 'I was disappointed that Vincent didn't sing "Lonely" though, the album track is haunting and he has a lovely voice...' Perplexed she looked around, 'strange I haven't seen him here.'

'Ah Van-son, he has gone off to hide. He doesn't relish the whole backstage party scene and then he saw that awful woman...' He jabbed a finger in Jane's direction, 'and he was gone, how does he say. Ah yes like a rat up a drainpipe.' Delilah could sit and listen to that divine French accent endlessly.

'Bad history?'

'She's a bitch.' Straight to the point with barely a trace of a French accent and almost spat out. He was, she thought a bit of an old fraud as the accent came and went willy-nilly as it suited him. 'It's a long story, the strange looking girl Tash runs our fan club and she was very keen on 'im from the start though he wasn't interested in taking her to his bed, so she makes mischief for 'im. When we decided to reform the group she introduced her friend Jane who wanted to be a serious journalist and asked if we would let her break the story. But Vince and Teddy have already told an old friend in the business that the scoop is his. Vince told Tash in no uncertain terms that they needed to honour their agreement so the Jane woman she goes ahead and does it anyway. He was so mad I thought he would kill her. So he hides or I think he will do something he regrets eh?' He shuddered in mock horror.

'Ah that explains a lot. If that's the case how did Tash manage to stay in charge of the fan club?'

'Ah Roscoe he likes her and Seb, well I'm afraid he is not so fussy who he beds.' He tipped her chin up with a gentle fingertip 'Stay clear of Sebastian Delilah, he is a...Mutt.'

'Don't worry Seb's reputation precedes him with fanfares and bunting, Lena gave us all a heads up to that. Anyway there's something about him I don't like.'

'Sensible girl.' He held her there for a moment his eyes taking her in so completely that she felt a little like a lab rat under a microscope. 'You are very beautiful Delilah, very much 'is type I think.' She was totally confused now, but there was no time for Louis to explain as their intimate space was being invaded by some of the others from their tour. Time to move on, she leant over and kissed him fondly on the cheek. 'Merci Louis.'

'My pleasure Chéri.' Lifting her hand to his lips he kissed her fingertips delicately and she blushed furiously as she walked away.

It was about this time that the beer from earlier was beginning to outstay its welcome and she hunted about for the toilets. Eventually finding a sign she took herself off in the vague direction and after a good ten minutes finally found the antiquated Ladies toilet down a poorly lit corridor, which would have seemed less threatening in a dungeon.

Walking back out of the ladies she found that the lights had gone out and she tried to remember which direction she'd come from. She had got lost in this rabbit warren on the way here so getting back was going to prove an adventure she could do without. Why would what seemed to be a reasonably small theatre from the front have a bloody labyrinth behind it? She strained her ears to see if she could hear any noise from the party. There was nothing just an eerie silence that pervaded the air. An involuntary shiver ran through her body, 'hello someone's just walked over my grave' she thought teeth chattering in the darkness. 'Pick a direction', she mumbled out loud and started off to her left, it didn't go anywhere just came to a dead end. Turning around and heading the other way she muttered darkly 'next time pay more attention.'

The corridor swung to the right and she was faced with various doors, it was like being bloody Alice in wonderland, but she could hear muffled sounds now so this must be the right direction. At the end there was a door and the corridor turned again, so did she try the door or carry on, she vaguely remembered twisting and turning on the way. Panic was just starting to creep into the edges of her mind, what if she couldn't find her way back. She glanced at the small mother of pearl faced gold watch that always hung slightly loosely on her narrow wrist, she had plenty of time before the coach left but what if it went early? She doubted that Lena, who when she last saw her was already stoned would bother to count heads, she would just bellow at the others to follow and they'd all rush after her like a flock of brightly coloured chattering birds. She could feel her chest tightening, Delilah liked to be in control and at the moment she wasn't.

The door was fractionally ajar and for that reason alone seemed to be her best option and pulling the handle she moved into what seemed to be a storeroom full of racks of dusty theatrical costumes not dissimilar to the wardrobe into Narnia in *The Lion the Witch and the Wardrobe*. It was dimly lit by one naked bulb dangling from the ceiling that flickered occasionally, illuminating the discoloured paint on the walls and she guessed this room was not visited frequently. It was strangely hushed and the sounds that had led her here had just vanished. The soft thud behind her followed by a loud click told her that the door had in a fit of spite shut and locked itself behind her.

'Delilah Grace, you're an idiot, stop bloody panicking and concentrate,' she said crossly to the completely unbothered costumes hanging everywhere. 'Who the hell gets lost in a bloody theatre?' She knew that she wasn't far off bursting into tears, which she decided was really just very childish and certainly not helpful. The room had a slightly musty scent to it and wrinkling her nose she wondered exactly how long it had been since anyone had found their way in there and if this was where she was going to die, alone and undiscovered her body mouldering alongside the long forgotten costumes.

'Hello Delilah Grace, are you lost?' Came a booming voice from the far side of a rack of old military uniforms. God she thought, it's haunted. A huge apparition with wild grey hair dressed in a pinstripe suit, with a bright yellow cravat and spats on his feet strode out with a huge smile on his craggy face. 'Can I help you?' Delilah, startled took a step back, tripped over a trailing sword scabbard and started to fall her arms waving ineffectively in the air and her mouth fixed in an uncomprehending oh. Her camera flew out of her hand as all her thoughts turned to saving herself and in a fleeting second she watched it arc through the air to be caught by the wild haired man. Bracing herself for the floor that was rushing towards her she felt a pair of strong arms grab her firmly around her ribcage and lift her back onto her feet.

'Clumsy' the voice was soft and smoky 'that could have been a nasty fall, would have put our insurance costs through the roof.' It took her a few seconds to process the London accent and realise that she had stumbled upon the elusive Vincent. So Louis had been right her saviour had found the perfect hiding place. Standing with his arms locked around her waist, she could feel the warmth of his muscular body pressed firmly against her back. Only then did it occur to her that she was stuck in a locked room alone with two strange men, one of whom seemed to have no intention of letting her go.

'So lost Delilah Grace would you like some pictures, as I have your camera?'

'The poor girl has just had a near death experience Roscoe; she might not be in the mood.' She could feel his warm breath in her hair, smell his musky soapy scent and felt the first stirrings of butterflies in her stomach.

'Everybody likes pictures' the man now identified as Roscoe Martin the groups eccentric manager said sulkily, 'you'd like pictures wouldn't you Delilah?' He flashed her an impish grin.

Delilah was trying to control her breathing, her brain trying to digest the situation while her body was still telling her things she really didn't want to know. She felt like laughing hysterically and tried desperately to suppress the hysteria bubbling up deep inside. 'Why not, ok?' She said with more confidence than she felt, her brain screaming "RUN".

'Goody I like pictures, now stay like that and smile Delilah we're not axe murderers.' She found a tentative smile from somewhere and tried to keep it as the flash went off. 'Now for some fun next shot...'

Now she was worried. Vince's fingertips had moved in what she had felt was a deliberately suggestive fashion down her bare arms until he caught her hands in his 'relax, let it go' he whispered as he pulled her hands above her head. Delilah couldn't hold the nervous giggles in anymore and so dutifully she let go and allowed these two crazy men to manipulate her into various silly contrived positions.

'Tango time' beamed Roscoe and Vince his arm firmly around her waist moved her into a dramatic tango pose. Delilah finally had a chance to take in her "jailor" and he was far more handsome in the flesh than he seemed on stage. Jet black hair cut short apart from the top, which had been left longer and was quite deliberately streaked with silver fell over a classic perfectly symmetrical face. The outside edges of his brows slanted gently upwards above intense cinnamon eyes, which close up were flecked with green and reminded her of her cats. His soft mouth was set into a knowing and very impish half smile, which made her wonder what exactly was coming next. Still, those eyes...

'Ok now for the naughty ones...' For a moment lost in Vince's eyes she had forgotten that Roscoe was standing there with her camera. She must have looked panicky because Vince winked at her and squeezed her waist. 'Old school movie I think.' Roscoe sighed blissfully.

She found herself staring into those intense cat eyes again and noticed for the first time that they were framed with long dark lashes, lord they were incredible and God help her she wanted him to kiss her. With a wistful smile, his eyes never leaving hers Vince dipped her backwards with one arm supporting her waist the other under her shoulder and then his mouth was on hers. It was brief 'Nope, this is no good for my back Roscoe.'

'I don't care, don't spoil the moment... stop whining, again please.' Then with the wickedest smile Delilah had ever seen Vince had dropped her back his mouth against hers long before he had her in the pose Roscoe was looking for. Delilah lost herself in the depths of his eyes and the intensity of his soft warm mouth against hers whilst memorising the moment, as right now she didn't think she would ever have another one like it. Vaguely she was aware of the flash of the camera and she felt rather than saw Vince wave one hand behind him in the direction of the door that from this position she could now see on the far side of the room. Roscoe tiptoed light footed as a cat, laid her camera on a shelf and moved away and out the door.

Vince pulled her upright and kissed her again, his kisses were deeper now, a slight insistence in them and she couldn't stop herself responding. Fast giving in to her insistent tingling nerve endings, she could feel his desire and knew where this could be going if she let it. She was no innocent, but this was something way out of her comfort zone, she knew she should stop but she didn't want to. He pulled her closer one of his hands running long slender fingers through her hair his mouth raining small kisses on her eyelids, her nose and the curve of her throat finding the places where her overheating blood was pumping faster through her veins. One of those strong hands cupped her chin and his mouth was moving towards hers 'Delilah this is...' The door opened suddenly and loud voices cut through the moment. Startled Delilah disentangled herself from his arms and bolted for the door.

Vince watched her go 'bollocks' he uttered, a look of total dejection on his face. Roscoe who stood in the doorway mouthed 'sorry mate, they were there before I could stop them.' Vince shrugged, it went with the territory. He tried to force down the desire then smiling brightly he signed autographs and laughed and joked with the fans that had so unceremoniously interrupted his enjoyment.

Lena caught Delilah as she staggered out the door 'we'll be going in about twenty minutes I think the boys have had enough of the crowd' she wrinkled her nose 'they're such a rabble.'

'You invited them Lena, this is your party', she pulled back. 'What the hell have you been smoking?'

'Weed' Lena giggled. 'You should try some, loosen you up. Oh there's Teddy...Oh Teddy' she called as she skipped across the room golden hair flying behind her.

'Loosen myself up, I was doing just fine thank you.' Delilah said irritably to her departing back. She found a seat on a faded and it had to be said lumpy chintz sofa. What was she thinking? She wasn't Lena, who'd practically had her knickers around her ankles the minute she had seen Teddy. So what on earth had she planned to do, let Vince shag her in a bloody cupboard! She didn't think that's what her parents had in mind when waving her off to "have some fun."

'God this incessant being nice is exhausting isn't it?' Delilah jumped as Mia sat down heavily beside her. 'I dare say the slavish fans can take any amount of it, I just find it a real load of bullshit actually, what do you reckon Lola?'

'What makes you think I'm not secretly one of those slavish fans?'

'Cos you look totally pissed off,' she leant against Delilah and smiled in a conspiratal way. 'I prefer Lou myself, there's something very sad and just a little dark about him.'

'Hmm what, oh...' Delilah hadn't realised that she'd had her eyes fixed on Vince from the moment he'd emerged from the costume room. 'Oh not dark, angelic. He seems to bring out my maternal side, I think he needs a good hug.'

'He doesn't bring out mine; I think I'd quite like to lose my virginity to him.'

'You what!'

'That got you huh? I really wasn't sure about this trip, but I decided to come because I thought it would be a good way of getting rid of it. It gets in the way of things when you meet a guy, I thought that I could come on this trip, have sex with one of the group and of course never have to see them again, plus it'll make a great story for the children later.' She tucked her legs under her on the sofa and rested her head on the back her eyes closed. 'A friend of mine lost hers with a boy at school that she thought loved her and told me it was awful, but then she had to face him again and put up with the horrible comments he made about her. It was years ago and I've had plenty of boyfriends since and things have got hot and steamy, but that always seems to come back to haunt me, so I thought how about someone famous, I mean just be slutty because it doesn't matter who they tell and then walk away and never see them again.'

'That's really cold Mia.'

'So your first time was all angels and earth trembling then?'

'No it was in a caravan and pretty crap.' Delilah laughed remembering. 'I think that could be a plan if you can handle the consequences, because there are always consequences.'

'Like being caught out in a cupboard...' She let the comment hang in the air between them. 'I don't think he cares much about consequences somehow, looks more than a little pissed off though.' She grinned, a strange contradiction to the gloomy make-up. 'I Think I'll make myself scarce, chat later.'

'So who was the bastard?' She looked up at Vince slightly uncomprehending, 'the one who gave you such a low opinion of yourself.' He sat down beside her on the spot, which Mia had just vacated 'There must have been one because all of a sudden you looked like someone who didn't deserve that kind of attention.'

'What did you want me to do, carry on and give them a show or tell them to fuck off?'

'Would have made it interesting'. he raised his eyebrows. 'I wouldn't have taken it too far you know. I can't say that musty old cloakrooms do it for me.' He shifted along the sofa until their bodies touched making her feel decidedly uncomfortable. 'I prefer the soft sand of a lonely beach in the moonlight or a candlelit feather bed with a bottle of champagne chilling by the bedside.' He turned to face her, that naughty smile back again and Delilah tried to keep a stern face, but she was struggling. 'Or a woodland clearing, sunlight streaming through the leaves' he leant closer and whispered in her ear. 'Or pretty much anywhere with you naked.'

'Pack it in' she hissed 'stop, are you always this incorrigible?'

'Then tell me who he was...?' His fingers running absently along the length of the bone as he slipped his arm around her shoulder. She shivered at his touch and glared at him.

'Will it shut you up?'
'Depends!'

'He was my fiancé I decided to surprise him one day and found him playing dogs with my best friend.' She turned seductively in his embrace. 'I threw a bucket of ice water over them, then I decked her and cooled his ardour with my knee. Happy?' Vince roared with laughter.

'You think that's funny?'

Tears streaming down his face Vince looked her in the eye 'lucky escape back there then.'

'Thanks'

Suddenly serious Vince pulled her sharply back to face him, lifted her chin with one guitar calloused fingertip, looked straight into her eyes and kissed her briefly, but intently. 'We Delilah Grace will carry this on at a later date...' He got up and still grinning started to walk away, he stopped briefly and turned back '...And next time we won't be interrupted.' Delilah felt a touch of cold at the back of her neck and when she looked up saw Tash and Jane staring at her in a very unfriendly manner.

Thankfully Lena choose this moment to start calling her troops to order and like a herd of elephants following the matriarch they all stumbled blindly after her. Some had been hitting the free drink with a vengeance and some like Lena had found other more interesting things to imbibe. Delilah and Mia linked arms and took up the rear again, the only two sober ones in the group. They didn't talk just walked along in peaceful friendly silence, but each one had their minds on something. Delilah was trying to work out where the whole Vince thing was going, she guessed that tomorrow there would be another girl and he'd have forgotten all about her. She wasn't sure that she would be OK with that...Not at all. Mia on the other hand was formulating a plan. For both of them.

Vince stood in the doorway watching as the group left, a pensive expression etched on his face. Louis ambled up beside him, followed his gaze and passed over a questionable glass of brandy. 'Interesting group, no?'

'Hmm you could say that' Vince replied laconically. He took a mouthful from the glass and wrinkled his nose in disgust. 'Jesus what the hell's this, it tastes like someone pissed in a bucket of meths.'

'I despair, you drink rough wine from plastic tubs taken straight from the barrel and yet you have two hundred pound bottles of brandy in your drinks cabinet at home. You are a philistine and a contradiction and after all these years it still surprises me, eh?'

'I prefer the term enigma, sounds more romantic.' He took a sniff of the dark amber liquid and shuddered, but had another swig anyway.

'Bet Lena didn't expect those two to turn up.' Louis gestured in the general direction of the group who missing two of their number had come to a halt and were waiting for Jane and Tash who ambled slowly after them.

'How out of it was she?' Vince never took his eyes off Delilah who stood at the rear nonchalantly chatting to Mia.

'Totally, every time I saw her she had a glass of something in her hand and I don't think it was water. She spent the entire evening following them round like an unwanted shadow to make sure she didn't miss anything.' He grinned and nudged his friend. 'So I see you discovered the delightful Delilah, we had a brief chat, quite delicious.'

'Do you ever miss anything?'

'No. She reminds me of Amelie, she has it all but doesn't seem to know it.' Louis chuckled.

'Oh I think Amelie knows exactly what she has, always did. Thankfully no, she's nothing like Amelie Lou.'

'So how did that little meeting happen, you've been missing half the night?'

'She got lost and fell into my arms, literally, then Roscoe had one of his photo sessions...'

'Oh God, not the dirty photos?'

He sighed 'I kissed her Lou and it was like someone put a match to a Molotov cocktail, I very nearly got a little too carried away. I can't even remember the last time a woman made me feel like that.'

'Other than Amelie?'

'Amelie was always yours my friend.' He shoved Lou playfully.

'Ah yes, such memories. Still delightful Delilah is quite the beauty, what man wouldn't want her?'

'Her ex fiancé it seems. Not treading on your toes am I?' He glanced at Louis.

'Not mine. I think you might have trouble with the two witches though, you could end up with a hex on your head, no!' He laughed 'On a more serious note you are going to have to be cruel and tell Tash to fuck off, it's the only thing she'll understand, stupid woman.'

'I might leave that till the end of the tour, I think a toad would have trouble with the guitar.'

'Would make a handsome addition to the band...' his laughter was infectious and Vince soon joined him.

'Am I missing something funny?' Teddy had walked over and standing between them stretched an arm over each of their shoulders. 'I thought I caught something about toads and guitars...'

'Private joke mate.' Vince said warmly 'Are we ready to make a move?' And as the door closed behind Delilah and the "rent a fan's" the three of them turned like the three musketeers and walked away.

~

FIVE

~

"I long to undress you, the way the autumn breeze blows the trembling leaves from the trees with a gentle breath. I long to awaken your bare skin like a raindrop softly caressing each naked branch. But you're not here and so I'll just lay on my cold lonely bed and lose myself in my fantasy..." Vincent's soft smoky voice delivered the words of "Lonely" whilst his eyes seemed to be fixed very firmly on Delilah.

'Couldn't be more blatant if he tried,' whispered Mia in her ear. 'I think he's pretty sure how he feels, but has he persuaded you yet?' Even in the darkness of the auditorium Delilah knew that her new friend had a wicked grin playing across that smart mouth of hers. Delilah though was unbelievably tired after the long journey up to Amsterdam and she longed for her bed. Sleep had been a stranger the previous night as her mind replayed the incident in the costume room, each time with different endings, each time with her body wracked with unsated desire. Then when eventually her mind switched off and she had begun to slip into blissful nothingness, Lena had started to snore. She'd dozed briefly on the bus before arriving at the third rate hotel Lena had booked and once there had barely found time to shower, change and grab something in a nearby café. Now she just wanted to stop.

Lena gathered them behind her for the backstage visit and Delilah was aware that she wasn't the only tired one as she knew one or two of the others had been partying long into the previous night. The backstage area was packed and yet again she struggled to locate Vince, but he'd seen her and made a bee line through the crowd.

'You look exhausted, what were you up to last night?'

'We didn't have the luxury of a quick flight', she said tartly 'and I didn't sleep well.'

'Thinking of me!' He said with a chuckle.

'Lena snores.' She said with what she hoped was a poker straight face as she followed Vince through the horde to a padded bench under one of the beautiful old windows. She yawned 'Kick me if I start to doze, I'm not normally this dopey.'

'And there was I planning a night of passion...' He rolled his eyes.

'Found a suitable broom cupboard.' She said with a lazy smile. 'Or perhaps a windmill full of mice with clogs on as we're here in old Amsterdam?' She struggled against her heavy eyes. Vince was warm, his arm was around her shoulders holding her close and he was absently toying with a strand of her chestnut hair. 'I think a girl would feel safe curled up next to you in bed.'

'Hmm, "safe" that's what I was going for.' He replied a mock hurt expression on his face. 'Where are you staying, walking distance?'

'Well we're the other side of the Rossebuurt and it didn't seem too far on the way here. Why?'

'Thought I might walk you home, get some fresh air unless you wanted to stay here and sleep through the party, if you could call this a party. What do you think Delilah Grace?'

'I think I will take you up on that offer kind sir, I was debating heading back now anyway.'

'On your own, through the red light district, over my dead body.' He stood pulling her to her feet 'Do you need to tell someone that you're leaving before we skulk away.'

'I don't need to.' She said waving at Mia who was watching from the other side of the room and gaining a thumbs up in return. 'Mia knows.' He cast a casual eye across to her little Goth friend.

Nobody paid them any attention as they walked out the stage door into the sultry night air. The cool air blew away her previous drowsiness and she took in a couple of good lungful's as they walked along in an easy silence in the general direction of her hotel. She had made a very careful note of the route on the way here, getting lost she decided remembering the previous evening, got you into all sorts of hot water. It was Vince who broke the spell as they wandered past a lively café where a bohemian looking chap was playing folk songs.

'Fancy a coffee?'

'Why not, this guy sounds good, not that I understand Dutch.' They found a couple of chairs on the edge of the narrow cobbled street and ordered a couple of very aromatic cups of coffee. They sat for a while listening to the music before Vince broke the easy silence.

'Delilah's an unusual name, do you ever shorten it.'

'That's pretty much what Mia asked. I think people find it a bit of a mouthful but I like it. My dad wanted to call me Lola and that's the only short form I accept. And you "Van-cent"' she copied Lou's French pronunciation 'Just Vince...?'

'Vinnie to my friends. That makes us Vinnie and Lola, cute, what do you reckon?'

'Sounds like it came straight out of a 50's American sit-com.' She chuckled.

'So what made you choose this trip? You don't strike me as being as devoted as some of your lot and there have to be more reliable people to travel with than Lena, bless her. She's a bit of a nutter, always reminds me of a loopy springer spaniel I had as a boy.'

'That's probably a good analogy, big sad eyes, not a nasty bone in her and endless energy with no off switch. As for me I've been packed off by my parents to have a summer of fun, they think I'm a workaholic.' She sighed for dramatic effect and clutching her coffee cup in both hands took a sip.

'Are you?'

'A workaholic, no I don't think so. I've worked since I was in my early teens, we're not rich and I've always had to work for what I want. I ride a couple of times a week, it's not a cheap hobby and I like the theatre, that's not cheap either. My parents have had a rough time of it until recently so I've paid my way. I moved out when I was twenty, put a deposit down on a little garret flat that you couldn't swing a cat in and loved the independence.' She shrugged, 'then mum had an accident at work. She was invalided out of her job and eventually got compensation, but in the meantime I sold my flat and moved home so I could help with the finances. I guess I got a bit carried away as at one time I was working two jobs, it wasn't intentional. So anyhow Lena wrote to me out of the blue about this trip and I couldn't make up my mind, so I put it to one side.

We met at Dingwalls when we were sixteen and hit it off.' She smiled softly at the memory. 'For a few years we were close, but people change and I just couldn't cope with her obsession with celebrity.'

'Teddy?'

'Teddy, I told her that he was using her but she wouldn't have it, she reminded me of a child having a tantrum. So we went our separate ways. Anyway my parents thought this would be the perfect way to start the summer and so here I am, unloved and unemployed as I've just taken redundancy.' She pulled a sad face 'So I'm here for Scarecrow, but I remember a massive fall out first time around so what made you decide to get back with the group?'

'Hmm, changing the subject are we?'

'I'm really boring...and?'

'I was bored, simple as that. I don't like the whole celebrity thing, but I like gigging. We have some very loyal fans and every few weeks I seemed to come across someone who wanted to know when we were reuniting. Then Teddy suggested it, Lou wasn't keen and I wasn't entirely sure it was a good idea. Like you and Lena we've changed. Seb and I still just about tolerate each other in small doses. He wanted to be back in the limelight, be surrounded by plenty of women. I did all that first time around, the booze, the girls. This time it's all about the music, I don't need the rest.' He leant across the table in a conspiratal fashion. 'So when did the infamous "dog" incident occur?' He'd put full accent on the word "dog". She glanced across at him and there was just the smallest hint of a smile pulling at the edge of his mouth. 'Of course if it's none of my business...'

'About six months ago. To be honest I'm still feeling embarrassed about it all.' She grinned sheepishly at him. 'I was relieved, isn't that awful? I was planning on ending it when he went and proposed, I didn't love him. I loved the old cottage he was renovating and I must have got confused.' She chuckled at the thought. 'Then everything got a bit out of control. I wanted to turn him down, but everyone kept pushing me and in the end I didn't know what the hell I felt.' She shuddered at her own stupidity and Vince reached over and took her hand in his.

'And all the time he was screwing your best friend?'

'So it seems. Why on earth didn't I just tell him to fuck off, I'd done it once before and then took him back. So it was an embarrassment, a huge dent to my pathetically fragile ego.' He lifted her hand to his lips and planted a gentle kiss on her palm. 'Losing my best friend was a bit crap, but her betrayal finally laid bare a truth I'd refused to see and that made me even more of a fool and I really don't like looking stupid.' She sighed as even now it still annoyed her to talk about it. She thought about telling him the wedding story, but decided that might be an admission too far.

'Well I reckon I've got you beat' he said morosely. 'I've been on my own probably about the same as you. Her name was Julie, we'd been together for several years despite there being no spark and virtually no passion between us. But she was pretty, clever and she gave me some sort of stability in my life, which I desperately needed at the time. Deep down though I knew it was going nowhere. One day she suggested we move in together and I agreed, even though just like you I was trying to work out how to end it without bloodshed and tears. You'd think at thirty I'd have gained some semblance of common sense.' He glanced sideways at her and she smiled back in understanding. 'She'd started talking about the future, marriage and children so when Teddy suggested putting the group back together.'

'You jumped ship.'

'Not until the whole fall out over bloody Tash and Jane, Lou said he'd told you about that. Tash was her friend so my name was mud, though if she'd known what had happened a few months earlier she'd have felt a bit different. Still it festered for quite a while and just before the UK tour started it just blew, we had a massive row and she thought I had been in her words "a total shit and that I should leave". I took that as my cue and walked. She tried to tell me that she hadn't meant me to actually leave, but...It was the excuse I needed and I never looked back.'

'We're a right pair then, doomed if we did, doomed if we didn't. But what happened earlier with Tash?'

'Must I?'

'You brought it up and you can't mention something like that and just leave it hanging...' He sighed and rolled his eyes dramatically, 'I'm a flirt Delilah, you may have noticed...'

'Nope can't say that I have.' She flashed him her best coy smile.

'Roscoe took her on originally as a temp in his office, she's apparently very efficient at what she does.'

'So is a vulture.'

'Play nice or I shan't tell you. Anyway he asked Tash to take on the fan cub when Carol went off and married a farmer. We had to deal with her from time to time, more so when we were in talks about getting back together. I felt sorry for her, so I flirted and she obviously took it to heart. There was a party at Roscoe's and we were all a little pissed. She made a very clumsy pass and...'

'You laughed, oh God you laughed didn't you?'

'I laughed. I didn't realise how much I'd hurt her till Teddy pointed it out, so I apologised. But I made a mistake, instead of telling her I was flattered, but not interested, I bottled. I told her that I would never be unfaithful to Julie and then I split with Julie...'

'And now she fancies her chances again.' She gave an involuntary yawn and Vince stood and pulled her to her feet.

'Come on sleepy head time for bed.' He dropped an affectionate arm around her shoulder and they walked off along the cobbles. She marvelled at the faded facades of the old houses, which all seemed to be leaning at a peculiar angle and their reflections in the rosy glow across the dark water of the canal beside them. The place was buzzing and there were people of all nationalities bustling along, camera's flashing taking in the atmosphere of this ancient part of the Dutch capital. The gaudily decked windows with their legal prostitutes showing off their wares to potential buyers were a particular fascination to her. She looked sadly at an older cheaply dressed woman sitting in her shop window, her face impassive as she stared out at the passers-by. Delilah gave her what she hoped was a sisterly smile and was rewarded with a lovely smile in return, what a beauty she must have been in her youth she thought. Her feelings were impartial it wasn't her place to judge another's choices and idly she wondered what had brought her here to this life. Vince seeing her lost in thought turned to face her and she couldn't resist asking. 'You going to take Tash up on it?'

He pushed her hair back from her face and traced a gentle fingertip down her cheek until he was able to tilt her chin up and plant the softest kiss on her waiting mouth. 'I have other much more interesting pursuits in mind.' He kissed her again, the barest whisper of a caress. 'A woman who has no idea just how incredibly beautiful she is, who is kind to Lena, has survived betrayal and who smiles kindly at a sad whore in a window in Amsterdam. And who...' His mouth was just inches from hers, cinnamon eyes fixed on Sapphire 'I'm going to take back to her hotel and kiss goodnight because she needs some sleep.' Pulling her to him he kissed her again and Delilah lost herself in his warmth, returning his kisses like for like until the ghosts of the past and present disappeared. Eventually it was a group of young lads out on the pull that brought an end to it, their whoops and whistles pouring cold water on their fast brewing passion. 'Saved by the mob, come on Lola, time for bed.' Hmm, she thought bed was pretty much where her mind had been drifting to. But she could wait.

Her hotel had seen better days, like so many of the other properties in this quarter it lurched slightly to one side huddling close to the house next door. The shutters on the windows were much in need of a fresh coat of paint and one of the panes of glass in the door was boarded. An elderly doorman in a faded uniform cast a lonely figure at the entrance.

'Wow, Lena went out on a limb for this one.'

'It's not so bad, it has a kind of old school elegance to it. I've stayed in worse, at least here you don't lay in bed counting the cockroaches as they run over the walls.' She shuddered, 'I hate cockroaches.'

'I suppose you shouldn't judge a book by its cover.'

'No I suppose you shouldn't...'

'I'm an open book.' He said catching her train of thought. 'If I was playing games you'd know it.' Delilah yawned, suddenly feeling very weary. 'Well, Lola I think it's time to say goodnight.' With that he pulled her close and kissed her gently, but she could see something more in his eyes and she hoped the same was reflected in hers. 'I'll see you tomorrow?' He held her hands loosely in his.

'Until tomorrow, night Vinnie'

'Sweet dreams Lola.' And as her hand slipped away from his he turned and walked away. A few yards on he turned his head briefly then hands in his pockets he sauntered back the way he had come.

Walking into the Scarecrow party back at the hotel Vince wished that he'd been a bit more vigilant as he'd walked in through the foyer. He had still been preoccupied with thoughts of Delilah and hadn't spotted the ambush until it was too late and now he was in a room full of strangers where he was expected to circulate and make polite small talk. A woman appeared silently at his side and offered him a brandy glass. 'I'm assuming it's still your poison?' Vince looked at her blankly, she was vaguely familiar but he couldn't place her. She was handsome rather than pretty and a pair of fierce hazel eyes peered at him out of a slightly masculine face framed with nut brown hair.

'Hi Nicki.' That was it, their original drummer Hilly had met her at a party in Dublin in Scarecrow's early heady days and the pair had been inseparable, he though hadn't seen her since Hilly's problems. 'What brings you here of all places?'

'Lena. She called me a few months ago and said she was putting this "adventure" together. She wondered if I was interested. To be honest with you I said no to start with, but then Rob said his cousin Jane, that's her over there wanted to go and he thought it would be a laugh.' She stared quite meaningfully in Jane's direction and said, 'I have to admit the words laugh and Jane don't go together, she's a miserable crab.'

'You don't like her much either then?'

'Hell no, she's a poisonous bitch and you'd be less likely to get stung in a pit full of scorpions. She and Tash have it in for Delilah, you know?' She added archly. Vince cast her a quick sideways glance. 'I'm not blind, you've obviously got her caught up in your web. A word of warning though Vince, don't let her become another Lena.'

'What?'

'Don't play the innocent, you know what I'm talking about. The rest of you stood back and watched as Teddy took that naïve little mouse and teased and toyed with her like a cat till her head was thoroughly messed up. Then when he was bored she was just dumped out the back door like a piece of garbage.'

'She...'

'Don't go blaming her, what was she Vince seventeen, eighteen. She was a baby, overawed because her idol wanted to screw her. Teddy intoxicated her, even now she can't see past him although he barely notices her.' She pointed at Neil who was watching every move Lena made whilst knocking back a large glass of something alcoholic. 'She doesn't appreciate Neil and yet anyone can see that he's besotted with her. And you see the little round dumpy girl ...' She pointed out Fran, who was staring morosely at Neil. 'That's Lena's best friend whose bloody name I can't remember, who has to sit idly by and watch as Lena ignores the man that she herself is in love with but who will never notice her.'

'Bloody hell that's complex, but what's that got to do with Delilah, she's not Lena?'

'No perhaps not, but she's just a nice ordinary girl and I'd hate to see her treated the way you lot normally treat your women.'

'What kind of monster do you think I am? I'm not Teddy, ok so I was no saint back then, but that was a long time ago. That's not who I am anymore.'

'Well, I'm just saying that's all.' With a last wistful shrug, she disappeared into the mass of gyrating bodies moving to the techno beat that the DJ was playing.

Vince watched her go with a pensive expression etched on his handsome features. He remembered that she'd always been a bit judgemental, but she probably had a point. Teddy had treated Lena inexcusably and the rest of them had just stood back and watched as the little wallflower with the mousy hair and glasses had turned into a crazed groupie. Poor Lena, she had started making all sorts of possessive noises about Teddy and hoping to get back with his ex he'd distanced himself before dumping her unceremoniously. The trouble was that even after all that had happened, Teddy had still been only too happy to oblige whenever he saw her, which was frequently as she had stalked him mercilessly for a while. He rubbed the irritating stubble on his chin and his thoughts turned to Delilah. He'd lied to her about Tash.

That party when they'd all overindulged, well he'd not laughed at Tash when she'd offered herself, she'd been different back then, no plastic, nothing fake, pretty even and after a bit of drunken smooching he'd briefly considered it. The following morning when he'd sobered up he'd tried to put her off kindly, but it had backfired big time and all he'd ended up doing was giving her the impression that she was in with some sort of chance. Nicki was right, he couldn't let Delilah get hurt and so with mindful resolve he walked over to Tash, he'd have to take her aside and tell her a few home truths…

Delilah woke the following morning with a gremlin pounding her on the head with a sledge hammer and the universe putting on a vivid lightshow behind her eyes. It had been quite a while since her last migraine, but even so she wasn't surprised by this one. She could hear Lena crashing about in the bathroom and wondered not for the first time if the girl was ever quiet. Ignoring her pounding head, she struggled out of bed and groped around in her handbag for a couple of painkillers swilling them down with the last of her bottle of water. It would be a good hour before they kicked in so she lay back against the pillows and tried to ease it with some yoga deep breathing whilst working the tops of her fingers in what she hoped was useful reflexology.

She hadn't slept well again last night and despite defending the hotel to Vince she had soon found out that the walls and floors were paper thin. Someone in the room above had spent a good hour bonking judging by the constant banging of the headboard against the wall, perhaps her head had come out in sympathy. She could have kept a record of all the comings and goings in the hotel as she'd pretty much heard all of them, even the ones she guessed who were trying to be quiet. And then about two o'clock Lena had swept back into the room and had collapsed noisily on the bed with a deliberately loud sigh.

Delilah desperate for sleep had grouched angrily at her and had been rewarded with tears, which in turn had made her feel unnecessarily guilty. Apparently as they had all been expected to find their own way back to the hotel their group had split up and Lena's troops had been the deserters. She'd bellyached that Mia, Tom and Sarah had gone off to explore the city's nightlife and God knows where Delilah had gone, but she'd been left alone with "the others". Delilah knew that Fran and Neil wouldn't have left her so that probably wasn't completely true.

She had then started wittering on that they'd all gone back to the Scarecrow's hotel for a party and that "bloody Jane and Tash" were lording it over everyone, "like they were the queen bees." Having finished her tirade, she'd stumbled more than a little worse for wear into the bathroom and after throwing up noisily had muttered "and of course they then buggered off with Teddy and Vince, fucking whores." Obviously feeling better for emptying her stomach she'd then got into bed and within minutes had been snoring, blissfully unaware of the torment she'd caused.

Delilah rubbed at her still throbbing temple and remembered lying here last night with sleep once more being a stranger and her mind running around in ever more confused circles. She looked up at the yellowed ceiling of the room and wondered why she felt so depressed about that one simple statement. After all what exactly had "Vinnie and Lola" got going on? They weren't in a relationship, were they? They'd shared a few passionate kisses, so what, she thought. Small town girls like Delilah went out with guys like Tony or jerks like Nick, they didn't get romantically caught up with rock stars.

It was their lot in life if that sort of thing happened at all, to be the groupies, the meaningless quick thrill among many, so why was she so bothered? He'd told her that he'd turned Tash down, but of course he could have been lying through his teeth and why would she be surprised at that. Why else would Tash still be desperately clinging to ideas of Vince's affections, if nothing happened between them? Delilah closed her eyes and her inner demon reminded her that she hadn't exactly been a raging success when picking men in the past, so why should this be different.

Having finally felt able to get dressed she couldn't make her mind up whether breakfast was a good idea or not, her stomach was rumbling suggesting that she was hungry, but her spinning head was making her feel nauseous. Despite her misgivings she followed Lena down to the tatty dining room where a Spartan continental breakfast buffet was laid out. She'd made the effort and put some cold meat, cheese and a bread roll that probably could have broken a window on her plate. She'd also helped herself to a small bowl of dried fruit compote, which smelt surprisingly good and a cup of what passed for tea in the hotel. She'd sat down with Mia, Tom, Carrie and Sarah and the other three despite obvious hangovers were all watching her with what appeared to be concern, did she look that bad? She made a quiet effort to ignore them and had just asked about their night out around the bars and clubs when the witch and her flying monkey sidekick appeared by their table.

'Last night was amazing you lot don't know what you missed.' Jane said a smug smile on her thin lips. 'It was a really great party and then things got really interesting...' She looked straight at Delilah. 'Vince wanted a word with Tash and well, you know what we're talking about, don't you!'

'It came completely out of the blue, he's amazing.' Tash gushed, although her moon face was flushed red betraying what, a lie?

'I thought he hated your guts.' Mia pointed out her voice dripping with venom.

'Oh that was just a misunderstanding.'

Delilah decided that the ugly sneer on Tash's face was almost an improvement on the frightened deer look. 'Why don't you both fuck off because nobody cares who got inside your pants. Least of all me.' And with what she hoped looked like nonchalance she carried on eating her breakfast. That was when she made the snap decision, it was a sudden thought that as soon as it came into her head, mindlessly flew out of her mouth. 'Guys I'm not coming with you today, I've got a migraine and I feel like shit. I don't think I could cope with another two hundred odd miles in that noisy minibus.'

'Do you need a doctor, are you going to stay here?' Mia her heart shaped face scrubbed clean of the usual dreary makeup put a warm hand, fingers still sticky with jam on her forehead.

'No, I haven't slept properly since we started out. I don't like all this travelling and I get travel sick on buses so I've been taking stuff to counteract it, which just makes me even more drained. I'll be fine, although I'm certainly not staying here.' That's too much self-pity Delilah she thought 'I just need to catch up with myself, you know regroup.'

'Oh God that was my fault last night wasn't it, going on and on. I'm so sorry I'm a really shit friend aren't I?' She hadn't noticed Lena standing behind her and now her pretty face was etched with whatever was the nearest to concern that she could muster. 'You must have been so upset at missing the party.'

'You were pissed Lena, its ok.' And missing the party was not what caused me grief she thought.

'What will you do then?' Her dark eyes glittered in the harsh light.

'Simple, I'll go ahead, see if I can get a flight to Geneva and try and get a room at the hotel we'll be staying in and I'll meet you all there.' That gave her three days without distractions to decide whether she went on or went home and in her current irrational state of mind home was winning hands down.

'But you'll miss Germany and you wanted to see Germany didn't you? Oh Delilah you will let me know won't you, I shall worry terribly.' She gripped Delilah in a bear hug, which really didn't help matters.

'It's ok Lena, I'll sort things out.' Mia said confidently rolling her eyes at Lena's theatrics 'and don't look at me like that, I'm not an idiot. I can sort a few simple things out for a friend. Leave it to me Lola.' And with a petulant shrug and the briefest kiss on Delilah's cheek Lena was gone leaving her with the feeling that she was relieved to have passed the buck. 'Come on, you can give me your credit card and I'll go and talk to the concierge he seems really nice.' Delilah with some amusement let Mia lead her away as if she was a small child, it was nice to feel that someone cared. As they walked away Delilah told her how sweet Vince had been the previous night and what he'd told her about Tash and then she recounted Lena's bellyaching and how she'd felt. Mia listened making all the right noises, but decided that she would have to have serious words with Vincent Angel when she next saw him.

~

SIX
~

Goose bumps popped up across Delilah's exposed skin as a cool breeze wafted through the open doors, she glanced at the clock above the bar and it was showing quarter to nine. Picking up her cocktail from the small table she slipped through the curtain, and out on to the lakeside terrace. The day had been too hot and the early evening sultry so she took pleasure in taking in a lungful of the freshening air. The panoramic view from the hotel over Lake Geneva towards the mountains was spectacular and after the solitude of the last couple of days she could see why so many people felt the Alps calling them back.

Drinking in the scenery she could hear the storm that had been forecast for tonight rumbling around the mountains and moving ever closer. A sudden fork of lightning briefly illuminated a small boat on the far side of the lake and the accompanying thunder clap made her jump, even though she knew it was coming. Twitchy Delilah, she thought and taking another sip of her cosmopolitan wondered with a certain amount of trepidation whether the other storm predicted for tonight would materialise.

Mia had been as good as her word on their last morning together in Holland. Having strolled off with Delilah's credit card, she had not only managed to book a flight to Geneva, but had managed to get Delilah her lovely hotel room for an excellent price. After a long conversation with the hotel concierge she'd also arranged for an appointment with a local doctor just to be sure that nothing more serious was going on. Mia surprised her in so many ways, naïve, but knowledgeable, ditsy, but organised and she in the space of just a few days had come to like her very much. Delilah having hugged her new friend in thanks had waved Team Lena off in the mini bus with promises of updates.

She'd seen the very pleasant female doctor who had confirmed both her own diagnosis and the reasoning behind it and had prescribed some extremely effective pain killers that Delilah had never heard of. After sleeping through a short flight and a nice meal in the hotel restaurant she had slipped between the crisp cotton covers on the feathery soft bed in her pleasant room and closed her eyes. She had woken up feeling ready for anything after the best night's sleep that she'd had in months. The migraine had simply melted away along with the stress.

The first day here she had just chilled out on a sunbed by the pool and relaxed, topping up her tan until she looked like a bronzed goddess. Mia had rung late in the afternoon. The Hamburg concert the night before had been good, the band had been supported by a local group who she had raved about, apparently they were one of Vince's finds and Mia reckoned could be the next big thing. They had all gone backstage making the most of it as they wouldn't be allowed at the Berlin show. Jane and Tash continued to be thorns in everyone's backside, especially Lena's.

But 'I talked to Vince' she'd said. 'I explained the Tash business and he blew his top, a bit fiery that one is Lola,' she'd chuckled. 'He gave me a message for you, said you'd understand.' She'd sounded bemused 'he told me "I'm not some randy old dog that would jump the first bitch in heat just because she's there wagging her tail and barking." I assume you know what he's talking about, sounds like a line from a bad spy movie.' Delilah had laughed until her sides had hurt and she'd told Mia all about it and she'd laughed too saying 'wait till I see Tash I shall give her my very best "I know something you don't" smile'.

Then had come the second call, from Vince this time still smarting from Mia's revelation. He'd been worried about her, was she ok, could he do anything, did she need a doctor as he knew one in Geneva? She'd told him she was fine, she'd been tired and just a little stressed. The conversation had been otherwise indifferent, she'd told him about the hotel, he'd told her about the previous night's concert, but the elephant sitting on the phone line between them had kept to itself. That is until the end when unable to stop himself told her he was going to, "sort a few things out". She'd told him to leave it, she didn't care "let the others think what they like and leave Tash with her delusions".

His soft smile could be heard in his next comment "you're a much nicer person than me Lola". I'm not, she'd thought remembering all the unpleasant ways she'd come up with to avenge herself. Then he'd told her he had decided to forget the German wrap party after the TV show they were filming in Frankfurt and had managed to secure a ride in a friend's plane. He would be with her tomorrow and would meet her in the hotel bar at nine o'clock. There had been no time to argue as the line was dead and the decision made.

Five to nine and the storm was inching closer. She took a deep breath to quell the unwelcome butterflies in her stomach and finished her cocktail, probably a little quickly judging by the resulting brain freeze.

'Hi Lola.' She felt his arms warm around her waist and the softest kiss on the nape of her neck. Where had he snuck up from, quiet as a stalking cat?

'Hi Vinnie.' She smiled as she turned to face him, 'I still wasn't entirely sure that you'd be here, I wondered if the weather...?'

'It was still far enough away not to be a problem and I was always going to show...' She leant against him indulging in the warmth of his arms, his mouth planting soft kisses across her forehead. 'Come on I'll buy you a drink, the storms closing in fast they say it's going to be a violent one.'

'I don't like storms, especially at night, always get a bit jittery by myself.' Stupid comment she realised seeing the sudden intensity in his eyes as he misread her comment.

'See if we can't change that', he offered naughtily. Taking her hand in his he led her inside just as another clap of thunder rattled the doors and the sky outside continued its unparalleled light show across the lake. Delilah clutched his hand tightly, her eyes a little wild and realised she may have just sent out entirely the wrong signal as they were now walking out of the bar and there was no doubt in her mind where they were going or what was about to happen. They had to wait for the lifts and Vince never once let go of her hand, his eyes fixed on the arrow moving excruciatingly slowly down through the floors. The rising tension between them was intoxicating and she could hear the blood that was rushing through her veins echoing in her ears. The sudden loud ping that signalled the arrival of the lift made her jump, so intently had she been following its progress.

They walked casually into the lift and he pressed the button for his floor. Delilah could hear him trying to keep his breathing even as the doors swished shut. She was pulled into his arms before it began moving, his hands pressed into her back below her shoulders and his mouth against hers making all sorts of promises of what was to come. The doors opened on the fifth floor and both slightly breathless they stumbled out and along the deserted corridor. His hand was shaking as he tried to get the key card in the lock and Delilah was raining little kisses along his neck, which probably didn't help. Eventually he got the door unlocked and turning to her with a triumphant smile practically dragged her inside.

With her back in his arms he back heeled the door shut. Their kisses intensifying Vince roughly pushed her back against the wall, probably harder than he intended and she knew there would be bruises tomorrow, not that she was bothered. Her hands were pressed against his chest and she took advantage to clumsily undo the buttons of his shirt before throwing it on the floor behind him. She had guessed from the very first time that he had held her that he kept himself fit, but now the evidence a well-defined chest tanned by hours in the sun was there and in reach of her fingers. She sighed as his mouth moved down her throat and across her collarbone sending shivers of delight to her brain and in some dark corner came the realisation that she'd chosen to meet him tonight half naked. It had been so hot that she'd chosen a simple strappy summer dress without a bra and only a pair of pretty knickers to make it decent.

She groaned at what he must be thinking or it may just have been that he'd found a sweet spot, either way she was so lost in the moment that she really didn't care. Vince slipped the dress's simple straps from her shoulders and with a little wiggle she let it slip easily to the floor. He sighed with pleasure as he cupped her revealed breasts in his hands and swept his lips in whisper soft kisses down to her exposed nipples. With unsteady hands she got his belt and trousers undone and he kicked the very expensive Italian trousers off into a wrinkled heap. Effortlessly he scooped her up and they lurched across the room her legs wrapped around his waist, before they fell laughing breathlessly onto the bed. There was little need for foreplay as the waiting had driven both of them to a frantic need for release. At some point during the process with clumsy hands they'd managed to remove any last barrier to their desire and clutching desperately to each other lost themselves in their own furious tempest.

Outside Vince's open window the storm raged as violently as the one within, steaks of blue gold lit up the night sky and it was as if Thor himself was dictating the rhythm of their lust as the thunder crashed its passionate reply to the lightning bolts. It was car crash sex, need, want, have at its most extreme. Once was never going to be enough to kill the need and neither was disappointed, so it was well past midnight long after the storm outside had abated when their tired bodies drenched in sweat finally drifted into a contented sleep wrapped possessively in each other's arms.

Delilah woke just before dawn, Vince was laying on his front a casual arm laying across her and his slow and even breathing told her he was sleeping contentedly. She extradited herself from his arm and slipped out of bed. The floor of the room was littered with discarded clothes and forcing her eyes to adjust to the lack of light she found what little she'd been wearing the evening before and dressed quickly. She retrieved her bag from where it had been thrown and opened the door as quietly as possible.

'You know that you don't have to go ...' Vince was propped up on one elbow watching her.

'Perhaps another night?' Please she thought, please don't turn that offer down.

'Breakfast, about nine on the terrace?' He lay back on the pillow 'ok?'

'Ok.' She replied softly as she shut the door. Tiptoeing around the corridors she found her own room with its soft bed and cool cotton sheets and with her body sated from the night's passion she drifted peacefully back into a dreamless sleep.

Ravenously hungry the next morning she showered, dressed and worked her way down to the pretty terrace outside the restaurant. The Storm had long gone and the warmth from the early morning June sunshine had already dried the ground. Vince had taken a table at the far side overlooking the lake and he waved when he saw her. With a certain amount of bravado, she walked over to join him, but she needn't have worried as he rose and greeted her with a kiss.

'The bed was cold this morning...'
'It was the right thing to do.'

'Hmm, I'd dispute that, but then I'm just being selfish.' He raised an eyebrow, amusement twinkling in his eyes. 'I think we should move you in with me.'

'That's very presumptuous Mr Angel, what if I don't want to share a room with you?'

'Would you rather put up with Lena's snoring?'

'Touché.'

'Thought that would sway you.' He laughed leaning over with his hand on hers. 'Seriously Lola it does seem a bit silly to keep two rooms on the go when we're both sharing a bed, anyway what kind is Lena going to sort out, a stuffy little back room overlooking the bins? Why have that when you can stay in a little bit of luxury with me, please...' He gave her his best imploring look.

'I may have been going to keep the room I had with its lovely view of the car park. Ok, why not. But if it all goes tits up...' She left the comment hanging there. 'I'm not travelling with you though, that's the deal. We can start tonight if you like as I was giving up my room and going back to Lena's snoring.' He nodded and gave her a huge smile in return. 'It's agreed then, are we eating only I'm starving.' The breakfast at the hotel was excellent and over the last few days she had taken to having their creamy scrambled eggs followed by a plate of fruit all washed down with some of the nicest coffee she'd ever tasted. They ate in companionable silence other than the occasional comment about what they were eating or the views across the lake.

Vince had a busy day ahead of him, the rest of the group would be arriving mid-morning and after lunch they'd be busy getting ready for the show that evening, which was also going to be broadcast live on Swiss TV. He himself had various meetings planned and Delilah half guessed that he'd been planning to arrive early anyway and that she'd just been the cherry on top of the iced bun. Still not entirely convinced it was a good idea she'd moved her things into his room, was it far too early to do it or should she just take the chance whilst it was offered. She didn't know, so having done a lot of the sightseeing bits over the last couple of days she allowed herself the luxury of going to do some shopping before Lena and the rabble came to take her mind off her hastily made decision.

She was there waiting with a smile when the minibus pulled up and got an enthusiastic greeting from Lena and Mia. Lena's smile had faltered slightly when Delilah asked to share with Mia, but it seemed that Fran had been keeping her company while she'd been gone anyhow. Mia catching on quickly had chipped in with her agreement and so Lena had shrugged her shoulders and agreed. A little later the two of them were sitting in the small but comfortable twin bedded room that overlooked the road, pretty much as Vince had suggested, but without the bins.

'So would you like to explain where your things are?' Mia said a mock serious expression on her face.

'Vinnie's room. I thought you wouldn't mind the peace and it would prevent too many questions about what I was up to. You don't mind, do you?' Delilah asked hopefully.

'Course I don't mind silly. Anyhow I'm rather hoping I shan't be here by myself either.' She flashed Delilah a naughty grin 'I've been sleeping in Lou's bed the last couple of nights. I told you I'd get my own way in the end.'

'Groupie!'

'Whore!' Delilah struggled to keep a straight face before both girls collapsed on one of the beds in a fit of uncontrollable giggles. 'You wouldn't believe what else you've been missing tucked away here in your Swiss solitude.' Mia said raising her eyebrows in a conspiratal fashion. 'Little red faced Sarah and her mate Carrie have been involved in a threesome with Seb, can you believe it? Lou reckons he's trying to work his way through the whole bus and there's only you and me left so we'd better be on our guard.'

'When I spoke to Lou in Brussels he called Seb a dog and told me to stay well clear...' She stood up her eyes wide, 'even Lena?'

'Oh Lena's been there on several occasions, Jane, Tash, Nicki and even bloody Fran.' She chortled loudly. 'He doesn't like me though so I think I'm reasonably off his radar, you on the other hand are an elusive creature...'

'Now why would I want him when I've got Van-cent, I can do this all night long?' She purred in a breathy French accent. 'So tell me, have you finally laid the ghost of your virginity to rest, given it a good send off, wished it well in its journey into obscurity?'

'You mean was it all angels and stuff or did Lou fuck my brains out...?'

'Crude darling, crude...Did he?'

'Let's just say it was well worth the wait. Oh don't get me wrong though, that's all it is. I'm under no illusions Lola, none at all. It's just sex and there has been no mention of it carrying on here so I may well be by myself tonight. Now you and Vince, what's that all about? I mean, what are you groupie or girlfriend?'

'I haven't the faintest, I don't really think it's either, but I'm going to enjoy every minute and if or when it ends I'll at least have drowned in pleasure for a little while. Does that make any sense?'

'Just be careful, do you remember what you told me, there are always consequences!'

'I think I can live with them if last night was anything to go by...'

She was back in the expansive room she was sharing with Vince a couple of hours before the show. There was no sign of him, but there was a quickly scribbled note on the bed, which read *"Cut it a bit fine so have to run. Will find you after gig and we'll go grab a late supper, grab some room service if you're peckish. Xx"* Well I won't worry too much about food, she thought, but then she remembered the little cheese tart she'd picked up this morning while shopping, which still sat in its pretty paper bag beside her handbag. The creamy, aromatic filling inside the thin crispy pastry was delicious so she wolfed that down with pleasure, it would fill a hole until later.

She took her time getting ready, choosing a perfectly fitting pair of jeans and a loose silky floral blouse, casual but pretty was what she hoped she'd achieved. She met Mia at the room they should have been sharing and they made their way down to the lobby to meet the others. Lena was busy handing out tickets and explaining that after the show they'd meet in the bar before she took them off backstage.

Mostly everybody seemed to talk over her and she quickly gave up, muttering oaths under her breath as she led the way out to the minibus.

The show was nothing short of brilliant, the boys were on fine form and threw themselves into everything with gusto. Teddy had the boundless energy of the Duracell bunny whilst retaining his suave and carefully pretentious appearance and his voice purred and soared in totally perfect pitch. Vince prowled around the stage with the swagger of a big cat working his way effortlessly between lead and bass guitar. His soft smoky vocals at times tantalising and provocative and at others haunting, tormented, tearing at the heartstrings. Louis as always looked like he was on another plane of existence as his fingers danced across the keyboards, an ethereal smile set on his beautiful face.

Seb, well Seb looked to all the world like a human version of Animal the drummer in the Muppets band, basically just nuts and Delilah half wondered how his head didn't drop off the way it bounced around on his shoulders. The crowd had been on their feet dancing and had sang along with all the old favourites. The new tracks had been greeted with rapturous adoration, Scarecrow had rarely put a foot wrong in their music over the years. Delilah feeling shattered having been swept along with the flock singing and dancing, felt like she'd been up on stage herself.

Before they wandered down to the backstage area afterwards she had dived into the nearest ladies. She'd felt the need to check that she hadn't got too sweaty and surreptitiously had a quick sniff inside her blouse, nope that was ok just very warm Chanel number five. She splashed cold water on her face and having worn no makeup this evening applied a little mascara and a bit of lip gloss. Her warm Irish complexion that she'd inherited from her mother with its naturally rosy cheeks had no need of layers of slap to make it look good, well not yet anyhow. She'd had to run to catch the others, which rewarded her with a stern "keep up" from Lena. There was always that little gap before the boys appeared and when they finally arrived they were immediately swamped. Press, dignitaries and fans all pressing forward, all wanting a piece of reflected glory.

Vince had somehow managed to disentangle himself from the hoard and beckoned Delilah to follow him down a garishly bright passageway lit by harsh yellow strip lights. She as before waved to Mia to let her know she was leaving and she gave her the thumbs up and a wicked smile in acknowledgement. Clutching Vince's hand, they walked quickly through the narrow hallway to the side door of the theatre and escaped down a dark alley in the opposite direction to the crowd of fans waiting outside the stage door for the group to emerge. As soon as they had reached a safe distance, Vince with his hair still damp from the shower pulled her into his arms and kissed her fiercely, sending droplets of water cascading down her cheek.

'I've been thinking of you all day.' He sighed between kisses. 'It's been very distracting.'

'I bet you say that to all the girls,' she whispered laughter in her voice.

'Cynic. Are you hungry because I could eat a horse?' She nodded in reply and clasped his hand as they walked off down the road. Seeing a couple of policemen chatting outside a bar Vince walked over and after a brief conversation about good places to eat, police in any city always know the best places, they were on their way. The recommended restaurant turned out to be a small French bistro tucked away down a narrow side street. There were probably no more than a dozen tables in the rustic yet cheerful interior, but most were occupied suggesting good food. The very precise little waitress in crisp black skirt and white blouse found them a gingham clad table towards the back and offered them the set menu. They settled on a bowl of pea soup followed by confit duck with sauté potatoes and spinach to be washed down with a carafe of what turned out to be a very drinkable red wine. When the food arrived, it smelt delicious and Delilah suddenly realised just how hungry she was feeling.

The soup was served in small earthenware bowls with a basket of bread. It was smooth, silky and tasted sweet and earthy. Both of them ate without talking just occasionally offering each other a contented smile. The soup bowls had been quickly replaced by the main course, which looked mouth-wateringly good. 'Oh God that's lovely', she sighed happily as the soft duck slipped from the bone. 'Try the sauté, they're all crispy and fluffy, I think I've died and gone to heaven.'

'The sauce is pretty good too, excellent choice Mr Policeman I think.' He smiled at her over a fork full of spinach. 'So what was the gossip from the troops, there must have been some?'

'Well from what I've heard Seb has been working his way through them and only Mia and I are left.' She greedily shoved another forkful of duck into her mouth rolling her eyes blissfully. 'Mia thinks that he doesn't like her, although I imagine that he wouldn't be too bothered by that. She also let slip that she had managed to seduce Louis!' She raised an eyebrow waiting for confirmation.

'Yes, he told me.' He grinned and launched into a fair imitation of his friend's half Gallic accent. 'Van-cent I 'ave been seduced. The little Goth 'as destroyed my defences and I 'ave taken 'er to my bed. She tells me that she still 'as the virginity and I should take it away.' He waved his hand flippantly in the air. 'Mon dieu I could not refuse, no?'

'He's such an old fraud when he talks, proper Franglais. I'm sure he could have refused if he'd wanted.'

'Even Louis doesn't turn down an offer like that. It was only a couple of nights I think, I don't see it as any kind of longstanding arrangement, but you never know.' He picked up the duck bone and sucked it clean with gusto. 'Do I get the impression that she deliberately intended to get shot of it on this trip.'

'Pretty much. She'd had a bad experience at school and she was tired of it making her life a misery so hatched a plan. Can't say whether I agree or not as I think it may have created a monster. I saw her eyeing up Teddy this evening.' Breaking off a piece of bread she wiped the remaining sauce off the plate.

'She'll be disappointed, no good looking there as Teddy is pretty well loved up with his latest. So how old were you?' He leant forward conspiratally, 'fess up.'

'Nineteen, if you must know. Believe me you wouldn't have looked twice at teenage me. I was pretty invisible where boys were concerned, I had greasy hair and spots, was straight up and down, clumsy and painfully shy. I had boys as mates and I had no problem with that, but I seemed to be incapable of anything else. I stuck to horses they liked me.'

'So who was he?

'What's this the bloody Spanish inquisition?' She gave a short laugh. 'He was a boy I met on a camping holiday down in the Dordogne. His name was Walter and he was German and a couple of years older. I, like Mia was eager to "grow up", I seemed to be the only one of my friends who "hadn't". Fair enough several of them were married and whether or not they went to the Altar still virgins I don't know, but I just felt left behind. It was nothing to write home about and afterwards I wished I hadn't. At least Mia picked someone who'd give a damn.'

'He wasn't kind?'

'He was a nice boy, good looking and charming. The trouble was he knew it and he was used to having his own way and I just sort of caved in. What did he say as we were snogging in his Volkswagen camper...? "You can have it if you want it" only with a German accent. See what I mean charm personified. It was all a bit quick and rather rough, the only good thing was that he had condoms. Such a naïve creature I was then Vinnie, just like Mia only I actually stayed clear of blokes for a while after as it put me right off. So come on tell me?' She refiled their glasses.

He smiled fondly a faraway look in his eye. 'Well I can confess that Louis and I lost ours to the same girl, at separate times I might add. Her name was Amelie and she was the Mayors daughter. I used to spend my summers with my Grandmother in a little rural village in the Loire Valley. I was just seven when I first went, it was a lonely old experience to start with, but I had enough of the language and I made friends. Amelie was one of them. The summer before I turned fifteen, just before I went home we went to a local dance. Well we'd had a few sneaky drinks, we danced and on the way home she enticed me in to an old hunter's shack and well... I was full of bravado, but really hadn't got a clue.' He chuckled fondly at the memory. 'Amelie on the other hand knew exactly what to do, I was shocked I can tell you. I know I wasn't brilliant, but she made me feel like bloody Casanova.'

'Where did Louis come into it?'

'We met at a football club the following summer, his parents had just divorced and they had sent him to live with an Aunt who lived in a nearby village. We hit it off immediately, shared all the same interests and he didn't know anyone so I pulled him into our circle. Amelie and me, we didn't take it any further, but there was an instant attraction between her and Lou. He thought he was treading on my toes, I told him to go for it. He and Amelie were together six or seven years and they should have married if the truth was known.' His voice was wistful.

'So why didn't they, what stopped them?' Delilah said softly running a gentle finger down his cheek. He caught her hand and kissed her fingertips.

'Scarecrow and Lou himself. Amelie was the only thing that kept Lou sane a lot of the time, he didn't cope well with fame. There had been a lot of trauma in his life, his parents had more or less deserted him when they divorced. His aunt was a lovely woman, but she struggled having a troubled boy in her home and his uncle was a difficult man. Lou had support from the local priest and Amelie always said that he couldn't make his mind up who to marry, her or God. The meltdown came towards the end of the group and he took himself off into a Cistercian monastery in the foothills of the Alps. Amelie knew then that she'd be lucky to keep him and let him go. He accepted it with grace, if not a bit too easily and heartbroken she went off to lick her wounds.' He grinned, 'she ended up as my neighbour in France.'

'Do you live over there, in France?' She raised an interested an interested eyebrow as she thought he was a London resident.

'No, I'd like to, it's sort of a plan. I bought the place out there just before the group split up. I love the place and liked the idea of friends as neighbours, but I never seem to have enough time to spend there. That's where I'm heading after the last gig, a summer at the house. Lose myself in French life, just be me until we head off to the Caribbean to finish the album in October.' He smiled and Delilah waited for details. 'It faces south west on the edge of a hill and the sunsets over the valley are incredible. There is this ancient oak tree in the garden, must date back to the time of the Musketeers and I love to stand there in the evening watching the sun go down. The village is small but everyone knows everyone and the nearest town has anything you might need. God I love that place.'

'The plan hasn't gone away has it?' He looked surprised and shook his head. 'Sounds blissful.' Not that I'll ever see it, she thought sadly. 'It's one of the few areas in France that I haven't spent much time as it was somewhere we drove through on the way somewhere else. We did stop over a couple of times, once in a little place called Mesland, which was just over the river from Chaumont and the other time we stayed about fifteen miles east of Orleans.'

'Am I that transparent? My place is up the western end between Angers and Tours, very rural, very French. It's all fields of sunflowers, vineyards and acres of forest.' He smiled at the thought, 'the village is about ten miles inland from the river, perhaps a little more. You can walk or cycle for miles along country roads past chateaus and troglodyte houses and never see a car, heaven really or my idea of I suppose...' Delilah listened intently as he talked on about the area and his beloved house, the love in his voice was as joyful as a lark on a sunny day. The longer he talked the more she could imagine it all.

She could see teenage Vince being led into the hunter's cabin set in the vineyards by the lovely Amelie and in her mind's eye she herself was sitting with him under the old oak watching the sun as it fell away into the valley. Oh he said it was his idea of heaven and the more she heard the more she knew it would be hers. She would have to add the area on to her list of "must go" places, at least it was more attainable than some on it.

'Do you speak any French?' She was roused from her reverie by the change of topic.

'I'd like it to be a lot better, but I get by. It isn't used enough and I'm really lazy.'

'I get rusty although I was brought up bi-lingual as my mother's French.'

'Oh yeah, I read that somewhere, no wonder the place calls to you. Is your grandmother still alive?'

'No, nor my father sadly, I miss them both. They passed within a few months of each other back in 89, we'd just finished reeling from grand-mère when my dad was killed in a car accident. Your family?'

'My grandmother Hazel is still around, her husband, my grandad a retired army man died when I was small, but there are family skeletons there and the inevitable closet I'm afraid.' She grimaced remembering the trouble surrounding those.

'We all have them.' He swirled the wine left in his glass and knocked it back.

'My Welsh grandad worked in the mines, died when I was about ten. I'm lucky though I still have both parents.' From the distant expression on his face she guessed he wasn't listening and hadn't heard any of that.

'Are you going to have pudding or are you ready to go...?' Delilah saw the look in his eye and decided that there were other sorts of "pudding" and the variety he was suggesting didn't come with calories.

Unlike the previous night when lust had been all consuming they had managed to get back into their hotel room without pouncing on each other immediately. She'd had the luxury of a few minutes before Vince had pulled her gently but firmly into his arms and had begun to kiss her into submission. She'd just started to unbutton his shirt when they were unceremoniously disturbed by a shrill ringing. With a muttered curse Vince moved over to the bed and answered the phone and judging by the discussion she guessed it was Teddy.

She walked over to the mirrored doors of the built in wardrobe and watched him as he continued to undress while he talked, finally sitting there casually stark naked, Mr Romantic she thought with amusement. She scrutinised her own reflection and was happy with what she saw. From the chestnut curls and sapphire eyes to the pert breasts, narrow waist and sculpted bottom to her long shapely legs. So why was her brain still asking if Vince preferred Tash with her large plastic breasts. Foolish thoughts, the mirror didn't lie and Vince's eyes were fixed very firmly on her reflection. Knowing he was watching and keeping her back to him she slowly and she hoped seductively started to undress, her own eyes taking in the soft smile forming on his lips.

When the gossamer light summer blouse was unbuttoned she let it slither softly down her arms and allowed it to fall into a silken pile on the floor offering Vince's reflection a knowing look through lowered lashes. The designer jeans that fitted to perfection she wriggled out of and bending forward in a provocative gesture finished the move and threw them casually over a chair. She turned her head slightly and raised an eyebrow and was rewarded with a mouthed "don't stop now".

Turning back to her reflection she ran her open fingered hands through her hair exaggerating the soft curls and closed her eyes in pleasure as she imagined him doing much the same. She slipped the narrow straps of her bra one at a time over her shoulders and flicked the clasp open cupping her breasts with her hands before removing it in one smooth motion. She let her fingers caress her abdomen as they moved to the pretty matching lacy knickers and slowly slipped them off, the delicate material caressing her legs as they fell. She stepped out of them dismissively and hands on hips admired the end result, how could he possibly want anything else?

'Teddy, awfully sorry, but bugger off...' And the phone was practically thrown back on the side. Always lacking a certain amount of self-esteem she had never really been one to lead. With him it seemed different, this was not a man who would be disappointed. So naked and infused with new found confidence she sauntered sensually over to where he sat on the edge of the bed, exaggerating every fluid movement and launched herself at him like a big cat going in for the kill.

~

SEVEN
~

Delilah watched the dust motes as they danced in the sunlight flooding through the hotel window with fascination and raising a hand wiggled her fingers in the stream of sparkling particles absently wondering what or who exactly she was filling her lungs with. She glanced over at Mia, a small frown etched on her pretty face dozing on her bed and even after such a short time she knew that she wasn't telling her something.

Yes, they had talked as they had travelled down, but the conversation had mostly been about Mia's plans for the summer as when this tour was over she was going home to a dream summer job. Her sewing ability had been taken up by Barney one of Britain's bright new designing talents and she was going to spend her summer sewing designer clothes for celebrity clients. She was hoping that it would lead to something more permanent and then she wouldn't have to go back to university. But still there was something she wasn't saying...

Delilah's reality was clear in her own mind, in less than a week whatever this was that she had with Vince would be over. She thought back to the previous night's lovemaking with a soft smile, unlike the unhinged sex that had been the order of their first night together, last night had been less urgent, gentler. Good job too she thought rubbing at a bruise on her hip where on the first night it had made contact with an unforgiving wall. Vince knew his way around a woman's body and even sitting here thinking about his touch and what he could do with his tongue left her nerve endings tingling with pleasure.

Over breakfast this morning he'd bemoaned the weird schedule the group had been following as this current tour had meandered all over the place. He'd spent the UK leg fighting on and off with his ex-girlfriend Julie who seemed to turn up everywhere like a bad penny and so he'd been grateful for the three weeks hidden away laying the groundwork for the next album. He'd explained why the group were briefly separating the day after the Rome concert, Vince and Louis were heading to a charity ball in Venice and Teddy and Seb were drifting northwards to Milan so Teddy could fulfil a solo gig at a celebrity fashion show.

Up until this morning Delilah had assumed she'd be following Lena and her minions to Milan, but out of the blue Vince had asked her to go to Venice with him and she hadn't been about to turn down an offer like that. Anyhow Mia and Tom had family to catch up with in Rome while they were here in Italy and Mia was desperate to drink in as much of the fashion scene in Milan as was possible in their short stay there so Delilah would have been left by herself.

She'd been looking forward to Rome, below the window the eternal city was spread out before her like a mouth-watering smorgasbord and here she was unlikely to see very much of it at all if she didn't get going. Mia was stirring and Delilah decided it was time to find out just what was troubling her friend so that she could at least get out and see something this evening.

'So are you going to tell me where the sour face is coming from?'

'Hmm...' She slurred with a sleepy voice. 'Oh sorry did I look miserable? It wasn't intentional.'

'Really Mia? So just what happened last night because you've been really weird all day?'

Mia gave a short bitter laugh and pursing her lips tightly said 'I gave in to Seb, simple as that.'

'Oh I see...' She tried to keep the disappointment out of her voice and failed miserably 'I don't think I want to know why, but you'd better tell me if only to get it off your chest.'

'I wasn't intending to. I was chatting to Teddy because he looked really fed up whilst hoping that

Louis would turn up...' She held up a hand to stop Delilah in her tracks. 'I know it wasn't going anywhere and he hadn't made any promises, but I thought...' She gazed intently at her feet as though she'd never really seen them before. 'I thought, perhaps, just one more night. It was going to be my last chance and I wanted to shut that door with a smile.'

'Vince told me that Lou wasn't feeling great and had gone off back to the hotel straight after the show.'

'So Teddy told me, I didn't really want to be on my own so I thought I could charm him, for a comparison. God what do I sound like?' Her voice trailed off and Delilah pretty certain that tears weren't far away felt guilty for the condescending look she felt sure had been on her face.

'First time around he wouldn't have hesitated from what I've heard, but they've changed, grown up I suppose. Anyway what does it matter Mia, you're young for goodness sake. Why shouldn't you go out and have fun, why shouldn't either of us? Who's to judge, huh? I'm not exactly a sparkling example of good behaviour am I?' She reached over and patted her knee, lord she thought I'm turning into Grannie Hazel she does that. 'I mean first of all I get stuck in a bloody cupboard with Vince on the very first night and then a few days later when he suggests I move my stuff into his room I'm there like a bloody bitch on heat, his expression.'

'He never called you that...'

'No, but he's used the analogy and in this case it wasn't far from the truth and I'd do it again. We have no time to mess about, this time next week it will all be over. You'll be starting your summer job and I'll be officially unemployed and trawling the papers looking for work. Everything will be just as it was and what happened on this trip will be nothing but a memory.' She fixed Mia with a steely glare, 'so why Seb?'

'Teddy saw right through me and told me he was attached and he wasn't going to ruin it by messing about on tour and risking it finding its way back to her.' She smiled sadly, 'he told me he was flattered though.'

'Her name's Loris and she's a singer, Vince thinks she'll be huge. Strange, that first night when I saw Lena and Teddy together I thought I saw a spark between them, wondered if they'd end up together again. Looking back, I see now he was just being nice. Poor Lena it must have broken her heart, bless her. Sorry I'm digressing, you were telling me why you elected to throw yourself into Seb's apparently infinite web of debauchery...'

'He asked, well suggested really and I thought why not.' She gave Delilah a sheepish grin. 'Not one of my better ideas, he wasn't gentle like Louis. It was all over in a flash and I think if I hadn't dived out of bed and ran for the hills he would have kicked me out. This morning at breakfast I heard Jane boasting that he'd called her and they'd spent the night...Shagging like bunnies was the term she used. I admit I felt a bit deflated.'

'I don't think you should waste another thought on it Mia. Forget it and move on. Ok?' She glanced at her watch. 'Aren't you supposed to be somewhere?'

'Oh lord yes, my Aunt will have forty thousand fits if we're late. You sure you don't want to join Tom and me, there's always too much food and you'd love the family.'

'No, thank you.' She looked back out at the lengthening shadows. 'Rome is calling and I might at least get to see some of the sights tonight if Nicki and I can pick up a tour bus.'

'You're not going to the show tonight?'

'It's being televised so nobody is getting in backstage. It's going to be some big celebrity shebang and I don't think Vince is looking forward to it at all. So I'm going sightseeing with Nicki, because I don't think either of us can stomach another show right now.'

'She's a bit of a strange one, isn't she?'

'Hard as nails on the outside all soft and squishy inside. I like her.' She patted Mia on the arm as she passed. 'Go eat too much pasta, drink some wine and have fun. I'll see you later.'

Delilah was quietly pleased that Mia was otherwise engaged whilst in Rome as she'd had a horrible feeling that they would have ended up on an overly descriptive tour of Mia's favourite city. Delilah was an explorer, she liked to wander down little back streets and find hidden gems and when it came to the big attractions she liked to touch the ancient stones and try to imagine those who had lived before. Being given a detailed history lesson just didn't fit into her philosophy. Anyway she was looking forward to a bit of a silly girly night with Nicki who like her had never been to Rome before. Delilah ambled back to the spacious room she would share with Vince and found the note he'd left on the bed, short and sweet it simply said, "have a good time, I'll see you later. xx". That she decided was pretty much what she intended to do.

As they'd arrived at the hotel Nicki had spied a small trattoria down a narrow road just around the corner, which they'd decided would be their starting point and they weren't disappointed as the food was delicious. They'd started with fiori di zucca, mozzarella stuffed courgette flowers and finished with coda alla vaccinara, which was oxtail in a tomato sauce and had washed it down with an unmarked bottle of red wine. Having eaten far too much they had both felt totally stuffed when they eventually left. The hotel concierge had given them some information about the tour bus and a few minutes after they'd left the restaurant they were being driven around Rome by an Italian bus driver who thought he was driving a Ferrari.

As the whole thing was totally unplanned they settled on getting off at the Trevi fountain where they were accosted several times by handsome and very stylish young men as they explored. They took photos of each other by the fountain, threw coins in and made wishes that both of them doubted would ever materialise and finished by stuffing their faces with the most amazing cherry flavoured gelato.

Returning to the hotel they found a little café where they sat outside in the balmy evening and ordered coffee and a Sambuca, which the chap behind the bar had served with the traditional flaming coffee beans. The night was busy and both found themselves occasionally having to shout to be heard above lively conversations and the noise of the traffic. Their conversation for most of the evening had been deliberately kept away from Scarecrow and the rest of their party. Instead they'd talked about their lives and families, a little bit of the mundane in what both had decided was a surreal situation. Delilah had talked about Nick and Olivia; the first time she'd thought about them in weeks and surprised herself at being able to talk about the incident in such a totally detached way. Eventually though Nicki briefly explained why things had ended between her and Hilly, telling Delilah that it had been for the best.

Hilly had fathered a couple of children with different one night stands and being a decent sort of man had paid up happily for the children's care and upbringing. Nicki told her that it hadn't bothered her as he wasn't interested in the women involved and she'd been pleased that he'd taken his responsibilities so seriously. When Hilly had left the group after his breakdown he'd got himself a normal job and everything had been rosy with Nicki wondering if she'd found her soul mate. Then one day he'd got a tearful phone call from Marianne to tell him that their daughter Tansy had been taken seriously ill and that she might not survive, so he had rushed to her bedside. Nicky hadn't imagined how close Hilly would become to Marianne as they held a worried vigil at their daughter's bedside. Suffice to say by the time that Tansy had recovered Nicki had lost Hilly's affection to her mother. She was glad she told Delilah that she had lost him to the mother of one of his children rather than some random girl. He's still with her, Nicki told her "so it was meant to be, wasn't it?". They were just about to walk back to the hotel when she'd turned to Delilah and said darkly, 'in their world Delilah there is always another me, you or Marianne and you seriously need to keep that in mind.'

Vince lay on his back staring at the ceiling, the digital display on the clock set on the bedside table glowed a neon green one o'clock. Today had been manic and he ought to be knackered. He and Delilah had been lucky enough to have part of the day together and so they'd started out early on the Roman trail. It occurred to Vince that they'd managed to pack in an awful lot of the main bits of Ancient Rome and yet he felt like they'd actually only briefly skimmed the surface. He grinned into the darkness remembering that even the over exuberant Delilah had grown weary of her, "tangible history" by the time a blister finished their tour. It had been fun and he couldn't remember a day when he'd laughed so much for a long time. By the time he'd had to leave for the evenings big charity concert that Scarecrow were headlining Delilah had been in her PJ's sitting on the balcony with a book and a glass of wine. The blister on the sole of her foot was giving her a bit of discomfort and she'd decided against the long evening standing up in the stadium, or so she'd told him. He was more inclined to believe that it was more likely to be something to do with the altercation between her and Seb that he'd witnessed earlier on.

Delilah lay naked beside him her chestnut curls falling in wild array across his chest and blissfully lost in her dreams. Normally it was him that slipped easily into slumber, but not tonight, his body was bone weary, but his mind was refusing to switch off. He was grateful that Delilah had been fast asleep when he'd finally got in and she'd just snuggled up beside him when he'd slipped carefully into bed. God he hated touring, the endlessness of the road with sometimes dubious accommodation at the end of the day. When it started he was always filled with enthusiasm, even enjoying the scenery as the tour bus sped along through various countries. After a while it got boring, another mountain, field or river and that's when he turned back to work. The private planes filled in the longer distances, but it was still one faceless airport after another followed by another ride through a different town. He idly wondered how the aging rock gods managed it with seemingly boundless energy, because he sure as hell didn't see himself still doing it when he was older. He loved the music, the performance, their fans and that their music gave so much pleasure to others; he just wished that it didn't take quite so much out of him.

Angel by name, but by no means always by nature, perhaps it was his past catching up, some kind of weird cosmic punishment for his earlier misdemeanours. He closed his eyes for a moment, he hadn't thought about the first time around for ages, it must have been chatting about it with Delilah earlier. They had been crazy times and he often wondered how he had survived it all in one piece. Five years they'd been at the top, five years of endless, nonstop recording and touring. They had grown up fast and just a little too wild and Roscoe had liked it that way. The group had developed a reputation for being hedonistic and difficult, although what else would be expected of a group of boys just nineteen when they found fame.

His mother had been alarmed that her beloved only child who she had brought up with impeccable manners and had encouraged to be kind to everyone had turned into a monster before her very eyes. His father had tried to console her by telling her that Vince would, "find his own way", but all she could see was a boy hell bent on self-destruction. In the end they'd both been right. He watched a spider as it trundled across the otherwise spotless ceiling with its carved cornices. It stopped momentarily above his head and tested the air about it with a couple of long black legs before resuming what Vince guessed was a well charted path to the far corner.

He hadn't made life easy for his parents, had he? Like the spider he had constantly tested the air about him to check whether anyone would stop him and they hadn't. The girls, God there had been so many girls and most of them drop dead gorgeous and so very willing. He had treated most of them pretty badly and unlike Louis who was true to Amelie, well most of the time, Vince had not seen the point of any kind of attachment. Why bother when there was always some girl who was keen to throw herself at him.

Then there had been the alcohol, his poison of choice. His head almost throbbed at the thought of it, there had been more than one occasion that Vincent Angel had taken to the stage three sheets to the wind. Fair enough he'd never started on the booze too early in the day, but when he did he'd downed it with gusto. The wakeup call had come about eighteen months before the group split up in a cold spartan room in a German hotel. He'd woken up with a dry mouth and a splitting head next to a girl whose name he couldn't remember or even worse probably never even asked. He remembered the panic rising in his fast sobering mind when he realised how very young she looked, only vaguely subsiding when he saw that like him she was still fully clothed.

At the time he'd been grateful that he'd been so drunk that he'd obviously passed out and that she had probably been in exactly the same state. Before she'd woken he had slipped away and Mike one of the road crew had sorted out the situation, telling Vince afterwards that the girl had still been stoned when he'd roused her and had no idea of where she was, so he'd popped her in a taxi and paid the guy to get her home safely. Not one of his finest moments, but he'd been young and stupid and he'd learnt. A few weeks at the end of that tour spent in Louis's favourite monastery retreat had set him back on the right road, but it had also given him time to think and made him realise how much he wanted to get off the merry-go-round.

That had been the last time he'd ever got drunk on tour, yes sometimes he liked a glass of something after the show, but no more than that and most of the time he stayed stone cold sober. The girls had been shunned as well and he'd started to hide after the shows. His favourite way when approached by groupies was to tell them where Teddy was, that usually worked like a charm and he didn't have to get unpleasant. Delilah stirred in her sleep and kicked the rest of the covers off prompting a satisfied sigh from him as he took in the long sensuous lines of her body. She reminded him of Cherry, the looks were similar and the quick bright mind and easy sense of humour were exactly the same.

Cherry had been his answer back then; she'd turned up backstage at their Liverpool gig on what was to be their last tour. A popular page three model with a mass of red curls and laughing green eyes, she'd seen the advantage of following Vince on tour. Like him she wanted something more, wanted to be known for something other than her boobs. Cherry Bomb as she was known back then wanted to be on the other side of the camera and she had been good too.

She had solved his problem of the hangers on and she'd given him exactly the kind of stability he had needed. It was never destined to be a love match, but there had been plenty of chemistry and they had shared a lot of interests so had rubbed along well together. Neither had been under any illusion of what their relationship was and both knew that it would come to an end the day the tour finished. Vince offered the darkness a sad smile, he'd known almost as soon as they'd parted that he'd made a terrible miscalculation, although by then it was too late.

Even so he still carried fond memories of his time with "The Cherry bomb". Seb had been jealous, wanting her himself and having lost out to Vince he'd cruelly called her "Vince's bed warmer", pretty much what he'd now spitefully christened Delilah. Vince had seen the way Seb had looked at Cherry, knew that today he'd made a move on Delilah and had crashed and burned on both fronts.

Cherry had used her time with the group wisely, taking photos of everything and noting down anecdotes and quotes from anybody she could. The resulting book had made her name, "Scarecrow on the road to the Emerald city", she'd never posed topless again. He still saw her occasionally as he had introduced her to her husband, Stevie Grieves the lead singer of rock band "Hob nailed". They'd been together a while now growing an army of kids, while

Cherry was in demand as a celebrity photographer. At least something good had come out of such a shit time. He'd even gathered up enough courage a while back to tell her how he'd felt back then, she'd smiled and told him gently that she hadn't felt the same so the outcome would have been the same anyway.

Now he had another problem, bloody Julie wouldn't let go of the lead, how the hell did she keep finding out where he was? Tash he supposed. Since they'd moved onto the continent he'd refused to speak to her especially after all her simpering when she'd got hold of him at home. She might have made a mistake, but he hadn't. He traced the curve of Delilah's hip with his fingertips, she was worth ten Julie's. The classic notes of ylang-ylang and jasmine from her perfume, still warm from her body scented the air and he breathed in the memory of it from other nights.

'You ok?' Delilah's voice was sleepy as she nestled closer, Vince noted the deepening of the cleft between her eyebrows, which he hadn't noticed before, was their relationship causing her any stress?

'Brain on overtime, I didn't wake you?'

'No, I seem to have chucked the covers off and I'm bloody cold. Do you want some tea I've got chamomile in my bag?'

'So you have half of Sainsbury's in there as well as half the local chemist then.' He chuckled, her and her tea.

'It doesn't hurt to be prepared.' She said in mock indignation 'tea?'

'Go on then it can't be any worse than lying here trawling over the past.' He flipped the bedside light on and it bathed the room in a soft amber glow. Delilah slipped naked from the bed and paddled barefoot to where the tatty kettle sat on a very old mahogany table with beautifully hand turned legs. She walked with the grace of a big cat and Vince marvelled at how she could be so totally unaware of how naturally sensual she was. He watched with pleasure as she rummaged around in the ethereal light for her box of tea, such a simple act, lord it shouldn't be allowed he thought.

Delilah waiting for the kettle to boil and totally unaware of Vince's growing desire couldn't resist running her fingers over the soft calfskin of her small dark blue Harrods travelling case. A steal at twenty pounds it was one of her favourite auction buys and it travelled everywhere with her. She poured out the boiling water and stifled a yawn before heading back to bed and handing Vince his tea. 'Who was she?'

'What makes you think it was a woman?'

'That far away smile'

'Cherry bomb?'

'The photographer?' He laughed, pleased that she saw her that way.

'Most people call her that tart.' He told her, but she shrugged unbothered.

'Weren't you two together before she married...' She racked her brains for a name 'Stevie Grieves.'

'I introduced them.' A smile, 'you remind me of her.'

'I'm going to take that as a compliment, I think. She's quite stunning, wasn't she a model before she released that book? I've got it at home, any self-respecting Scarecrow fan went out and bought it, I thought she was an incredibly clever photographer. Her photos of Seb made me smile he always looked like he wanted to punch someone, knowing what I do now, I'm guessing you'

'She turned him down, women don't turn Mr Casanova Seb down.'

'I did!'

'Yeah he didn't like that either!' Vince flashed her a smug grin, leant over his cup and breathed in the vanilla scented steam rising from the tea. 'Did he turn on you tonight? I saw that look of sheer exasperation on your face when he cornered you downstairs.'

'I did wonder if you'd been watching, but you didn't say anything. I didn't want to cause any trouble, you and Seb are hardly the best of pals.'

'What did he call you?' Vince felt the normal irritation bubble up when he talked about Seb.

'He said "you're just another one of his fucking bed warmers and in a few days he won't even remember you". I'm a big girl Vince and it probably wasn't far short of the truth so why would I waste time worrying about it.'

'Bastard, that's utter bollocks. I'm sorry Lola you shouldn't be subjected to that. I can't say I'll miss his endless drivel when we finish this leg of the tour. God I'm tired, I feel like an old man.'

'Hmm, as your current bed warmer I can't say I've noticed.' She flashed him her best coquettish smile and lay seductively back on the soft down filled pillows, 'and as we're both awake and I'm really cold...'

'You're an incredibly bad influence Delilah Grace.' Vince didn't need to be persuaded tired or not and the cold night air blowing in through the open window like the freshly made tea was quickly forgotten.

EIGHT

~

Venice, Delilah had never been before and quite frankly might as well not be here now for all she was going to see. Despite her lack of sightseeing opportunities other than the water taxi ride across the lagoon from the airport, she was glad to be free of Lena and the posse for a few hours as their petty jealousies and endless bickering were getting on her nerves The flight here from Rome on the private jet had been a fabulous experience and oddly she had felt less panic on the little Gulfstream than she normally did on a bigger aircraft. The inside had been sumptuous with huge leather seats that you could drown in and Delilah not normally jealous of others wealth quietly envied Francesca the planes owner. It was a whole new experience and offered a small insight into what life might be like living in Vince's world.

Just before lunch Vince, Lou and Delilah had been picked up at the hotel by a small limo with blacked out windows for the short drive to Rome's Leonardo da Vinci airport. They took the VIP route through the busy and vibrant airport where to Delilah everyone looked like film stars. Vince and Lou had cast her the odd surreptitious glance as they'd walked along exchanging amused grins over her astonishment at the marvels that they took little notice of. Eventually after the umpteenth stop to gaze at something or someone Vince lost patience and catching hold of her hand dragged her along. The flight was just over an hour and they passed their time on board discussing Delilah's sightseeing trip the evening before while playing trumps, which Delilah had always had the luck of the devil in, so she won more often than not. This caused some disquiet as Vince she'd discovered had a strong competitive streak, which Lou having known him for so long played on for his own ends and there were various lively discussions about cheating. Actually though, the only one cheating had been her.

Delilah was keen to know all about their host Francesca and between them Vince and Lou were happy to fill her in. She had been married and widowed twice, both times to wealthy older men and after Nicolo the second husband died in a terrible car accident she had briefly lived with Lou. There was a young daughter, who called Lou dad although he wasn't her father, it was complicated they told her. Francesca herself had created a fortune of her own from her highly successful business as a gifted interior designer, which her first husband had encouraged her to start. Lou had described her as beautiful, funny and clever and Delilah got the impression that he still harboured feelings for her. Vince seeing her worried expression had told her not to worry as Francesca was very down to earth and everybody loved her.

Neither of her companions were wrong, Francesca or Cesca as she introduced herself was everything they'd told her. She was older than Delilah had expected being closer to forty than thirty, but that did little to dampen her beauty. There was a touch of just about every famous Italian actress about her, lovely bone structure, hour glass figure and a long lustrous mane of mahogany hair. She had greeted Delilah sincerely, like a long lost friend and had wrapped a long slender arm around her shoulder as she led her inside. The house was magnificent with long sweeping staircases leading upwards and a myriad of rooms opening off the mosaic flooring of the hall. Antiques happily shared space with modern pieces wherever the eye travelled and there was something astonishing around every corner. Delilah complimented her hostess on her décor and was greeted with a nonchalant shrug and the comment, "It is a house, not a home."

Lou had told her that the house in Venice had belonged to her second husband and that she much preferred her villa on the Amalfi coast. That aside this house was beyond Delilah's wildest dreams. They were served coffee and the ubiquitous delicate cake that seemed to be served everywhere in Italy in what Delilah guessed was Cesca's main reception room. Vince had asked about the order of proceedings for that evenings charity ball and Cesca had told them that she'd put them on first before dinner if that was alright as she had a wonderful quintet from the local music school to accompany the dancing later on. As they nodded their agreement she'd added that it would allow them time to actually enjoy the rest of the evening. Delilah was certain that she'd seen the older woman wink slyly at Lou with that comment.

With time moving on Vince and Lou had wandered upstairs to the ballroom to start their preparations leaving Delilah alone with her hostess.

'So Delilah you must tell me everything, how did you two meet?' Her voice was laced with honey. Hmm Delilah thought, this will be interesting.

'I was lost backstage in Brussels and then I tripped and fell into Vince's arms…literally. We've been together since.' Short and to the point she hoped that would be enough.

'How fabulously romantic, apart from Brussels as I can't say I'm a fan. I can tell that he's besotted with you though, his eyes never left you for a moment in here.' Was that a touch of Americana creeping through her Italian accent? 'I can't say I blame him as you're gorgeous.'

'Thank you.' Now that was probably the most direct compliment she'd ever received. 'You don't think it was an odd way of meeting?' Ok Delilah go and dig yourself a hole, she thought.

'You mean do I think you're a groupie?' She raised a carefully shaped eyebrow. 'If that's how he saw you then you wouldn't be sitting here. And no I don't. I am no hypocrite Delilah.' She leant towards her conspiratally. 'Did they tell you anything about me?' Delilah shrugged. 'Darling girl I am what my fellow American's would call "trailer trash". I got lucky, men find me alluring to look at so I made use of that to my benefit.'

She smiled and purred on. 'I was nineteen when I met my first husband, I had gate-crashed a party in Manhattan with a friend and I caught his eye. He was a widower thirty years older than me, Italian nobility with a portfolio of successful businesses and I took my chance.' For a moment there was a touch of sadness in her big brown eyes. 'I came to love him very much in the ten years we were together, he gave me everything, encouraged me to become someone else and taught me to spread my wings and fly.' She fixed Delilah with a direct stare and she waited for the lecture that she felt might be coming. 'Be careful Delilah, his world is full of predators and you'll be on their menu, you understand?' She nodded, understanding totally.

After much discussion about what she'd bought to wear Cesca decided that she could find her something much better and she readily accepted as the long slinky black number that she'd stuck in her luggage just in case, would look horrendously cheap in these palatial surroundings. She and Cesca were sort of the same size although she couldn't compare with her generous bosom, but no matter as she was soon clutching a beautiful midnight blue gown that had looked stunning on. Delilah could only imagine how much the couture dress had cost, certainly more than she would ever be able to afford.

Vince gave a soft whistle when he came out of the shower and told her that she looked incredible and that he'd be the envy of every man there. The look on his face had been priceless and her confidence skyrocketed. The diamond jewellery she chose to wear had been her grandmothers and although the stones weren't of the highest calibre, they were real and they complimented the dress perfectly. She'd put them in her bag just in case as well, hoping that they'd stay safe as people would assume they were fake. Vince offered her his arm and at his side she descended into a dream world that before she could only have imagined.

This was Delilah's *Cinderella* moment. In the inky depths of the canal she could see the full moon and a million glittering stars reflected as they shone down from the indigo sky above. Behind her a hundred sumptuously dressed people whirled about the ballroom to a waltz played by the sublime quintet. Her fairy godmother had waved her magic wand and here she stood a fairy tale princess dressed in a gorgeous designer gown on a sweeping balcony, its marble palisades smothered in purple bougainvillea in full bloom.

Her prince, the top button on his shirt open and his bow tie hanging free stood before her with his arm outstretched, inviting her to dance with him. With a smile she took his hand and held in his careful embrace let the music guide her feet in a dance she remembered learning as a child. Vince never stopped surprising her. She'd never had him down as a ballroom god and yet here he was leading her with expert timing. As the music waned they slowed to a gentle smooch and she rested her head against his shoulder her hand resting over his heart, which seemed to be beating as fast as her own.

'Vince I can't breathe...' She whispered urgently as her eyes sought his.

'I haven't been able to breathe since the first time I saw you.' He leant down raining tender kisses on her forehead, eyelids and the tip of her nose before finally finding her lips. He'd never kissed her as if he meant it, as if he felt something more than just the overwhelming attraction between them. Delilah knowing that soon this would all be just a moment in time, lost herself in the moment responding with a desperation she had never known before. Soon just like in *Cinderella* the clock would strike midnight, the magic would disappear and she'd be plain old small town Delilah Grace, unemployed and alone.

She pulled away from his embrace and walked a few feet away, it hadn't bothered her before. She'd always treated it for what she thought it was, a lovely holiday romance nothing more. That kiss just now, well that had told her in no uncertain terms that she was falling for her enigmatic lover and that hadn't been her intention. Way to go Delilah you're about to get your heart broken, she thought gloomily as she closed her eyes and fought off the threatening tears that seemed to be just moments away of late.

Vince wondering whether he'd done something wrong watched her move away with a pensive expression on his face. There were times when he felt that he could read her like a book and others like now where she left him completely flummoxed. He'd never had that with a woman before. Cherry had been honest to the point of cruelty, so he'd always known what their relationship had been, even if he hadn't been happy about it after it had finished.

Amelie had been a surprise, but even so he'd quickly learnt to read between the lines with her and had got out in the nick of time. Julie, well poor Julie despite her protestations otherwise had been incredibly naïve for a supposed successful woman of the world. He glanced across at Delilah, now she was complicated, a contradiction and he couldn't imagine her not being at his side. Now he understood and he needed to act.

So lost in her thoughts she hadn't noticed him walk up behind her so that when he clasped her shoulders it momentarily startled her. 'It's a beautiful night isn't it?' She said wistfully leaning back against him. 'There's almost a magic in the air, it must be the harvest moon, I haven't seen one so spectacular for years.'

'Hmm. Delilah don't go home.' She twisted in his embrace her face a mixture of emotions. 'Stay with me in France for the summer. No questions, no promises and no consequences. If it doesn't work, well then at least we'll know, but right now I can't just let you walk away from me without doing something.' His face was earnest, his eyes intent and she knew this was not a decision to think about. If she went away and thought about it, she knew she would find a hundred and one reasons not to go for it. He hadn't told her that he loved her and she thought more of him for his honesty, but the inference was that one day he might. 'Think about it, that's all I ask...'

'Yes. The answer is yes Vince. I know I overthink things and when I do I make the wrong decisions, so yes.' With all my heart yes, she thought.

The music that floated up from that magical balcony below was intoxicating and Delilah feeling giddy from drinking just a little too much champagne felt like she had wings on her feet. Back in the room she kicked off her heels and blister or no blister danced around the bed laughing. The room was full of shadows where the light from the full moon didn't reach and here Vince watched as she joyfully danced with an invisible partner in the ethereal glow. Vince drank in her pleasure and rejoiced in it, he had no regrets about his spur of the moment suggestion and loved that she had answered without hesitation. He wasn't sure how it would work, but thinking ahead was hoping that a discussion with Cesca over breakfast would put a few arrangements in place. Desire washed over him as she sashayed sensually towards him and he pulled her intently into his arms.

'No regrets?' Gently he pushed escaping tendrils of chestnut out of her eyes and planted a whisper soft kiss on her forehead. 'Tell me if you have...'

'None.' She cupped his chin in her hands and fiercely pressed her lips to his, 'believe me you'll be the first to know.'

Unzipping the expensive gown, he caressed sensitive skin as he ran expert fingers down her spine making Delilah wish she could purr with pleasure like a cat. She allowed him to slip the silken fabric from her shoulders and sighed as it slid with a whisper into a molten puddle around her bare feet. With practiced hands she unbuttoned his shirt and eased it over his shoulders tracing her fingers down the taut muscles of his arms and chest. She paused for dramatic effect at the waistline of his tux trousers keeping flirtatious eyes fixed very firmly on his. In return he offered her a sly half smile waiting for her to make the next move.

As her fingers curled around the black leather belt she leant in for a kiss, which he responded to with almost a cool indifference. She offered him a coquettish grin and pulled the belt free letting her fingers linger briefly on the top of the fly before pushing the zip down with a fingertip letting the expensive trousers slide to his ankles where he kicked them dismissively to one side.

Picking her up as if she was made of gossamer he took her to the moonlit bed where he gently lay her down. Vince leant in to kiss her whispering into her ear, 'trust me'. She nodded in reply, 'close your eyes and let the music consume every sense.'

A familiar *Paganini* piece wafted through the open windows as it began in the ballroom below and a soprano started to sing. Delilah tried to control her breathing and racing pulse and slowly the music filled her mind. The intensity of his caresses left her breathless before imperceptibly he entered her and an unbidden sigh escaped her lips as their bodies found their rhythm against the black satin sheets.

Delilah kept her attention on the poignant familiar story of love and loss and as the violin soared so did the intensity of her pleasure and all the time Vince followed the ever changing rhythm. Not once did his eyes leave hers and as the intensity increased their hands locked together tighter as if at any moment one of them would slip the chains to this existence completely and disappear. She longed to close her eyes and let go of the world, but the thought of losing their current bond was more than she could bear.

Each moment sent yet another exquisite shiver of pleasure through her body and she wondered just how much more she could take. The room echoed with their collective moans of delight as the soprano's exquisite voice rose and fell and they gave themselves totally to the glory of Paganini and each other. The piece reached its inevitable conclusion and their cries of ecstasy echoed the soprano note for note and they clung to each other until their trembling subsided. She'd never ever reached such euphoria before and it was some time before her body came down from the dizzy heights. Their lovemaking had seemed timeless and seamless and she was shocked when she looked at the clock, which signified that it had drifted in waves of pleasure into the early hours.

Beside her Vince was sleeping soundly his breathing deep and even and for the first time since he had asked, she contemplated the offer he'd made and she'd so quickly accepted. Laying here on this gloriously soft bed, her body still aching with pleasure and a cool breeze playing across her cheek the first seed of doubt raised its unwanted head. What had she been thinking? Forcing it back into the deepest recesses of her mind she snuggled closer to her enigmatic lover and closing her eyes let sleep wash over her.

Vince was talking to her from the bathroom, but she was watching the antics of the gondoliers on the canal below and he might as well have been talking to himself. He stood in the doorway a toothbrush in his hand and watched her for a moment. 'Did you get any of that?'

'Sorry I was miles away. What were you saying?'

'I was wondering whether you were going to accept Cesca's offer...In a nutshell.'

'I don't know, it's very generous, I mean I've only just met her and the dress must be worth a fortune. Oh you meant taking the private jet with her?'

'Uh huh. It's your choice honey, but Cesca's coming to Turin with us before she heads to Paris so it makes sense really.' He paddled barefoot across the cool tiled floor and gathered her into his arms. 'So decisions my dear one.' He leant down and kissed her tenderly and Delilah remembering the night before fought the urge to respond to the longing racing through her veins.

'She'd be really hurt...?'

'She would, and it'll be dead easy to get the train down to Saumur from there...' He hesitated a worried frown settling on his face. 'Unless you've changed your mind.'

'No, I've not changed my mind, God help me.' She touched his face lightly hoping that she looked more confident in her decision than she felt. He beamed then and with a quick naughty slap on her bottom he went back to get ready.

'Oh and the dress, put it in your bag. She'd really be pissed if you didn't accept that.' He grinned leaning back out the bathroom door. Delilah watched him with a sly smile wondering if there was enough time for just a little bit more naughtiness before they set out for Turin.

Delilah saw about as much of Turin as she had of Venice and by the time she was standing backstage after the show she totally understood why Vince hated touring. The few days of peace in Switzerland had given her a break, which had been denied everyone else on the trip and the effects on the others were now impossible to ignore. Vince had intimated that there were ructions within the group too and half the time they weren't speaking to each other, so he was glad they were reaching the end. Mia was grouchy, Tom had decided to stay with his cousins in Rome and she was feeling abandoned. The fashion show that she'd been itching to go to in Milan had been a let-down as there had been no tickets for anyone other than Jane and Tash, a fact that Lena had neglected to mention.

'If I'd known I would have stayed in Rome with Tom and we could have got a train down here together and if the bloody flight wasn't already booked from Turin I could have flown back from there. Lena couldn't organise a piss up in a bloody brewery. "I thought you'd all like the atmosphere..." There were a few moments there when I thought they were going to lynch her.' She passed Delilah a glass of Limoncello. 'It's all gone a bit pants really.' She sighed.

'Glad I didn't go then...' The Limoncello tasted artificial and she wrinkled her nose.

'Come on then spill how did the romantic night in Venice go or did that go wrong too?'

'Vince asked me to spend the summer in France with him.' Mia spluttered on her drink. 'I said yes.' Delilah shrugged. 'It seemed like a good idea at the time.'

'Oh my God, that's crazy, what were you thinking?'

'I was thinking, oh a nice summer in France...with benefits.' She flashed Mia a wicked grin.

Nicki stalked over and flopped down on a nearby chair with a dramatic sigh 'I really need to go home.'

'That bad huh?'

'Bloody Rob. He's just gone off on some weird jealous rant at me. I mean he's a friend, well that's all I've ever seen him as.' She took a glass of the luminous yellow liquid from Mia and knocked it back in one go. 'Shit, where the hell did that come from Mia, it's vile?' Realising that Delilah was standing beside her trying not to laugh she poked a red taloned finger into her ribs. 'And where did you bugger off to yesterday De-li-lah?'

'Venice in a private jet.' She cocked her head to one side, 'I went to a ball.'

'Been there, done that...yawn.' Nicki grinned. 'But, Cinderella, did you lose your Prince at midnight or was he still there in the morning?'

'Oh he was still there.'

'He's asked her to spend the summer with him...' Mia chipped in worriedly hoping that Nicki would talk some sense into her friend.

'Bloody hell Delilah, going back to his castle as well. Good luck with that.'

'See, I told you it was a bad idea.' Mia murmured chewing a fingernail absently.

'Oh, I didn't say it was a bad idea.' Nicki chipped back. 'I just meant that Delilah has just crossed the line and now she's going to have to learn to deal with everything that's lurking in the shadows of the enchanted forest. The thorns, jealousy, hatred and that bloody awful place of Vince's in the middle of nowhere.' She leant in conspiratally. 'There are dragons!' Delilah looked nonplussed. 'His mother and his neighbour, don't say I didn't warn you.'

'You've been there?'

'The French place, once. I went to a party with Hilly just before we parted company.' She smiled at what Delilah guessed was a fond memory. 'I didn't know the end was as near as it was. Sorry, digressing. I had it in my mind that it was going to be some huge castle, boy was I wrong. Amelie, his ex, she's the dragon next door persuaded him to buy the adjacent house, apparently she can be very persuasive, told him she could keep an eye on the place when he wasn't there.' She snorted with derision. 'More like so she could keep an eye on what he was up to. Watch that one Delilah, she's sly.'

'Who's sly?' Lena had appeared out of nowhere her face tear streaked.

'Your mascara's running Lena, who's upset you now.' Nicki asked tersely.

Delilah looked at the others and wondered what she'd missed in Milan other than the non-event.

'Fran. I never realised, am I so very shallow that I couldn't even see how my closest friend felt. She's just read me the riot act over Neil. She told me that I only wanted him now because Teddy doesn't care. She went on and on about how I was going to hurt him and that she could have made him happy.' She looked at each of them in turn. 'She's loved him for years, why didn't I know that, am I stupid?'

'You are inclined to ignore anything that doesn't involve you Lena.' Delilah hoped that she sounded like she was being sympathetic. Lena's big brown eyes filled with tears and she sniffed loudly. 'You're not stupid. You're beautiful and funny and when you want to be, you're really kind...' It had to be said, sometimes the truth needs to be told. 'It's just that sometimes you can be a little selfish and a little bit blind. I mean, you've not said anything to me...'

'What about?' Lena hadn't cottoned on and it wasn't as if she and Vince had been secretive.

'Vince has been shagging Delilah.' Nicki offered nonchalantly and shrugged her shoulders. 'You haven't noticed, have you?'

'Since when?' Lena's tone had a hint of petulance to it, 'you never said...'

'I dropped hints the size of elephants, you kept changing the subject, kept wittering on about Teddy and Jane. And there's nothing going on between them because he's shit scared that he'll lose her.' Delilah pointed at the stunning coffee coloured woman wrapped around Teddy. Lena's expression suggested that she hadn't even considered that Teddy already had another woman in his life.

'Oh, I didn't know, who is she?'

'Her name's Loris and Vince says that she's going to be the next big thing, played me a demo of hers and her voice is bloody amazing. It would seem that Teddy discovered her, got Roscoe involved and he's going to launch her into the world just before Christmas.' Delilah wasn't a big fan of the female voice, but Loris had such tremendous range that she seemed to be able to inject depthless emotion into every word.

'Who's the frightened looking girl chatting to them?' Nicki asked. Delilah shrugged she didn't have a clue. She guessed she must be a friend of Loris as they were very easy with each other.

'Her name's Lucee,' piped up Mia. 'She's a model, just crept onto the scene in the last few months, she'll be big too. I wish I had that kind of fragile beauty.' Adoration glowed from Mia's heavily made up grey eyes. Delilah had noticed something else about Lucee that she didn't like much, the girl's eyes hadn't left Vince. She was chatting away to Teddy and Loris, but her attention was fixed on him and as he passed she drew him into the group with a smile. Nope there was no adoration in Delilah's eyes, just jealousy, now where did that come from?

~

FRANCE SUMMER 95
~

NINE

~

Mesmerised by the dark brooding landscape as it slipped past the fast moving car, Delilah struggled to keep her eyes open. Today's journey had been long and by the end of it had become tedious beyond belief, so she had been relieved when the train had pulled into the station at Saumur. Cesca had been distracted on the flight from Turin as she had a presentation to new clients within a couple of hours of landing. She'd made small talk and had been very gracious, but Delilah felt guilty about taking her from her work and so had feigned weariness. Even so when they landed Cesca had enclosed her in a bear hug and told her that hopefully they'd see each other at some point during the summer, if it lasted thought Delilah. She'd also echoed Nicki's warning about Vince's world, which was now beginning to worry her a little too much.

Vince had arranged for one of his French neighbours, a lady called Jeanne to pick her up at the station. Jeanne was waiting where she'd been told and had greeted her with a warm smile and the necessary kiss on each cheek. A homely woman with short blonde hair, huge brown eyes and a ready smile who Delilah guessed was no more than a couple of years older than her. She had threaded a strong arm through hers and steered Delilah to a smart MPV parked outside. Too tired to take much notice of the passing scenery her weary brain struggled to convey her fragile French, so she just listened as Jeanne made what she hoped was polite small talk.

Her new acquaintance soon lapsed into an uneasy silence and Delilah struggled against the sleep that was screaming to take over. Entering the outskirts of a small village Jeanne told her in halting English that they had reached St Clair, she had pointed out the bakery and the bar before turning away from the sparsely lit main road into pitch darkness. About half a mile out of the village Vince had said, and a bit she thought.

Vince's large farmhouse sat amongst four other properties at the end of a lane, which petered out into a track that disappeared up the hill and into a dark brooding forest. Jeanne pulled through an open pair of intricate wrought iron gates onto a large circular gravel drive in front of the last of the houses on the right and with a gentle smile said simply 'home'. Delilah stood outside the house and glanced about her with more apprehension than she would have liked to admit. It was very dark, there were no streetlights here and although there were lights twinkling in all of the nearby houses

it was a lonely location. Jeanne led the way inside and Delilah let out the breath she had subconsciously been holding, the house was at least welcoming. In one corner of the large square entrance hall on a beautiful old table stood a large bunch of stocks and the sweet scent from the tall pastel stalks filled the air. Beside the table sat a battered old wooden trunk with a pile of post on its rough much used lid. Jeanne told her that the room on the right side of the front door was hers. Hmm she thought, I have "a room", but her tired mind couldn't be bothered to question the situation further. Jeanne gestured to follow her through a pretty stained glass door and she followed without argument into a traditional French living area, which opened out across the whole of the back of the house, stunning she thought vaguely.

Jeanne had reverted to French, but was now speaking slowly enough for Delilah to keep up. There was a baguette, a pot of homemade soup and a small plate with a ripe camembert on the side in the kitchen if she was hungry. In the fridge was milk and butter. There was coffee, hot chocolate, homemade strawberry conserve and local honey in one of the cupboards for breakfast. She eyed Delilah worriedly, would she be ok? If there was a problem she and her husband Eustache were just opposite and she gave her a piece of paper with her phone number on. She passed her the keys and pointed out that the car key on the ring was for the Clio in the garage, Vince had already told her that it was insured for anyone to use. Delilah smiled and hugged the older woman thanking her for all the trouble she had gone to, but hopefully she'd be fine. She waved to Jeanne from the door before shutting out the night, now what?

She wasn't hungry so she tucked the food away, but she felt the need for something soothing, so she rescued her tea and made a cup of camomile to drink in her room. Pretty and probably recently decorated as the smell of fresh paint still lingered, her room also had a small on-suite. Delilah undressed wearily and turned on the shower hoping that a quick blast of hot water would make her feel better. Closing her eyes, she let the water wash over her and wondered what had she in her haste had agreed to? Afterwards laying afraid and alone in the strange bed with its crisp cotton sheets she felt overwhelmed by home sickness, but sweet oblivion was calling and finally she allowed it to sweep her away in its arms.

She was awoken early by one of her neighbour's roosters who was greeting the new morning with gusto, no lay ins here she thought as she got up to open the shutters. She was greeted by an endless blue sky and the warmth from the fast rising sun enveloped her as she stood looking out. The forest looked less foreboding in the sunlight and now she could see that below these four houses were at least another two so not so isolated either. It hadn't been the best night's sleep ever, there had been noises, mostly easily explained, but enough to scare her at the time alone in a strange place.

There had been owls chatting to each other quite close by and about two o'clock several large somethings, deer she guessed had trodden across the gravel. Something small had scurried under her window just as the first light of dawn had seeped through a gap in the otherwise tight fitting shutters and that had been about the time the birds had started, a dawn chorus like nothing she had heard before and she had been unable to do anything other than lay there and listen to it drinking in the voices of the birds as they gave thanks for another day.

Once up she had been able to explore the house more thoroughly. The ultra-modern kitchen flowed into the dining area and in the middle sat a large oak table surrounded by comfy looking chairs. In-between the patio doors and the first of two large picture windows sat the most beautiful dresser, probably very old she guessed. Photos adorned the shelves and two vases and a large bowl in what she recognised as Milano glass sat proudly on the main surface. The lounge area looked cosy with a leather sofa and two arts and craft type arm chairs, which bordered an inglenook with a wood burning stove. A television sat in one corner and a very expensive music centre in the other with an acoustic guitar propped up at the side. The floors were flagstone and the large windows although draped to the floor in heavy tapestry curtains let in an abundance of light. Jutting out of the kitchen was a large well stocked utility room and Delilah ever practical put on a load of washing. She started a pot of coffee and while it percolated she decided to investigate Vince's domain upstairs, what she found took her breath away.

Light poured into the room from a dormer window above the huge bed and she could imagine star gazing though it at night, which she guessed was the idea. This faced double doors in the centre, which opened out on to a balcony with wicker chairs. The view was amazing and Delilah sat on the end of the bed with her mouth agape in awe. The house had been built on a hill and as such it maximised the stunning vista that spread out below it. Delilah took in the way the garden swept casually down to a magnificent oak tree heavily hung with bright green bunches of mistletoe, past a walled vegetable patch, which dipped away as if in deference to the stunning valley below. The late June sunshine poured down onto open farmland interposed with little copses of trees and the occasional house or barn built with the soft creamy Truffeau native to this area and glinted off quaint twisted church spires.

Vince had already told her about the amazing sunsets over the valley and she could imagine sitting on the balcony marvelling in the beauty with a crisp glass of wine in her hand. The panorama fascinated her as she remembered the Loire as being flat and boring as they'd passed through on their way down south on many family holidays. That had been travelling on the motorway out of Paris, where the views either side of the long virtually straight grey ribbon that skirted Blois and Orleans had been of huge flat stretches of arable fields, which the wind swirled and skittered over pulling at their old camper van as it travelled along. But this end was undulating with long gradual climbs out of pretty valleys with breathtakingly beautiful views of farmland and seemingly endless forest.

Bread from the bakery had been her next task, but as there was still a stick left from the previous night she made toast instead smothered with the local honey that Jeanne had left. After washing up she hung out the clothes on the line and set off to explore the garden. It sloped more sharply than it had seemed to from upstairs and she came to the conclusion that it was probably the first flaw she'd come across so far. At the other side of a high wooden gate she found a swimming pool set in a large courtyard with a pretty summerhouse at one end. Lifting a corner of the cover she wiggled a couple of fingers in the surprisingly warm water and decided this is where she'd spend her afternoon. There was a profusion of equipment in the summer house including loungers, a cupboard with towels and a small fridge, for beer she guessed, how civilised.

The vegetable garden was well planted and there was already a good supply of salad ready to eat, won't have to buy that she thought. A large chicken coop with a secure long run stretched down one side and when she lifted the roof someone had already set it up ready for some occupants. She'd always wanted chucks, but they'd had too many foxes at home so this would be a pleasure. What looked like an old stable was on the other side and she found a good store of chicken feed inside an old chest freezer, rats a problem, probably.

The garden dropped away into fields and for a few minutes she stood watching a buzzard lazily working the thermals soaring higher with each circle and every so often it called, its cry like a cat's meow. The sky was full of swallows and house martins all chattering amongst themselves and every so often one would swoop down and into the old stable where she assumed it had a nest. For the first time since she'd decided to take Vince up on his offer she was glad she had.

A movement at the far side of the nearest field caught her eye as several red deer emerged from the forest to feast on the grass in the field left fallow by the farmer. She subconsciously held her breath as she stood rooted to the spot watching them and hoping that she didn't disturb them. A narrow face turned in her direction, the hind's large ears flicking this way and that as she hunted for danger. A captivated Delilah watched for what seemed ages before the deer moved on and she was able to move away. Her tour of the garden finished back at the top peering through the windows of a renovated barn. She knew from what Jeanne had told her the night before that it was a garage at the front, but Vince had turned the back half of the building into a small music studio. Hmm not totally an escape from work then, she thought.

After a quick recon of the kitchen cupboards Delilah grabbed the keys to the Clio and Jeanne's roughly jotted directions and was soon on her way to the shops in the nearby town. It was all really quite straightforward and after fifteen minutes of effortless driving she was parking outside the local Intermarché. She dug out a coin for the trolley and strode with what she hoped looked like confidence into the shop. As always with these French stores there was an eclectic mixture of small shops before reaching the actual supermarket and she made a particular note of the yummy looking bakery.

Where to start, hmm better focus on what she needed, if she could find it. With great resolve she walked past the bargains that were laid out at the entrance, mostly a hundred and one things you never realised that you needed. She could see an extensive fish counter at the back of the store, so that was her first port of call. That led to the deli counter where she bought delicious salads, pate and cheese and the butchery where after much gesturing and hesitant French, she picked up chicken and some veal mince.

The green grocery section was full of seasonal goodies and she stocked up on a couple of items that were missing from Vince's blooming veg garden. She whizzed about the shop picking up bits and pieces, some lime syrup, a decent chunk of Normandy butter and most important a couple of bottles of wine and some beer. On the way out she bought bread and an incredibly beautiful calorie ridden cake to celebrate that she had completed the whole endeavour in French.

Lunch was Jeanne's soup, some bread with sharp creamy Neufchatel cheese and a sweet juicy white fleshed nectarine eaten on the patio in the shade of a large umbrella and all washed down with a glass of crisp rosé wine. This was the life. She thought it again that afternoon as she lounged on a sumptuous cushion watching as the sunlight sparkled on the water in the pool having just stuffed herself full of her delicious cake. And again that evening as she sat in the fading sunlight eating her whiting filet and waiting for the spectacular sunset she'd been promised. The mosquitoes that drove her indoors she could have done without, especially the huge and very loud ones that seemed intent on biting her. Much later tonight Vince would be home and with that thought the panic set in again, this was his territory.

Eight am and the house was cloaked in silence, so tiptoeing round like a thief Delilah got herself sorted and grabbing her purse set out for the bakery in the village leaving Vince to sleep. He had got back just after midnight and although he'd tried to creep in quietly the car on the gravel had betrayed his arrival. The walk down to the village was longer and steeper than she expected and she found herself not looking forward to the return trip. Still it was an interesting exercise and she'd be more than ready for breakfast when she got back. Once past the little clutch of houses she was walking with a huge field of sweetcorn to one side and a pasture with creamy white cows up to their chests in grass on the other. She stood leaning on the wall watching them for a few moments and was rewarded with indifferent stares from a dozen deep brown eyes before they went back to their grazing, their heads occasionally flinging back in a spray of spittle to deal with a biting fly.

In the distance she heard the call of another buzzard and looking up she could just make it out, a large dark speck against the blue sky flying high above the distant forest. The chattering of many different species of birds came from bushes and trees as she passed, some she recognised and some she didn't. A lark flew up from the cow's field with a shrill cry of alarm, rising higher and higher into the sky its sweet song designed to distract threats from its nest on the ground. Delilah smiled drinking in her surroundings as she walked.

Two thirds of the way down to the village sat a thoroughly dilapidated house surrounded by an overgrown garden where insects of all kinds revelled among the myriad of flowers left to their own devices there. No matter how hard she looked she couldn't make her mind up whether it was empty or occupied although she had a tingle at the back of her neck that suggested she was being watched. Whatever the circumstances she walked quickly on, just in case. There were a few people milling about the village, some she guessed were heading for church and others had been to the bakery for their bread. There were baguettes stuffed under arms, boules in baskets and a couple of long crusty flutes being used as swords by two young boys much to the annoyance of their mother.

Opening the door to the bakery she was immediately assailed by several interested faces and a pleasant chorus of "bonjour mademoiselle" and she replied with what she hoped was a confident "bonjour" in reply. She waited for the inquisition, which she was certain she was about to be subjected to, but it never came. Instead she was quite deliberately served before the others choosing carefully from the array of bread and cakes on sale whilst the delicious smell of freshly baking bread filled her nostrils and made her salivate. Having paid, she made a hasty exit remembering her manners and offering a polite "au revoir", leaving behind the ladies who were obviously very keen to discuss the new arrival. On her way out the door she almost ran into the archetypal French woman who stunned her by greeting her by name.

'Delilah?' Her face must have been a picture.

'Yes...'

'Hello, I'm Amelie. Vince must have told you about me.' The emphasis was on the "must". Her English was perfect and no Vince hadn't told her much at all and he certainly hadn't told her just how attractive the woman was. 'I think we will be neighbours and such good friends, I hope.' She smiled and Delilah thought that it was the kind of smile a praying mantis used to find its next victim. 'We must have lunch, my treat. I have Wednesday free is that ok for you?' Like she would have a full calendar of social events.

'That sounds very nice, I'd like that.' Delilah said cautiously not sure she meant it.

'Bon. I have an old friend who has this amazing place, the food is divine. I will let you know the details ok?' And swirling in a cloud of Dior perfume she was in the bakery and Delilah was left outside wondering what had just hit her. She put her head down and hurried back up the hill half worried that Amelie would catch up with her in the car and offer her a lift. She needn't have worried as she had the road to herself and the reason for that she guessed was that the little gaggle of women in the bakery were having a good old gossip at her expense.

The smell of brewing coffee and frying bacon assaulted her senses as she walked in ravenous.

'Lola is that you?' Who else would it be she wondered with amusement.

'Uh huh, I've been for bread.'

'I guessed that.' He pulled her into a bear hug as she walked into the living area. 'I heard the door...'

'And there was me trying to be quiet.' She allowed him to pull her closer. 'Sorry, I didn't mean to wake you.'

'You know me; I don't sleep late no matter what time I fall into bed. Also I didn't want to leave you twiddling your thumbs for another day.' She pulled out of the hug and offered him the basket containing the bread.

'I'm really hungry and that smells lovely.'

'Knowing that you're always hungry I thought you'd like some bacon and eggs, well no actually I've been dreaming about them for weeks. Silly isn't it?'

'Not really. Do you want a hand?'

'Nope, you're a guest so kick back and relax and I'll cook for Mademoiselle.' He made a mock bow and swung his hand in the direction of the table. There was butter and a variety of conserves 'Jeanne's, she makes her own and they're delicious.' Not Amelie's then she thought, not that she could imagine the chic slender woman at the bakery standing in front of a bubbling jam pan.

Later after eating Vince's delicious breakfast Delilah stood mindlessly drying dishes as she gazed out the kitchen window. Vince his large callused hands surrounded by soft foamy bubbles considered the lost expression on her face and a deep frown crept across his own. 'Sometimes Delilah something worth having is worth waiting for.'

Delilah stopped, her mind momentarily caught between her delight in the view and the sudden concern in Vince's voice. 'Sorry...?'

'I didn't want to push, wanted you to feel at home...'

'Oh, the separate rooms.' She said suddenly understanding. 'I was a little confused about that, after all that particular horse has bolted. But it's ok, really.'

'You looked lost just now, not having second thoughts?' He reached up to brush a stray chestnut curl from her eye with a gentle soapy finger leaving a trail of bubbles trickling down her cheek. She took in the intensity in his cinnamon eyes, he was looking at her in a way that no man had ever done before and for those few precious moments Delilah knew that she never wanted him to stop looking at her like that. He brushed the bubbles away with a soft smile and kissed her forehead. 'When you're ready Chéri, I can wait.'

'In that case...' she said flashing him a coquettish smile and throwing him the tea towel 'I shall keep you apprised.' He laughed and all the tension melted away.

If she was to describe the next few days as anything it would have to be normal or as close to normal as her current situation was. After a lively discussion where Vince insisted she was a guest and she put her foot down and insisted that she contributed to everything they eventually laid down some ground rules. Having settled that and got it out of the way she helped Vince in the garden and did her share of the housework and the cooking.

At the nearby market on the Monday despite the consternation of the wizened elderly lady selling them, they chose six chickens and a small rooster. As they walked away with their new charges in two cardboard boxes Delilah heard the woman making comment to her next client, another elderly woman about the crazy English choosing hens when they all looked the same. It made her smile. Once settled into their new home the russet coloured chickens were all given names, which was going to prove interesting as the woman was quite correct...they all did look the same, well apart from Henry the rooster anyway.

Lunch with Amelie on Wednesday arrived all too quickly and Delilah walked the short distance to her neatly kept house with a certain amount of trepidation. Vince's neighbour had insisted on driving, although Delilah had seen Amelie behind the wheel of a car and it was more than a little unnerving. Vince off to catch up with some business dealings had left her standing in her bedroom in her underwear chuckling to himself at the variety of clothes she'd tried on and discarded. She had given him a playful shove out the door and had turned panicked eyes back to the mounting pile on the bed.

She wouldn't get the rest of her stuff until her parents drove past on their way to the Vendee in a few weeks' time and despite having bought pieces here and there her options were dwindling. "It's just Amelie." He'd said, exactly, it was Amelie. The woman had known him forever, had been his first, had dated Louis and what was worse, she was French. Effortless glamour, that's what most French women oozed. They just threw any old thing on and looked brilliant, when she did that she looked like a bag lady. In the end she settled on a plain green shift dress that she'd bought in Italy and a pair of simple gold sandals.

Amelie had seen her coming and sashayed out to meet her with a lovely smile and open arms. Delilah took in her new acquaintance with fresh eyes and felt totally inadequate in comparison to the stunning woman crushing the life out of her and kissing her cheeks in greeting. She was tall and willowy with long mahogany hair loosely plaited to hang casually over one slender shoulder and big brown eyes framed with dark lashes. She wore a pair of perfectly fitting navy Capri's and a simple silk top finished off with a jaunty floral scarf and a pair of ballet pumps. Now if she'd gone in that direction she would have looked like she was trying too hard.

Amelie's brand new Citroën eased around the narrow winding lanes past apple orchards and fields of bright yellow sunflowers until they reached the gates of the nearby Chateau and drove up the long twisting lane that followed its boundary wall. Eventually the car turned up a neat driveway and parked on a small rise, which had a view through the parkland to the imposing façade. The small restaurant barn roughly translated as "Chateau view" that Amelie had chosen had been open for a couple of years and the owners were a Parisian couple fed up of the rat race who had moved back to the area where the chef Marie had grown up. Amelie was careful to park in the shade of a large tree as the noon sun was beating down and while she waited Delilah stood and watched a kestrel hovering above the fields opposite, its attention fixed on some poor little creature on the ground. Her companion broke her reverie and threading Delilah's arm through hers walked her through the heavy oak door and Delilah had to take a moment to adjust to the change in light inside the cool interior.

All the original creamy Truffeau stone work had been lovingly restored as had the oak beams that crisscrossed the high ceiling. The restaurant was tastefully decorated and was filled with wooden tables covered in jaunty, brightly coloured tablecloths. As they walked in the majority of other diners greeted them with a pleasant "Bonjour". An attractive middle aged man with the most glorious moustache threaded his way through to them and greeted Amelie fondly.

His name was Jacques and when introduced to Delilah he had rattled off a small poetic eulogy to her name, quite the ladies' man. The delicious smells pervading the air was making her stomach rumble and she was grateful when he finally directed the two of them to a small table in a bright corner next to a window. He poured them a Kir, local Samur sparkling wine with just a splash of Violet syrup and put a small plate of delicate canapes on the table. Fizzy Palma violets thought Delilah as she sipped the pale lilac liquid, the bubbles fizzing and popping refreshingly on her tongue, scrumptious.

Amelie hadn't spoken much on the way there other than to point out the odd landmark or to drop a small anecdote about the area or a local personality. She leant over the table and smiled.

'So what do you think?' Amelie asked seeing the surprise in Delilah's eyes.

'About?'

'This place? Très jolie, no?'

'It's been beautifully done.' She took another sip of her Kir trying to ignore the sudden triumphant look on her companion's face.

'I helped with the renovation.' Lord was this woman good at everything? 'There's no menu at lunchtime by the way, it's just a set meal and you get what you get, I hope that's ok.' She was happily talking in excellent English, which made Delilah feel guilty for not trying out her French. 'The food is brilliant, Marie has worked in some wonderful kitchens in Paris, I'm so glad she came home. We were such good friends at school.'

'It certainly smells good.' Delilah felt there was something coming, but was unsure what.

'I have to tell you Delilah, because I know Vince won't, we were lovers...' She waited, but Delilah decided to let her carry on. 'The first time was after a dance when I was just fifteen.' So far nothing Delilah didn't know. 'I began dating Louis when Vince returned to England to start college, but I never stopped loving him.' A bit theatrical Delilah thought waiting. 'So, Louis he loved the church more and so we parted. Vince came back here when the band split up and we just, well we just became lovers again. It was never going anywhere though, so I told Vince it was over. I thought I might have broken his heart as he told me he couldn't live without me. I hope, I am not...a jinx?'

Hmmm, she looked like she believed what she was saying. Now last night Vince had told her that he had always harboured feelings for Amelie and so when the group crumpled he had turned to her for support. He'd said "careful what you wish for" as he had quickly realised that he didn't feel how he thought he would, she'd been an unattainable fantasy that had disappointed in reality. So who was telling the truth?

'Thank you for being so honest Amelie.' She said calmly keeping her face unreadable.

'I think we shall be great friends Delilah, no?'

'I'm sure we will.' Delilah smiled but she wasn't so sure. There had to be a reason why Nicki had labelled her a dragon and Julie had loathed coming here other than Vince's explanation that she "just hated the place". Did Amelie still keep herself firmly planted in between Vince and any woman in his life, even to the point of frightening them off? She decided that she would keep a very close eye on her.

Marie the delightful chef was a small attractive woman with a shy smile and soft eyes who spoke halting, heavily accented English. Her delicious food did her talking for her and Delilah who had enjoyed the lunch felt comfortable enough to tell her in cautious French. She had tried to be involved in the conversations going on in the restaurant and she was pleased that her halting French had held up. She couldn't say that she had warmed to Amelie, but she was happy to keep an open mind.

Jacques had surprised her as she left by asking whether she had any plans to work during her summers stay and had offered her a few hours a week working for him. Delilah gobsmacked by her good fortune had readily agreed, it would give her more opportunities to improve her French, give her some pin money and it would get her out from under Vince's feet.

Back at the house she made the decision that it was about time she moved back into Vince's bed. During lunch Amelie had let slip that it had been her idea to put Delilah into her own room, to take things slow and reluctantly Vince had agreed. Well, thought Delilah we'll see about that and she set about filling the empty spaces in his large walk in wardrobe with her stuff. Hot after her exertions she showered in his bathroom with the glorious picture window over the valley, glorying in her nakedness in front of the uninterrupted view. Wanton creature she thought as she threw herself on to Vince's bed where a cool breeze blew through the open window sending goosebumps racing across her naked flesh. Happy with her exertions, she dozed contentedly.

'Now that's a sight to come home to...' Vince's voice drifted into her consciousness. 'I guess this means you've decided to move up in the world.'

'I'd have been here from the start if I'd had a say in it...' He sat on the edge of the bed, his eyes drinking in her body. 'But it seems others had a different idea.'

'Ah Amelie...'

'Amelie has a big gob when she's had a couple of glasses of wine.'

'Charming.' He slid down beside her and gathered her into his arms. 'She probably meant well.'

'I don't think she did at all, I think Amelie and I have a difference of opinion where you're concerned, she thinks you still belong to her and I don't.'

'Hmm, that's what Julie hinted at.' A quizzical look had crept across his face. 'But she's married to Henri and like I've said, I see her as a friend...no more.' He ran his fingers absently up and down her spine bringing the goosebumps back in a much more pleasurable manner. 'Anyway if she winds you up like this perhaps you should see her more often.' He chuckled moving in for a kiss and finding her holding back.

'I'm actually very miffed that you listened to her. I mean it was a bit like shutting the stable door after the horse had bolted, wasn't it?'

'You talk too much...' This time he was a little more forceful about his intentions and Delilah having missed their intimacy decided that perhaps it would be better to shut up.

Later that afternoon Vince stood watching Delilah as she cycled off to discuss her new job properly his face full of pride over her decision. He'd had few Girlfriends who hadn't taken advantage of his money and he loved that she didn't want to. There was a tatty old Renault van coming up the lane and Vince waited as it headed his direction belching black smoke into the clean country air. It pulled into the drive and Eustache, Jeanne's husband and one of his oldest friends heaved his bulk out of the driver's seat a mischievous grin beneath his moustache. Vince didn't move but just stood there with his hands on his hips and with what he hoped was a suitable rebuke written in his eyes. Eustache shrugged his shoulders looking like a naughty child who'd been doing something he shouldn't.

'I guess that this job had something to do with you...' It was a statement not a question, spoken in accusing French.

'Ah, but Vincent would you rather she had been left to her own devices?'

'She's bright, might have surprised us, but some warning of your plans would have been nice. I must have looked at her as if she'd just dropped in from Mars when she told me. Beer?'

'I thought you wouldn't ask, I brought some of Jeanne's pate, if you have bread…'

'Well when you put it like that. Eustache, thank you.' Eustache threw a friendly arm around his shoulder.

'You are welcome my friend. Anyway it will be useful for Jacques to have such a pretty girl working there and Jeanne says that Delilah wants to improve her French.'

'As long as they don't monopolise her. Anyway, how did you know she wasn't another Julie, who just wanted to sit on her arse and vegetate?'

'You said she wasn't the sort to just sit about catching the sun and anyway this way everyone's happy. She has her own money, you get some space and Jacques gets a lovely new employee, Voilà!' He threw his hands up in delight at his own initiative.

'Hmm, I guess. Now let's find that beer and you can tell me everything.'

~

TEN
~

Up on the potting shed roof under a darkening sky a black redstart was singing his strange song with the rustling paper notes at the end and the endless chatter of the swallows and house martins filled the air as Delilah fed the chickens expectantly gathering around her feet. Surreal, that's what her situation was she thought absently, as to all intents and purposes she and Vince were living together as partners and yet she still felt like she was just a house guest with benefits. Fair enough their relationship or whatever it was, felt solid enough and they were very easy with each other. She was learning to read his moods and now knew when to give him his space, just as he knew when she needed hers, even so what she craved now more than anything was normality.

About the nearest she'd come to reality were the few weeks she'd spent working for Jacques in the restaurant before she'd become some sort of local talking point and had given a grateful Jacques her notice. Vince bless him, had overcompensated wanting her to see everything and now she was on tourist overload. They'd visited just about every Chateau within a fifty-mile radius and now she felt that she'd be happy if she never saw another one again. They'd done the zoo twice, explored the local Troglodyte village and watched Ospreys fishing from a boat on The Loire. She'd lost count of the number of local vineyard's that had been visited and wines that had been tasted and now all the different varieties were jumbled together in her mind.

She had been in France for just over a week when she'd finally summoned the courage to tell her parents that the friend she was spending the summer with was actually one of the group that she had been following. They'd not been overly impressed. Still as Alice had pointed out she was a big girl and perfectly old enough to make her own decisions, right or wrong and live with the consequences. What she hadn't told them though was that she'd made a backup plan and if everything had gone horribly wrong their arrival on their way south would be her opportunity to jump ship and leave. It hadn't though, had it?

Fate in the end had also conspired with a compliant Vince that he was conveniently away when her parents had dropped in, so they hadn't had the opportunity to meet the shadowy new man in her life. Delilah had ended up wondering if he hadn't just made her life even more difficult by appearing to avoid the situation. He'd bloody well be there when they came back, whether he liked it or not, she'd make sure of that.

Later in the week glancing at Vince's calendar hanging on the wall Delilah realised that not only had she lost touch with reality, she'd also completely lost track of time. July was nearly over and August was fast approaching, her bizarre summer was flying by. Outside the rain that had been threatening for the last week was dropping in sheets shrouding the valley that lay beyond the window in cloud and although the temperature had probably only dropped a couple of degrees it felt chilly. A cloak of melancholy had settled around her with the arrival of the rain two days ago and for the first time she doubted the romance of living somewhere as remote as this.

At home when it rained there were normal places to go when not at work, like down to the town centre for a bit of retail therapy or to the pictures. Here the nearest town had limited shopping opportunities and the bigger ones were far enough away to be inconvenient. She could go to the pictures, but the films were all in French and although hers was improving it wasn't good enough for that and she had already braved the weather this morning and gone for a walk so that was out of the equation as well. She sighed and stared morosely back out at the rain, a small niggle at the back of her mind, which wouldn't go away. This house just refused to feel like home.

Something dropped through the letterbox and she retrieved it half-heartedly, wrinkling her nose at the lingering aroma of Amelie's expensive perfume wafting from the envelope. This was another one of her little games, regular little notes to Vince in perfumed stationery all designed to put her back up. So far he had never offered to tell her about the contents and she hadn't asked, but they still rankled. With another sigh she made Vince a coffee and Amelie's note in hand headed for his studio at the end of the barn at a brisk walk.

Music drifted out from the building, sweet yet haunting as Vince tinkered with the main theme song from a film score he and Lou had been producing. There was a deadline coming up and Vince ever the perfectionist was keen that this piece was the best it could be. Delilah knew it intimately so often had she heard it and yet she never tired of the melody, trademark Vincent Angel.

The film was his young protégé Frenchie's first Hollywood outing, a film about love and loss called simply "The Beachcomber". Vince had told her the tale and then played her the beautiful score and she'd been able to picture the whole thing in her head. The incredibly handsome Frenchie played a young man who spends a summer by the sea and has a summer romance with a local girl he meets. At the end of the summer they say a sad goodbye and he leaves, but he can't get her out of his mind. Years go by and desperate to find her again he goes back only to discover that she went missing just after he left so he moves there and waits, but she never returns, heart breaking stuff. Vince was lost in his work and Delilah put the coffee down out of the way and stood quietly listening for a while. Then leaning over his shoulder draped her arms around him.

'Hi Babe, everything ok? He planted a soft kiss on her cheek.

'Uh-huh, just fed up with the rain.'

'It is pretty miserable out there. I'm sorry I feel like I've just deserted you.'

'Work's work, I knew what I'd signed up for. Oh I nearly forgot you've a note.' She pulled Amelie's message out of her pocket as he swung the chair around and pulled her onto his lap. 'Another love letter?' He chuckled quietly.

'I wondered when you'd start showing some interest. It's all pretty much meaningless drivel you know? She's just trying to wind you up.'

'That, I'd realised and actually I have no interest in what's in them at all.' That was a big fat lie, it was killing her. He ripped the envelope open and read for a moment.

'Ah, now this is one you'll be interested in.' He passed it to her and she half tried to push it back. 'Just read it and tell me what you think.' Delilah took the piece of rich velum and read the elegant hand inside.

'A party, I...'

'...Could have organised it. I have no doubt about that, but this has become a regular affair if I'm here and because of the time of year it needed to be sorted in advance...'

'And Amelie offered.' He nodded with a small shrug. 'So what happened when you were with Julie, surely she...?' He shook his head. 'She didn't, why?'

'Didn't want to. She was only too happy to let Amelie do all the leg work and then all she had to do was play hostess and anyway if Amelie hadn't made the arrangements Julie would have hired someone else to do it.'

'With your money.'

'It was a complicated relationship.'

'Doesn't sound complicated to me. I'd say it was very simple, you had money and she was happy to spend it.' He laughed softly and pulled her closer.

'You are far more complex than any of them, that much I do know.'

'No I'm not, I just know the value of money.' She thought for a moment wondering whether to share something with him about her family as it would she thought enlighten him about what he considered her complexities. 'I'm going to tell you something that I've never told anyone...' He waited and taking a deep breath she told him.

After her Grandad's death her mum and her Nan Hazel had fallen out. She'd been five and too young to understand the intricacies of adult relationships and she was in her teens before Alice had sat her down to explain the circumstances behind the estrangement with her own mother. Delilah had already worked out that Hazel didn't approve of Bryn, as she had thought a boy from the valleys to be far below what she had expected of Alice. That though had not caused the rift, it turned out that the pleasant elderly man who Delilah had called grandad, had not in fact been her granddad any more than he'd been Alice's father.

She'd been told that shortly after moving to Sussex from Ireland with her wealthy family, Hazel had become romantically involved with a young man and Alice had been the result. He had been killed in the war leaving Hazel in a proper pickle and so she had run away from her straight-laced family afraid of what they'd do.

When she'd arrived in London she had taken a job as a secretary to a retired general, a widower. Eventually her condition couldn't be hidden any longer and she had tearfully confessed to him expecting to be sacked and sent home to her family. He though had offered to marry her and offered to bring the baby up as his own and Hazel had eagerly taken him up on his offer.

Hazel had foolishly chosen not to tell her sparky daughter the truth until after his death, which had been the final straw in a difficult relationship. Bryn had been the peacekeeper, he'd made all the arrangements for Delilah's visits to her nan's rambling Bayswater home and had tried over the years to reunite his wife and her mother to no avail. When told the truth Delilah had taken her mother's side and so the hostility had intensified with both daughter and granddaughter being estranged and Bryn eventually giving up trying to fix things.

When Alice had the accident that changed her life she had refused to ask her mother for any financial help, which unfortunately piled the pressure onto her husband and daughter. They'd managed and anyway Bryn was a proud man and would probably never have accepted help. So just after finishing school Delilah had packed her dreams and plans for further education into a file marked "can't afford" and had taken the boring job in the local bank. She had just turned twenty when the ice had finally started to thaw and this time she had been the instigator of the peace talks

Vince was sympathetic. 'Families are funny things; one day I'll tell you about mine. Anyway as you well know, blood isn't everything. You and I are so alike, both come from working class backgrounds where money's been tight and that explains a lot.' He kissed her softly, brushing a stray strand of hair away with his thumb. 'Amelie, Julie, both of them have always had Daddy's money or a man to get them out of the mire and unfortunately neither of them sees any problem with that, because they see it as their right.' He pushed her to her feet. 'Just makes me love you more...Now I have work to do otherwise I shall be in serious trouble. Go talk to Amelie and put her nose out of joint, eh?' He slapped her playfully on her backside as she walked away wondering if he'd meant the "L" word.

Vince watched her go with a deepening frown on his face. He found Amelie's note where Delilah had dropped it and felt a familiar irritation prickling at the back of his neck so screwing the piece of paper up he threw it dismissively in the bin. She was writing notes because they weren't talking since he'd read her the riot act. She'd turned poor Delilah into something of a freak show for her snooty friends and had probably ruined poor Marie's restaurant business in the process. Delilah had felt so uncomfortable being paraded as "That Groupie that Vincent Angel had brought home", that she had reluctantly given up her little job.

She hadn't known that Amelie was the one sending her friends in to cause problems, or that they in turn were slating the restaurant, but Eustache had and he'd told Vince. So Vince had torn Amelie to shreds wanting to know what poor Delilah or Marie had done to her to deserve such inexcusable treatment. Amelie had resorted to tears and when Vince had refused to discuss it further had moved onto the pathetic consolatory notes.

He now understood why Julie had eventually flatly refused to come to France with him as he assumed that she had suffered similar poisonous attacks from Amelie and he felt guilty about that too. All in all, his plans to make this house his base were becoming less attractive as the summer wore on. But what to do with Delilah? She needed to be useful, she liked to work and he knew that he couldn't interfere as she didn't like being helped either,

Eustache had discovered that the hard way. Another bloody Cherry, fiercely independent and stubborn, but with a vulnerability that his ex-girlfriend had never had. Hmm, now perhaps Cherry could have a word... He binned the next note that came through the door without reading it although he guessed it was probably a moan about Delilah. Amelie had been miffed that she had wanted to interfere in the party arrangements, but had reluctantly agreed that she could help much to his amusement as he knew that once she was no longer the centre of attention Amelie would lose interest.

Stevie Grieves, Cherry and their three small children arrived unexpectedly early on the Friday lunchtime on the day before the party, which caught Delilah by surprise. She was put even more off balance when with the two men settled by the pool watching the kids play, a heavily pregnant Cherry suggested that they take a walk. She needed to stretch her legs after the drive she told her hostess and tucking her arm firmly under Delilah's steered her out the gates and down the lane.

They had only walked a few hundred yards before running into an elderly chap who lived down the road. He looked the pair up and down and asked Delilah if her companion was her sister and for the first time she realised just how much alike they were. Cherry looked at the shock on her face and laughed raucously the light breeze blowing through her russet curls.

'Your face is a picture Dee. You do know that he has a type?' Delilah wasn't sure about the "Dee" aspect, that had always been Livy's pet name for her.

'He did say we were a lot alike. But I thought Julie was blonde and fluffy, so...'

'Julie was girly like Amelie, but I think he prefers a tomboy with a touch of red in their hair, makes us interesting. After Amelie he took up with a German doctor, she was a red head too.' She grinned at Delilah her green eyes sparkling with good humour. 'Seriously, most men have a certain type, didn't your ex have previous?'

'Yes, but I stupidly changed to suit him, the real me wasn't his type at all.'

'Nah, you don't want to do that.' She waved casually to a couple of boys in a tatty old fiat who'd whistled as they drove past. 'So how are you coping with the whole famous boyfriend business?'

'I haven't experienced a whole lot of it, but what I have has been a mixed bag. We were out in the chateau gardens at Villandry and ran into a group of Japanese tourists who recognised Vince immediately. They were really lovely and very respectful. And you know Vince, he likes to give back to the fans, so we were there for ages with the autographs and photos and there was an awful lot of bowing.' She thought back to that afternoon, it had been such an enjoyable day and she had loved Villandry. 'The strangest thing was, they wanted photos of the two of us together, there have been other fans, but I've always been ignored as if I didn't exist, so that was really sweet.'

'Nice people. It was the way I was treated that I found the hardest and I was relatively well known myself, so I can't begin to imagine how difficult it might be for you. You're going to have to develop one hell of a thick skin.'

'Surely it was the same for Amelie and Julie.'

'Amelie never experienced it, Vince is part of the furniture around here and they never went too far away. Julie, well she loved it, all of it. She has such a high opinion of herself that one, it probably never occurred to her that those people didn't give a monkeys about her.'

'Did Vince put you up to this?' The truth had suddenly dawned on her. 'A little pep talk!'

'Of course, but I would have done it even if he hadn't.' She smiled wickedly, 'because I'm like that.'

'Thank you. Really. I don't know if I'll have to think about it much when the summer is over though'

'Gosh, you're very insecure aren't you? Believe me if Vince wasn't interested, you wouldn't be here. He is so anal about his privacy and bringing you to his "bat cave" kind of throws that out the window.' She dragged Delilah to the ditch on the side of the road and pointed excitedly. 'Look at that butterfly, how beautiful. I never have my damn camera with me when I need it, you'd think I'd learn. Anyway Teddy and Seb are the two that crave the fame and the adoration of the masses, Vince and Lou are more grounded and don't need it. Stevie is the same, he'd rather be up in the Highlands up to his ears in a river fishing.'

'Well we'll see, I just feel the need to have some kind of lifejacket, just in case.' Cherry offered her a small smile and wrapped an affectionate arm around her shoulder. Delilah found that she couldn't help but like the woman.

'Well shall we head back? I'd like to say that they're talking about us, but I know Stevie and Vince when they get together it'll be football or shop.'

'They've been friends a long time?'

'Since the beginning. The two groups both started with Roscoe at the same time and those two hit it off on their first meeting. It's good for them to have friends outside their respective group who understand.' She shrugged 'Hobnailed still have the same line-up, have never stopped recording or touring, but they give each other space. Now Scarecrow, they have issues, with Teddy it's all about the group or all about Teddy and they should have ditched Seb when they had the chance as he just continuously winds Vince and Lou up.' She shrugged 'if they'd kept the original line up I don't think they would have called time on it. Has Amelie given you problems?'

'Just a few, but I can handle her.'

'Watch your back, that one would stab you in the back soon as look at you.'

'So I've already discovered. To be honest she's not going to be a problem for much longer, Henri has taken a permanent post in Paris and they'll be gone by the end of August.' For a few minutes they walked in silence their little chat over before spending the rest of their walk talking about normal things like the baby girl who would join Cherry's expanding brood and why Delilah really wasn't interested in having children just yet.

The morning of the party dawned with wall to wall blue sky and thirty degrees, which meant that the evening was warm and temperate. Lou and Cesca had arrived the previous evening and genuinely pleased to see her Lou had wrapped Delilah in a huge bear hug and Cesca had greeted her like an old friend. The wine had flowed and it had been a very pleasant evening with the group of old friends talking about old times while always keeping her included in the conversation. Roscoe and his wife Niamh had arrived just a few hours before the party and that had been a completely different situation.

Roscoe had greeted her coldly and his wife had ignored her completely, which had thrown her as Roscoe had been really nice during the tour. Later after overhearing what was probably supposed to be a private conversation between the two of them and Vince Delilah had been left feeling indignant. Roscoe was less than pleased with his friend's summer "companion" and his wife had gone further and dismissed her as "that groupie". Vince had been livid and had made his opinion well known before stalking off muttering under his breath. Still they'd be gone tomorrow and that'll be the end of that, she thought gratefully.

Amelie's arranged hog roast smelt delicious and even Delilah had to admit that her choice of caterer was nothing short of brilliant. People came up to her and congratulated her and she was only too happy to tell them that it was all down to Amelie, praise where praise is due. In fact, she had arranged for a beautiful bouquet of flowers and bottle of very expensive champagne for Amelie in thanks for all her time and effort and they were waiting for the perfect time in the evening to be given.

Vince spent most of the evening hovering protectively at her side until she'd reminded him that she was a big girl and quite able to look after herself. He'd taken that moment to crush her laughing in his arms a huge silly smile on his face before kissing her fiercely leaving her breathless. Roscoe she noticed looked sullen and his wife looked like she was chewing a wasp so Delilah helped things along by flashing them a triumphant smile.

Cesca flopped down beside her on the grass under the oak tree as the last of the guests were leaving. Tonight she had dressed down in jeans, probably very expensive jeans with a crisp white shirt and she still looked effortlessly glamourous. Her hair was caught up in a soft chignon and with a relieved sigh she pulled it out and shook it loose. 'That's better. I don't know why I put it up, habit I suppose.' All traces of the Italian accent that she'd been using all evening had disappeared and she was all American. 'Are you ok Lola?'

'It's been a surprisingly easy evening all considered. I had been having a bit of a meltdown over it.' Delilah glanced across to where Amelie stood talking to the caterer. 'I can't make my mind up Cesca, is Amelie glaring at you or me or both of us?' Cesca followed her gaze.

'Oh I think it's probably me, I'm the devil incarnate, can't you see my horns?'

'Just what's her problem, I reckon she needs to get over herself.'

'Oh poor Amelie is a very troubled young woman. Has Vince not told you anything about her?'

'He dismisses it as jealousy, finds it humorous I think.' Delilah leant back against the tree a worried frown on her face. 'I struggle to like her, she's incredibly selfish and yet other women fall over themselves for her attention. Is it me?'

'Nope. I don't like her either and I pretty much try to see the best in everyone. She doesn't like me because she thinks I stole Lou from her.' Delilah raised a quizzical eyebrow. 'She dumped him because he wouldn't marry her and she thought he was heading for the church. So you can imagine her disgust when just a few months afterwards he took up with me, a widow ten years older with a small baby. It must have been a real dent to her ego, no?' She smiled. 'If she knew the truth she would be horrified. Lou and I met at a party in London about eighteen months earlier, my second husband Nicolo was still alive then. We had a brief liaison and then went our separate ways. I had told him I was unhappy and he'd told me that so was he, but my darling we weren't brave.'

'Is Ornella Lou's?' Delilah asked wondering if that was the complexity the boys had spoken of. Cesca heaved a sigh deciding to be candid.

'To be honest Lola I don't know. Although she looks like me I see traces of both of them so...'

'What does Lou think?'

'She calls him Papa. She was still a baby when Nicolo died so he is the only father she has known. He doesn't ask and treats her as his, so perhaps one day...Anyway we've changed the subject, we were discussing Amelie, were we not?' Delilah nodded, that door was obviously shut. Lou choose that moment to arrive with brandy and after offering the women a glass sat down between them.

'So, my two favourite girls together, what poor soul are you ripping to shreds?'

'Amelie, Lola wanted to know what her beef is?'

'Ah, poor Amelie.'

'Come on Lou you know her best, spill.' He exhaled dramatically before leaning in to them in a conspiratal fashion.

'Amelie was her parent's princess, she could do nothing wrong and was told from an early age how clever and pretty she was. So understandably that is how she sees herself. When Amelie looks in the mirror she doesn't see ordinary, like I know Cesca does and I imagine you do, she sees a desirable sexy woman that every man wants and every woman wants to be.' Cesca rolled her eyes. 'She doesn't understand when a man doesn't want her, or when he prefers someone else. That's why she no longer talks to me, she desperately wanted a ring on her finger and babies in her belly and I didn't see myself being with her forever, then I met Cesca.' He reached out and stroked her cheek. 'Her parents divorced when she was nineteen and I stayed with her then because she was unhappy, but really she wanted Vince, she always wanted Vince.'

'He didn't want her.' It was a statement rather than a question.

'Not then, no.'

'You know?' Delilah put her hand over her mouth and glanced over at Vince.

'Of course I know, she made sure I knew. He'll tell me one day when he stops feeling embarrassed about it. You mustn't be concerned, he is my dearest friend, it means nothing to me. Perhaps one day I will tell him, but not yet eh?' He grinned like a Cheshire cat, he enjoyed holding that over Vince thought Delilah. 'Amelie, she didn't understand why her parents parted and she was confused why her father would prefer a struggling painter to her elegant Parisian mother. Life doesn't touch her, daddy was always there to dig her out of any financial problems and now she has Henri and God help him if they ever part she will take him to the cleaners, no?'

'Would she leave him if Vince…?'

'In a heartbeat, but you need to understand.' He shrugged. 'Our group was never up there with the greats, we had our successes and we made good money despite the charlatans who robbed us blind. Teddy and Seb are broke, but Vince's uncle was a financial advisor so we made some good investments, this makes us perhaps a little more attractive to some women. If Vince was penniless Amelie would have no interest, he could do nothing for her, money is everything to her.'

'It's not made her happy though has it?' Cesca chipped in.

'She lives the life she believes she deserves and it gives her no problem that someone else is supplying it. She considers herself a success and yet everything she has either comes from her father or Henri. If she knew Henri had a mistress...C'est la vie, no?' He chuckled mischievously although it came as no surprise to Delilah as Vince had already told her about Henri's other women.

Delilah was dizzy. Vince, like her only knew how to waltz and now he was spinning her around Viennese style across the grass as The blue Danube echoed on the night air across the garden. Both had kicked off their shoes and were laughing like a pair of tipsy teenagers after too much champagne. Most of the guests had left and just those staying at the house remained, it had been a wonderful evening, a great success.

Stevie and Cherry had joined in the dancing doing what looked suspiciously like a disjointed highland fling, although that might have had something to do with Cherry's pregnancy. Lou and Cesca clapped in time to the music before being dragged up to join in the dancing. A waning crescent moon lay on her side in the sky and the heavens were full of stars as they enjoyed a few precious minutes of total abandon.

After everyone else had finally headed to their beds Delilah and Vince chilled from the rapidly cooling night air retreated to a warm bubble filled bath. Delilah lay wrapped in his arms with her head against his shoulder staring out the huge window across the valley with her thoughts lost in the star filled sky. 'You never realise how many stars there are until you lose the lights. It's just like an intricately woven carpet, absolutely stunning.' She whispered contentedly.

'It was one of the things that attracted me to this place, that and the sunsets.'

'Not the woman next door?' It was said as a playful comment and in Delilah's pleasantly tipsy brain quite meaningless.

'I can't lie it gave it an extra attraction...then. Unfortunately, she ended up being the reason why I didn't come for so many years. You're not still worried about her, are you?'

'No, I think Amelie and I finally understand each other.' She pointed out at the sky where a satellite whooshed briefly into view. 'Do you ever wonder what's out there? Somewhere in the distance there must be two other lovers laying in a bath full of bubbles staring at the sky and asking the same question.'

'Always have, must be the whole *Star Trek* philosophy. It's all too vast for this to be the only planet with intelligent life on. God Lola that's deep for this time of night.' Her hair was bundled into a loose pile on top of her head and he freed it from the clip holding the curls in place. 'About Roscoe...'

'What about him?' She really didn't want to hear excuses about his manager's behaviour.

'It's a habit with him. I think he still thinks we're just a bunch of kids starting out that he can boss about and control. What we do, who we see, how it will affect the group.'

'And his income I dare say.'

'Cynic. Fair enough he ripped us off something wicked when we started out, but...Our relationship changed over the years and he's a mate Lola, a surrogate dad.' Hmm, debateable she thought. He shivered briefly, 'waters getting cold.' Reading his mind, she smiled and got out wrapping herself up in a big fluffy towel before handing one to him. 'It's strange,' he said as he rubbed himself dry, 'but I always feel at home here. I can see it all mapped out this house, wife and hordes of kids running about.' He cast her a sly sideways glance. 'You thought much about the future?' She didn't answer immediately as he led the way to the bed and slipped under the duvet pulling her with him. First Cherry and now him, it was a bit like the Spanish inquisition.

'Sometimes.' She tried to word her answer carefully. 'I'm not the most maternal creature in the world. Don't get me wrong I'd like children one day, it's just that I'd like a bit of a life first. You know, see some of the world and perhaps have a job that I really enjoy.' She wriggled closer snuggling into his arms with her head resting against his chest. 'When I have children I want to be a proper mum, watch them grow up and not have any regrets or what if's, does that make sense?'

'Perfect sense. I've often thought that's been half my mum's problem. She had no adventures and no life with dad before I came along.' Delilah could hear the slow steady beating of his heart and knew that her own was racing.

'So she has no immediate desire for grandchildren then?'

'Oh she has that, hence the whole obsession with Julie. The longer we were together the more she thought all her Christmases and Birthdays had come at once. Julie's biological clock was ticking with a vengeance and mine wasn't. If we'd stayed together any longer I don't think I would have had any say in the matter, it would have made mum happy though.' He buried his lips in her hair and she felt an involuntary shiver run through her body. 'Cold?' He pulled her closer 'I think we can do something about that...'

Laying there later with sleep alluding her she was hit once again with the same premonition that had been plaguing her since arriving here, this house was never going to be her home. So if Vince saw a future living here with a family, she would be no part of it.

~

ELEVEN

~

Bryn Grace leant his lanky frame over the orchard gate, settled one foot casually on the bottom rail, lit his pipe and watched his daughter. She was fussing over Jeanne's elderly grey cob, discussing the pony with the older woman and had one feathered hoof elevated across her knee. The French summer sun had bleached gold highlights into her hair and as the curls blew in the gentle afternoon breeze they sparked and glittered in the sunlight. This was a Delilah that Bryn hadn't seen for years, toned, tanned and totally carefree involved in a conversation about one of her favourite subjects.

The Gelding reached back and nudged her with his nose and absently she stroked his soft muzzle muttering a gentle word to settle him. I should have saved up and bought her a pony he thought, she'd always wanted her own, but as soon as she'd gone out to work and had the money to do it, she'd not had the time. He should have given her the opportunity when she was younger, poor Delilah, they'd never really had the money for anything, not that she'd ever complained. She'd had a spartan wardrobe as a child only starting to fill it when she discovered the delights of charity shopping in her teens. The occasional stab of guilt crept into his heart as he'd always done his best for his wife and child and this moment was no different.

Now though his guilt was over something else entirely, Nick. He had always been the instinctive one out of her parents, Alice was always happy to see the best in people no matter how they behaved, nevertheless Nick had been his mistake. In private bedtime chats with Bryn, Alice had confided that she didn't trust the young man, although she'd been nothing less than enthusiastic for Delilah's benefit. That had been a mistake too, perhaps if she'd voiced her misgivings their daughter would never have taken him back when they'd first separated.

The blame though was his, he'd really liked the lad and he was pretty much exactly the sort he wanted Delilah to end up with. A hard working outdoors boy who'd bought his own place and who was keen to extend his knowledge within his profession. He'd had good looks, nice manners and charm by the bucket load and Bryn had been completely sucked in. Well until he'd cheated on his Lola and tried to embezzle their money anyway. Although Alice told him he was being hard on himself, the remorse over the hurt caused to his daughter still remained.

Bored with standing still, the pony trotted off across the field to talk to his donkey friend in the field next door while the two young women watched still deep in their own private discussion. They might have been watching the pony, but Bryn was pretty sure the conversation was about something else, Vincent Angel. He straightened up and knocked the pipe out into a nearby sand filled flower pot that he'd been using as an ash tray. He liked the man, what wasn't there to like. A Chelsea supporter like himself, personable with an easy dry sense of humour and despite his profession remarkably normal. But then he came back to Nick and he'd thought the best of him too. Alice had hit it off with Vince straight away giggling like a schoolgirl when he flirted shamelessly with her, women Bryn decided liked Vincent just a little bit too much.

There hung the problem really, he was worried that Delilah would get hurt again. There seemed to be too many other women desperate for his attention, not that the guy seemed remotely concerned about any of them and that to Bryn made them dangerous. On the up side Vince seemed genuinely fond of Delilah and had been quick to defend her to those who it appeared disapproved of their relationship.

It was Vincent's world that bothered Bryn the most, he wasn't sure that his gentle easy going daughter would cope with the pressures of his fame and the problems that came with it. Alice had told him that she needed to find that out for herself and that she might surprise them all, Bryn though had a horrible feeling in his gut that he couldn't quite shake.

'What you thinking dad?' Delilah was standing on the bottom rung of the gate a silly childlike grin on her face.

'I was just wondering when my little girl grew up and became such a beauty.'

'Aww, no you weren't.' She climbed athletically over the gate and smoothed down her totally impractical summer dress. 'You were fretting about Vince...' When, he wondered did she learn to read him so well. 'I know what I'm doing dad. I have absolutely no illusions, if it lasts I shall be happier than you could imagine...'

'...And if it doesn't?'

'Then I'll have to get on with it, won't I?' Leaning over she planted a gentle kiss on his cheek, 'you'll always love me so what does anything else matter. Anyway do you remember that time I asked Nana Rhianna how long forever was, I think I was about eight?' He nodded remembering his serious faced daughter, her hair in bunches deep in conversation with the grandmother who'd raised him after the death of his mother. 'She said that forever was however long you wanted it to be. So if it's ok I'll take this as my own personal forever, even if it's only for the summer.' Bryn watched dumbstruck as she skipped with childish glee over to where Alice sat deep in discussion with Eustache.

'I'm your dad, I'm allowed to worry.' He whispered to her departing back.

Delilah watched Vince with her parents and smiled, he was in full flow about an old fishing trip he'd been on with Stevie in Ireland and there was a lot of hand estimation of sizes going on. She was quietly pleased that they all seemed to be getting on so well, as that immediately took the pressure off her if they liked him. She'd meant what she'd told her dad about being realistic about her situation as she still didn't see herself as Vince's partner, girlfriend call it what you like.

This summer had often felt like it'd had a fairly hefty touch of fantasy about it at times so during her practical moments she fully expected the bubble to pop when autumn came. Ever the pragmatist Jeanne had just said as much and that meant that Eustache had dropped some kind of insinuation about Vince's feelings during their normal run of the mill conversations. She'd meant no offense and Delilah hadn't taken any after all why would Vince see her as anything more than a summer romance.

Her dad kept glancing over at her with a slightly worried frown and Delilah flashed him some of her best "I'm fine" smiles in reassurance. She knew he felt guilty about pushing her at Nick just as she knew her mum hadn't liked him, but she had been a big girl and quite capable of making a total pigs earhole mess of things all by herself. Strange how she no longer thought of Nick, Livy and the baby due in early Autumn with anything more than a detached interest. Her parents had told her that her other old friend Holly was now expecting her first child and that didn't surprise her as Holly had always been quick to copy Livy.

When Livy changed her hair, her style or her makeup then so did Holly even if those choices made her look silly and Delilah who hadn't cared what her friends got up to had just smiled and had gone her own way. She smiled fondly at the memory of her teenage years, how far away they seemed now. Looking up she realised that Vince was watching her with eyebrows raised and she guessed that he was wondering what she was smiling about.

Still she had other things to worry about, Vince's possessive mother Vivienne was coming to stay for a few days the following week and she was not looking forward to that at all. He'd explained on more than one occasion that Vivienne was very keen for him to get back together with Julie his ex as she considered her friend as perfect daughter in law material. Delilah had already had problems getting the seemingly perfect Julie who everybody had loved out of her mind. Vince had rarely mentioned her, as like Amelie he had already consigned her to the past, but even he admitted his mother wasn't about to give up on their relationship easily. It had crossed her mind that Julie was the reason for Jeanne's negativity as according to Amelie the two women had been "how do you say...thick as thieves".

Strangely enough it had been Amelie over a cup of coffee a week earlier who'd filled in the gaps where Julie was concerned, rather than Vince, probably Delilah had thought at the time to wind her up. She'd only brought the subject up because Vince had explained that he was meeting her during the week he was spending back in the UK when he took his mother home. To all intents and purposes, it was to be a very innocent meeting to discuss the splitting of their joint assets, but that didn't ease her mind.

This though had opened the floodgates as Julie was not Amelie's favourite person. She'd brought out a picture that she'd taken during a Summer barbeque and Delilah now had a face to put to the name. The nasty green-eyed fear that took root in her mind following this revelation shocked her. How could Vince have told her that there had been no spark, Julie was stunning. Her blonde hair was perfectly tousled, her skin flawless and her body would have done any glamour model proud. Amelie had suggested that Julie was only interested in Julie and looking at the smug face in the picture Delilah had found herself agreeing with her nemesis on that point at least.

Anyway, she thought watching Vince pull his guitar onto his lap, what did it matter? Her sixth sense was still telling her that she would never live here, not in Vince's beloved house and not in this village and the longer the summer wore on the keener she felt it. Her lover a mischievous smile playing on his lips had just launched into one of his favourite numbers "Girl" by the Beatles, which he teasingly serenaded her with in the evenings. The irony in the lyrics about the girl who came to stay were not lost on her in the slightest although his version of "Lola" by the Kinks was a thought provoker. The song was her cue to re-join her family before he dug any of his other favourite ditties out of his bag of tricks for the rest of the evening sing-along. It was her parents last evening in France before returning home and Delilah was not about to waste any more precious moments than she had to worrying about what would or wouldn't be.

Strangely, considering how they met it was the Scarecrow fans that were becoming Delilah's albatross. She was beginning to feel a certain amount of anxiety when faced with the aggression towards her that some seemed to feel was obligatory. There had been a number of occasions already this summer where they'd come into contact with people who recognised Vince.

Some had been alright, like the various groups of Japanese tourists that they'd met at Villandry and on a long weekend at Versailles. They had been delightful, polite and patient they'd all wanted photos with Vince and one or two had even wanted her in the picture, although she had declined and when they had finished one of them had kindly used her camera to take a couple of pictures of her and Vince. Then there were the others.

They'd been in Angers walking through the cathedral square after they had just trekked through the Chateau and its ancient Tapestry of the Apocalypse when they had been approached by a group of four tipsy young British women who recognised Vince and had upset Delilah enough that she had got out of the way. Vince was rankled by them, but had handled it all in a pleasant enough fashion until one of the girls a large brash brunette started making aggressive overtures towards him.

She had very loudly proclaimed that if he wanted a real woman when he got back to the UK he should call her and had thrust a piece of paper with what Delilah guessed was her phone number on it very calculatingly into his trouser pocket. Then she had turned and smirked at Delilah slurring maliciously as she shoved past her, 'you've got no chance love.'

Delilah waited for Vince to empty his pockets and dispose of the offending article only he didn't and as the afternoon ground on, so did her annoyance. She was surprised she'd kept her temper as long as she had, but it blew once they arrived back at the house. Despite the fact that her feet ached from the huge distance they'd covered she had turned tail and gone out for a walk, unfortunately the resulting pulsating feet didn't improve her temper. When she got back he'd asked what was wrong, which was a big mistake and she'd launched at Vince and obviously suffering as well he'd bitten back. With his mother arriving the following day it wasn't the best time in the world to have their first real stand up row, but with her apprehension rising about that meeting and her annoyance about the phone number she had just exploded.

Vince waved sheepishly to Delilah and Amelie as they drove off for their shopping trip. Once the little Fiat had disappeared from view he retrieved his spade and returned to planting the row of lavender and rosemary plants in the freshly dug red soil under the front windows. If Delilah was worried about his mother, Vince was more so as there were some very solid reasons why so far Vivienne Angel had only met some of his girlfriends.

His mother at fifty years old was a very difficult woman and even after all these years he still couldn't predict her moods or reactions. Rubbing his hand gently over the tiny rosemary plant he breathed in its spicy fragrance before tucking it carefully into its new home, it brought back fond memories of his late father who'd always smelt of the herbs he'd lovingly grown.

His dad would have adored Delilah, she was similar to Cherry and Simon Angel had liked Vince's ex very much. He'd never been brave enough to introduce his ex-glamour model girlfriend to his sometimes prudish mum because he'd known that she wouldn't have approved. When their break up had hit the tabloids, she'd given him a lecture about "women like that" despite having never met her and he had a horrible feeling that Delilah was going to slip regrettably into the same bracket in his mother's eyes. The groupie he'd picked up on tour and stupidly brought home. Then of course there was the Julie issue, his mother just refused to accept the end of their relationship and Vince was certain that she was behind Julie's endless chasing.

He had boasted before his dad's death that his parents had a fairy tale marriage, although the truth he knew was somewhat different. They had been very different characters and often fought like cat and dog, Vince was like his dad, normally easy going with an occasionally sharp temper and an often inappropriate devil-may-care streak. His father had liked nothing more after a hard week's work than to watch some sport on TV, or to be up to his eyes in muck in the garden. Vivienne was unable to sit still and relax and needed to be doing something all the time.

Regardless of a long working week and often tired, her long suffering husband had been continually nagged to do this or do that and if she didn't have anything for him to do, she'd insisted that they went out somewhere to do something. Inevitably this usually ended in a row because Simon had told her no!

Simon Angel had met his unfortunate end in a pile up on the motorway on the way home from work less than a week after Vince had met his oddly morose dad for a pint. Already confused by his miserable dad, Vince had been completely flummoxed by his mother's reaction after his death. He'd expected grief, but she'd not wanted to see or talk to anyone, including him.

Of course they say "the truth will out" and it did. She had eventually broken down and told him that she had asked his dad for a divorce the week before his death. She'd explained that despite still being in love with him, she had wanted to jolt some sort of reaction from the always laid back Simon. And so it was guilt, Vivienne believed that his death had been her fault and he'd died thinking that she no longer loved him.

Vince had been angry with her and they'd hardly spoken for months until his grandmother became ill. After her death Vivienne had become increasingly possessive of Vince wanting to constantly interfere in his life. Then she had met Julie and began plotting how she could have this wonderful new friend as a daughter-in-law. When they had split up she had been livid. He sat back and took in his efforts, nope he wasn't looking forward to this at all.

It didn't help either that he and Delilah had been tiptoeing around each other this morning as they'd had one hell of an argument last night and it had blown up out of his own short sightedness. That bloody girl in Angers. Delilah had been off with him for the rest of the day and had stalked off for a solo walk when they'd got home. He'd been bewildered by her change in mood until he'd asked her what was wrong and that started the row.

She had been obsessed over the telephone number the girl had given him, telling him that he should have thrown it away in the first bin he'd come to. Well he'd disposed of it when he'd come home, so he didn't understand why she was being so neurotic about it. Things like that came with the territory, didn't they?

There had been telephone numbers offered at other times in the past and previous girlfriends hadn't been so wound up about it, but that was when it hit him. Amelie and Julie had been supremely confident in themselves, as far as they were concerned no man would ever cheat when they had something so wonderful in their bed. Delilah though had been crapped on by her fiancé and best friend, so all she saw was Vince holding onto the number for when he went back to England at the weekend. On top of that she hadn't been too happy that he was seeing Julie either. Normally she was the pacifier in their occasional disagreements, but this time he'd been the first to stand down. He'd shown her the meaningless screwed up scrap from the bin and told her that he didn't want anyone else. That was one thing Vince didn't do, he didn't cheat on the women in his life, might have been tempted at times, but so far had never followed through.

Nothing quite like a bit of serious retail therapy to ease a troubled soul and so Delilah returned to the house later that afternoon armed with an array of bags and found a very stressed Vince in the kitchen, his hands on his hips and his eyes a little wild.

'She wants bloody fish, I'd got chicken, she always eats chicken, but no, she wants bloody fish. Sorry love did you have a nice day.'

'I spent lots of money.'

'That's nice' She looked at him with her nose wrinkled in amusement, he wasn't listening.

'With your credit card...'

'Lovely, what?'

'Hah, that got your attention, didn't it?' She threw her arms around him and he rested his head on hers. 'Well you bought me a very nice handbag anyway.'

'Does that mean I'm out of the doghouse then?' He breathed in the apple scent of her hair.

'Hmm, you weren't really in there, it was my fault I blew it up out of all proportion, sorry.'

'No it was mine. I forgot, it was insensitive of me. So it's me who needs to apologise.'

'You already did, you bought me a very expensive bag. Thank you.' She grinned, 'so where is your mother?'

'At a gathering of the coven in the village. Discussing you in great detail I would imagine.'

'Did you just refer to your mother as a witch?'

'Yes, I suppose I did.' He let out a resigned sigh. 'I really wish she'd go out and meet a new man then perhaps she'd keep her nose out of my life. Come on Lola, what on earth am I going to put with this fish?'

It hadn't been the best of evenings for Delilah, the fish according to Vivienne was overcooked, the skin had been left on the peppers and there hadn't been enough herbs. Then for good measure Vince's mother had spent the rest of the meal telling Delilah just how perfect saint Julie was and that she would have got the Provencal cod just so. Vince had quietly snarled that actually he'd cooked it and if she didn't like it, she could eat elsewhere. By the time they'd finished the meal she was wishing she'd cooked and put a whole heap of herbs in because then Vivienne wouldn't have tasted the henbane that grew in the forest that she could have added. As she cleared away the dishes an inaudibly seething Vince suggested that she went down the garden to put the chickens to bed and Delilah didn't need asking twice.

She'd barely got out of the door before Vince exploded. He told his mother in no uncertain terms that she had been exceptionally rude to Delilah by endlessly talking about Julie and should apologise. He then read her the riot act about his ex-girlfriend making it very clear that it didn't matter how much she wanted them to get back together it was never going to happen. Delilah wondered if Vivienne had guessed that she'd be listening as she added something that would have been hurtful if Delilah hadn't already known about it.

Vince was meeting Julie at the end of the week when he was back in the UK to in his thoughts "amicably" sort out a few loose ends. Vivienne and Julie it seemed had the idea that it was some kind of reconciliation. Vince put her right and suggested that if Julie had any different ideas, they could just as easily sort it out in his solicitor's office. Delilah took this as a good time to disappear and headed off to deal with the chickens and by the time she had finished with them Vivienne had retired for the night and Vince spent the rest of the evening apologising for her behaviour.

Thankfully the old dragon had only stayed three nights and after the first disastrous evening had duly apologised and become the perfect guest. She had even praised Delilah's abilities in the kitchen and had asked for the recipe to the "scrumptious" lemon drizzle cake that Delilah had made on the last afternoon. Mostly though the pair of them had kept out of each other's way. Vivienne had come to France to catch up with some of her old friends and seeing her son was just a convenient extra. Strangely her visit had accelerated the thawing of Delilah's troubled association with Amelie as Vivienne had been staying in Paris with her mother Marie and had travelled down with her.

Amelie didn't have the best relationship with her mother or Vince's so she and Delilah had found a certain amount of solace with each other. They would never be close friends, but bitching about the two older women had made them both feel better. It was during one of these sessions that a despondent

Amelie had confided that they would be closing her beloved house up and moving to Paris sooner than she had first thought. She was struggling with the idea of moving away from her support network of close friends and extended family to live in Henri's Grandmothers old house in the road where he had grown up, somewhere that she would be the outsider.

Vince meanwhile had been overly attentive during his mother's stay and it had made Delilah uncomfortable. It brought back disturbing memories of Nick and the way he had so obviously overcompensated with her while cheating with Livy. She hadn't realised how much that situation would continue to raise its ugly head in her life no matter how much she thought she was over it and as she waved her lover and his mother off her mind was already fighting fleeting shadows of the past.

It was ridiculous really, he'd explained why he had arranged dinner with Julie, hadn't he? They had legal stuff to sort out and he had wanted to keep it civil, but did he need to take her to one of London's most fashionable restaurants? And yes he'd argued the point with his mother, but that could have been an act put on because he'd thought that she was listening. What it all boiled down to was the simple fact that their crazy summer hidden from reality was nearly over and her own personal forever was coming to an end. She sighed sadly and walked back inside the house that no matter how hard she tried, she just couldn't think of as home.

~

TWELVE

~

Vince had been driving for longer than he should have when he pulled into one of the myriad of stopping areas on the almost deserted French motorway and getting out of the car rubbed the weariness out of his eyes. The September sun was deliciously warm as he ambled around the peaceful picnic area before sitting in a sunny spot behind a hedge with a sigh. He'd been gone longer than he intended and although he felt guilty about leaving Delilah by herself he was pleased that a week away had helped him sort out his jumbled mind. He leant back against the hedge and turning his face to the sun closed his eyes and drank in the warmth.

The journey back to the UK had been intolerable. Vivienne had bleated on and on about Julie and when she wasn't talking about her dream daughter in law she was waffling on about the newly arrived grandchildren of various of her friends. The only subject that hadn't come up had been Delilah. Vivienne had treated her badly and Vince had been pleased that her stay had been transitory or else he imagined there would have been all out war. In the end he was grateful to drop his mother off at her home in Hampshire before zipping off up the M3 to the welcome sanctuary of his London flat. The dinner with Julie had been a colossal disaster. She had walked into the restaurant like it was an everyday occurrence, clad in what looked to be a very expensive skin-tight dress that was fractionally too short and cut way too low. She had looked stunning and the sight had left him cold, which told him all he needed to know about any latent feelings he might still have had.

She'd been charm personified, all coy smiles and girlish giggles, well up until the space between the starter and main course when he'd slapped the legal paperwork in front of her. She'd looked at it inanely as if it was some strange alien that had somehow found its way onto the table. He'd explained that the house they had bought together was hers, but that was all she was getting out of their breakup and she had until the end of the week to take it or leave it.

The tears had come then, she hadn't realised that they were over, she'd thought that he just needed some freedom while he was touring. Briefly she had excused herself to sort her face out before coming back calmer and back in control. Weirdly she'd behaved then as if nothing had changed, chatting about her new job and what she'd done to the house before leaning over the table with an adoring smile to kiss him. Disgusted, that had been his cue to leave. He'd paid the bill and left her sitting there with a slightly amused expression on her face. What the hell had that been about, he'd thought at the time?

It had been just after ten when he'd got back to the flat and completely flummoxed by the evenings events he'd poured himself a drink and phoned Delilah to tell her what had happened. He'd heard the relief in her voice and knew that she'd been fretting about the meeting. He discovered exactly what Julie had been up to on the day that he'd originally planned to head back to France.

Teddy and Roscoe had conned him into staying a few extra days, as they wanted him to help promote the re-release of one of Scarecrow's early tracks that was being put out to raise money to help the people of Montserrat. Teddy had a home on the island where he spent a fair amount of his free time, thankfully for the moment it was far enough away from Soufriere Hills not to be affected by the volcano's current eruption. Even so he wanted to help the displaced locals who had lost everything. So Vince found himself booked onto one of the morning magazine shows with Teddy.

He hadn't seen the papers. He'd spent the previous evening with Stevie Grieves watching

Chelsea play, followed by a late night Indian and numerous beers so just getting up in time to get to the studio had been a major achievement. The interview had started well enough, they'd talked about the group, their forthcoming new album and Teddy's reason for wanting to do something for the Islanders. Then they'd asked Teddy about his relationship with Loris and he had chattered on about their wedding plans for the following year, all pretty innocent. That was when the front page of one of the tabloids was pushed in front of Vince and their hosts quizzed him about its contents. There were two pictures, one was of that baffling moment in the restaurant when Julie had kissed him and the other was a somewhat dishevelled looking Julie leaving the hotel in the early hours of the morning and so now he knew.

Julie had played him. She had known what was coming and she'd made sure that she'd taken her revenge. He guessed that by now his mother or Roscoe had been on the phone to Delilah to "warn" her about the photos, knowing full well what reaction it would cause. All of them knew his reticence when it came to his private life, he liked to keep it just that, private. Teddy played his life out in front of the world because he couldn't handle life without the adoration and the fame, but Vince preferred to actually have a life, with no interference. He looked at the pictures and for all the world the story they told was unmistakable, he and Julie had rekindled their passion over a romantic meal and had followed it up in the bedroom of the hotel where he must have been staying. Only he hadn't been staying there.

Unlike Delilah, who he'd discussed money with, he had been very cagey with Julie about his finances when they'd been together making sure that she only knew what he wanted her to know. When they'd met he'd been sharing Teddy's Battersea terrace, not because he didn't own his own place, but because he'd been mostly living in France and his Bayswater pad was rented out. Technically most of his property portfolio was owned by a holding company, which in turn belonged to him. Hiding it away to make sure others couldn't get their hands on it had been on his uncle's advice and he'd never regretted taking it.

So dilemma time. He hadn't hesitated and with a casual chuckle he'd told his hosts that he had a girlfriend waiting for him back in France and he'd been talking to her from his London flat for about an hour or so before the photo was taken. Thank god for Delilah thinking she had an intruder and using the speed dial on the phone to call him, he'd thought.

Revenge for being dumped he'd told them with a shrug and the ensuing shock on their faces had given him a great deal of satisfaction. The interview went a bit flat after that.

Vince got up, stretched and walked back to the car slipping easily back behind the wheel to finish his journey. He was back at the house just before seven and opened the door to the glorious smell of a beef casserole creating its magic in the oven, which made his stomach rumble in anticipation and reminded him just how long it had been since lunch. Delilah greeted him as though he'd been gone for months rather than the five days they'd been apart, her arms thrown around him and her lips glued to his.

Hungry or not there were other needs more pressing for both of them and he picked her up and carried her to the large fluffy mat in front of the fire. Afterwards as they lay naked in each other's arms Vince recognised the feelings that burnt in his chest and accepted that what he'd felt under that full moon in Venice was love. He loved this gorgeous creature more than life itself and the idea that this magical bubble they'd lived in would come to an end and she'd disappear into the cold mist of day was more than he could stand, so he told her without hesitation or doubt. Time to put plan A into action.

Delilah had been as grateful for the break as Vince and needing her own space she'd fast come to the conclusion that actually you can have too much of a good thing. She'd put the time to good use making plans for her future, creating a game plan that she could put into action when she went home. She had phoned Mia, as she often had during the summer only this time they had discussed the possibility of her moving up to London to share her new friends flat in Shepherds Bush. She knew that the likelihood of her getting a decent job where she lived was remote as the recession of the early nineties was still biting hard locally. So a move up to town sounded the best option especially as she had the choice of two places to live.

She was fairly certain that if she wanted she could probably stay at her grandmothers rambling old house just a few roads back from Bayswater and although she didn't know it, a short bus ride from Vince's London home. She didn't exactly know what she wanted to do, but was sure that once she was settled and had found herself a job everything would fall into place. Then Vince arrived home and she'd realised just how much she had missed him. Then totally out of the blue, he'd said those three magic words, he loved her…

The two weeks since his return had been quite frankly amazing and Delilah started to disregard some of her more negative concerns. Even her annoying niggle about the house seemed to dissipate in the rosy glow of Vince's revelation. He'd told her the Julie story and had been quite startled when she said that nobody had spoken to her about it.

She'd lied, Roscoe had called and in quiet, honeyed tones had asked her not to worry about it. She'd not wanted to upset Vince about his friend and Manager, although she wondered if she might regret that at some point in the future. And the future was what Vince wanted to talk about, the autumn he'd be spent hidden away in the Caribbean recording the new album, the charity gig in London when he got back and the last part of the tour during the first half of the following year.

After that, he'd said that they'd finally have time for each other and she believed him. Laughter filled evenings had been spent under the oak tree with Vince playing his guitar while the sun put on a stunning light show as it slid below the horizon. When darkness fell and the mosquitoes forced them indoors they had spent long nights wrapped in each other's arms with their bodies aching from their lust and their rejuvenated hunger for each other feeling like it would never fade.

With just a couple more weeks left until work pulled them apart Vince took her to a nearby village that was holding what had become a regular festival held just before the grape harvest. The narrow, twisting medieval streets decorated with thousands of fairy lights echoed with the sound of music and the night air was filled with delicious aroma's that wafted upwards from the dozens of food stalls dotted about.

Delilah was awestruck, she had never been part of anything so magical back home and yet everyone here seemed to be completely at ease. Her feet ached from dancing and her throat was hoarse with laughter, but she didn't want to stop and drunk on such enchantment all her worries about the future melted away. All thoughts of this pleasant corner of France not being her home were pushed back into the part of her brain marked "ridiculous" as she allowed the pragmatic part of her to dismiss the paranormal.

Laughing, Vince pulled her into a shadowy doorway and kissed her until they were both breathless with desire. She knew it was one of those moments where they really ought to stop, but tonight she didn't care and the devil inside was urging her on. The little side street was deserted, the doorway secluded and this was a scenario that she had never experienced, so trusting Vince completely and totally lost in the moment she let herself go. Briefly he stopped, his eyes asking if she was sure and she answered his question by hooking her fingers inside the waistband of her delicate lace briefs and letting them slide to the floor before grabbing the front of his shirt pulling him roughly back to her. Delilah had been astonished at how casually she had just given into Vince's suggestion and indeed just how exhilarating the experience had been. Senses heightened at the thought of being caught at any moment had intensified her arousal beyond anything she could have imagined and certainly the old Delilah wouldn't have even considered doing anything so risqué.

After as hand in hand they walked back into the village, Vince stopped to exchange pleasantries with somebody he used to know and as she didn't expect to be included in the conversation she looked about for a snack to quench a sudden pang of hunger. A stall selling small pots of mussels and fries was a few yards up the street and she found herself drawn to yet another new experience. Vince had been teasing her all summer about the fact that she had never tried mussels and she had wrinkled her nose up every time he had tried to tempt her. So as she was feeling bold she bought a pot. The smell of butter, wine and garlic with the faintest scent of the sea was delicious and she tucked in with delight smiling with pleasure at the crunchiness of the little skinny frites. Vince had an amused expression on his face when she turned to walk back to him, if he said "I told you so" they'd fall out, she thought.

The mussels came back to haunt her at about three o'clock the following morning and after crawling downstairs to her own room she spent the rest of the night talking to God down the large white telephone amongst other very unpleasant symptoms. Vince waking up alone at about six found her collapsed in a pile on her bathroom floor and set about cleaning her up before tucking her up in bed. Sometimes people surprise you and the tenderness that Vince showed her over the following twenty-four hours certainly surprised her. The local doctor wasn't too worried telling them that the symptoms would soon subside and giving out the standard instructions about the importance of trying to keep some fluids going in. Whatever the doctor said Vince was an ever present sentinel sitting beside her bed until the worst of the symptoms subsided.

After a couple of days, she started to feel better, although the thought of solid food made her stomach curl and so Vince made chicken broth, most of her ex's she thought would have left her to starve.

On the third day she was well enough to sit out on the patio in the September sun, but even so he insisted that she was wrapped in a blanket. Sitting beside her after bringing her tea he told her about the private auction coming up on the coming Saturday, which Cesca had asked him to go and bid on a couple of pieces for her, as she was working out in the States.

Apparently a wealthy Spaniard had bought a long abandoned chateau about two hours south from St Clair and had set about restoring it to its previous glory. At some time in the distant past one wing had been left in ruins after a fire and it was here he found a secret hiding place behind a bricked up fireplace filled with the magnificent collection. The hauntingly sad story behind the sale was about a tragic love affair that Delilah found a little too close for comfort.

The lady of the house had played Columbine in a travelling troupe just before the start of the French revolution and had met the youngest son of a local Marquis in Paris during a rainstorm when they had both sheltered in the same doorway. Against all the odds they had fallen in love and defying his parents had married moving into a distant aunt's home when she died. Then the revolution took hold and afraid for their lives they had paid off all their staff except his loyal valet and her maid and made plans to flee. Unable to take anything other than what they could carry and not wanting to be noticed they put everything of value into the inglenook fireplace in a little used wing of the house and concealed it by making a false wall, planning to come back when it was safe. They then left the house separately, planning to meet up again at a pre-arranged safe rendezvous some time later. The young man turned up and waited, but his wife never came. Eventually he learnt that his lady and her maid had both contracted the plague and had been lying sick and dying at the time of their planned reunion. Nobody knew what befell him, but he never returned to the house.

Looking through the catalogue there were some glorious pieces, a striking teardrop ruby pendant and a tiny Japanese black lacquer box with gold inlaid artwork of a samurai and a geisha under a cherry blossom tree, both of which she found herself secretly coveting. The exquisite engagement ring, one of the central pieces of the collection called to her from the glossy pages, demanding to live on her finger. A band of Welsh gold embossed with tiny stars set with a flawless sapphire carefully fashioned into the shape of the crescent moon with three perfect diamonds nestled within its curve, stunning.

With a sigh she decided that she was getting expensive tastes as these were all way out of her league, not that it stopped a pang of envy that both Vince and Cesca could afford anything on the list that took their fancy. Having already dropped a few hints in recent weeks that her birthday was coming up at the end of the month she'd asked Vince if he was planning to get anything himself and he'd shrugged pointing to a lovely set of pearls that he thought he'd get his mother for Christmas. Oh well she'd thought.

The phone call that was to change everything came on the Wednesday night. Vince had taken it as she'd been ushered off to bed early as her temperature was up yet again and his face was gloomy when he came to pass on the news. Her Grandmother had just had a stroke, although her parents had been quick to point out that she was stable and it wasn't life threatening, but as she was due to have surgery to bypass the blockage they thought she should come home as soon as possible. Her immediate reaction had been selfish, as she knew that she would have to leave Vince prematurely and she hated that she felt that way.

Then the terror that her nan would take a turn for the worse overwhelmed everything else and she started to panic about getting home. Vince had eventually managed to calm her down and after talking to her parents she'd felt a bit more composed. They, like Vince felt that she should give herself a couple more days to recover and he said he'd ring the next morning to get her on the first available flight home, so all she had to do was get well. In the end the flight he booked was on the Saturday of the auction and he offered to phone Cesca to cancel, but despite her inner reluctance Delilah couldn't ask him to let his friend down and told him she'd be fine.

Roughly flinging up the lid to Vince's old trunk in the hall, Delilah was briefly startled by a small soft thud as something slipped off and fell down behind it. She was just about to investigate when the phone rang and she heard Vince answer in a quiet voice. It was enough of a distraction for her to lose interest in the probably unimportant object as she strained her ears to hear the conversation. Vince obviously didn't want to be heard and what she picked up was suitably cryptic for her not to be able to pick up the subject.

    She pulled an old blanket roughly out of the trunk a look of pure frustration written across her face and stalked outside and down the garden. The small delicate Chinioserie address book filled with just about every contact number and address for him and his circle, which Vince intended to give her lay under the trunk forlorn, forgotten and unaware of its future importance.

With the blanket dropped in a pile under the oak tree, Delilah stood barefoot on the soft mossy camomile lawn and tried to make sense of the maelstrom of thoughts swirling through her mind. The last couple of days could only be described as puzzling. Both of them had drifted mechanically around as though guided by some unseen metronome putting the house to bed like a couple of zombies. They had barely communicated as both of them seemed unable to frame the words that needed to be spoken and even the address book he'd promised had failed to materialise increasing her anxieties.

Perhaps he'd changed his mind, perhaps he'd seen her nan's illness as some kind of omen that they were on the wrong path and decided to end whatever this summer had been. They had been so close up until that point especially since he had returned from the UK at the beginning of the month and told her that he loved her. If the thought of going home scared her, the thought of losing him was worse and it was tearing her apart.

The night was muggy and already Delilah could see the bank of ominous black clouds moving up from the south on the horizon and could almost smell the forthcoming storm in the static air. Ironic she thought that there had been a massive storm the first night they'd made love and there would be another on the last. She glanced up through the gnarled branches of the old oak tree to where the night sky was still clear, a full moon shone down, its silvery glow glistening on the bunches of parasitic mistletoe hanging above. The sight brought back fond memories of her dad's Welsh grandmother who he'd always jokingly inferred had been a witch, but Delilah hadn't cared a jot as she'd loved the old woman's wealth of wisdom and endless sayings. She had been the one to tell her that forever is however long you want or need it to be and this summer had been Delilah's forever. If it was about to come to an end, then so be it.

She'd also explained to her great-granddaughter that the moon was her goddess and that she should always pay obeisance when the lady was at her fullest, so that was what she did. Undressing carefully in the ethereal light of her deity until she proudly stood naked and bathed in moonbeams. Taking a deep breath, she spread her arms wide and tilted her lovely face up to the heavens bowing deeply. She turned slowly and her eyes met Vince's across the garden, he'd been watching and stood silhouetted in the doorway his hands on his hips and stark naked. Temptation, that's what Delilah offered as she felt a triumphant smile form on her lips, she would make sure that this would be a night he'd never forget. To her stomach, bubbling with butterflies it took him a lifetime to walk the short distance between them and the mischievous vilja driving her onwards became ever more impatient.

Who needs words? Just like that first night in Switzerland it was a lust driven by quite simply need, want, have and every nerve ending in her body responded with pure naked desire. Laying together on the grass with the scent of camomile filling their senses their bodies moved with a rhythm born of familiarity. There was something incredibly elemental about their love making as if they were inherently connected to the earth beneath and the heavens above and neither made any effort to conceal or hold back anything. In the distance the first rumbles of thunder could be heard above their shared cries of pleasure and the glow of the lightning illuminated the night, but they neither noticed nor cared even when the first drops of rain began to fall.

When the rain became too insistent to ignore and the storm crept ever closer they took their still unquenched passion up to the bedroom that had been their own private sanctuary from the real world during Delilah's forever. During the long night with the thunder crashing overhead words of love were whispered and promises made, but as Delilah well knew a lot of things are said in the heat of passion and not all of them meant.

She woke at six o'clock alone. Vince had left early to get to the auction on time, which she had known, but even so she wished they'd had more time. With a heavy heart she'd taken a final shower looking down over the valley and a last breakfast of toast and honey before the driver Vince had booked turned up to take her to the airport. Having loaded the last of her belongings into the back of the Mercedes, she locked the door to the house that she knew she would never live in and slipped the keys that she'd no longer need through the letterbox. As the sleek black car eased effortlessly away down the lane she took a last look filled with longing back at where she'd spent such a happy summer.

There was no adoring lover waving a fond farewell from the slowly closing gate and her heart felt heavy with the loss of it all. Amelie and Henri had finally left for Paris two weeks earlier and Eustache and Jeanne had rushed to the side of her ailing mother not long after, so no new friends to see her on her way either, even the ever present buzzard had deserted her. Sadly, she turned away and blinking back her tears fixed her eyes on the long stretch of tarmac taking her on the first step back to reality.

~

ENGLAND AUTUMN 95

~

THIRTEEN

~

Reality hit as soon as Delilah's feet touched English soil. Her drained and distracted dad had picked her up at the airport and driven her home in virtual silence taking only enough time for a cup of tea before returning to her mother's side up in London. He explained that there had been a rekindling of old hostilities between her mother and grandmother during what Bryn called "a difficult summer". Her grandmother had suffered a series of minor falls due to the odd dizzy spell, but had refused to see a doctor leading to some heated discussions. Alice had brought these up with doctors after the initial stroke and a previously undetected heart condition had been found.

Hazel hadn't been happy that her daughter had interfered and now the cold war had set in, so Bryn was once more acting as the peacemaker. Weary and disheartened Delilah was left by herself in a home she barely recognised as it looked to all intents and purposes that her parents had started to pack away their possessions, perhaps they were planning the major overhaul that they had often talked about.

Thankfully her nan was stable following surgery so she had time to get stronger herself before going to visit the following week. Once she had psyched herself up enough she'd phoned Vince to tell him she'd arrived home in one piece. He'd asked after her nan and made all the right sympathetic noises. She'd asked about the auction and he told her that he'd managed to obtain the pieces he'd hoped to buy. The conversation was stilted and at times there were moments of silence when it seemed neither of them really knew what to say, almost like strangers she'd thought. After a few moments of guilty silence, he confessed that he was packing up earlier than planned after managing to get a flight out to New York first thing Monday and so would fly to Antigua from there. She had no answer to that and so tired and emotional she put the phone down, poured out a glass of wine and had a good cry. Several glasses of wine later and filled with renewed bravado she rang Vince again ready to sort things out, but there was no answer.

She had a fairly serious hangover when he rang the following morning. Sounding more relaxed he chatted away about the forthcoming album and how much he was looking forward to getting back with the boys and putting it all together. 'I'll ring when I get there' he'd said, but he reminded her that it would be their last contact for a while as the band worked best by locking themselves away from distractions. He gave her the name of the hotel if she needed him, but she got the feeling that he would prefer that she didn't, which was exasperating. Lena would have the backstage passes for after the show in December and he'd see her then. He told her that he missed her and wished that they'd had the extra week, Delilah wished it too, but they hadn't and now she wasn't sure about anything. 'I love you Delilah, you do know that don't you?' No, actually she wasn't sure that she did.

A short while ago he was holding her in his arms, making love to her and whispering his deepest feelings in-between kisses, so why did his words ring so hollow now? Standing under the oak tree that night she'd known beyond any doubt that she was never going to live in his beloved French house, so perhaps this was the way it ended. For the second day in a row she stood looking at the phone through tear stained eyes and reached for a bottle.

Her nan Hazel looked fragile when she finally got to see her halfway through the following week and her parents apologised for keeping her in the dark about her poor health. It seemed that they hadn't wanted to spoil her lovely summer and wouldn't have pulled her home at all if it had been anything less serious. They both looked weary and Delilah felt guilty about her selfish desire to have stayed on for just a few more days with Vince. Hazel had been lucky, the stroke had been relatively small and after the bypass surgery had left her with problems that would hopefully be mostly sorted with Physiotherapy. The heart problems though were considerably more serious and would probably limit her life expectancy, a fact that didn't seem to bother Hazel as much as it did her family.

Back at her nan's rambling Georgian house just off Bayswater her tired parents dropped another bombshell, they had sold their house, her home. The doctors had told them that Hazel would need care if she was to stay in her beloved old house and so her parents had made the heartbreakingly difficult decision to sell. Bryn had left his job and had already got himself a part time job nearby and Alice intended to care for her mother with the aid of a small team of carers.

Delilah was stunned by the news and immediately panicked that she hadn't had this information when Vince had briefly checked in on his arrival in the Caribbean, so he was totally unaware of her change in situation. After a lonely walk around the serpentine in a damp Hyde park common sense kicked in and she phoned the hotel in Antigua. They had been very polite when they had refused to put her through to him, but had told her that they would make sure that Vince got the information. Lots of explanations crossed her mind when she didn't hear anything back, but she knew that whatever the reason she could do little about it and so with a shrug she put her mind to a more pressing issue, work.

Even though she had already concluded during the summer that she had more chance of getting a decent position by moving up to town, she'd thought that she'd have more time. Now her previous optimism was becoming jaded and she began to have visions of spending her days trudging around various agencies through the autumn rain looking for any available post. Sometimes though life offers up a break and out of the blue she found herself talking to the Vascular surgeon who had briefly been involved in her nan's care. He did some private work in a small exclusive clinic and an attractive post had just arisen in the main management office and would she be interested.

Delilah had jumped at the opportunity and an interview had been arranged for the following day. It was an interesting and well-paid administration post and she immediately liked her new boss Leo. Work sorted, she went home to pack and to say goodbye to her friends. Armed with a pretty baby outfit, she even went to see Livy and her new born daughter. She'd cooed over the baby, despite having no real interest in babies and made small talk with her old friend. They would probably never get back the friendship they'd had, but it was a small piece of closure in a complex world and she felt relieved as she drove away.

Finally settled in her new home she had phoned the hotel Vince was staying at again and left another message for him to call, he didn't. So she had phoned yet again and this time had just asked them to pass on the number for her recently purchased mobile phone. Still nothing, not even a text, which re-enforced her nagging concern that "they" no longer existed. On top of everything else whatever bug she'd had that last week in France seemed reluctant to go away completely and she felt nauseous and weary at times. Still her new GP assured her after a blood test that she was stressed and a little anaemic and that with some iron tablets and a bit of relaxation she'd be fine.

Mia had crept seamlessly back into her life and as both lived close to each other she was soon dragged into the vibrant London social scene and if nothing else she'd had fun. She made new friends among her colleagues at work. Her boss Leo was a burnt out cynical ex lawyer who she had hit it off with at her interview, Lisa the other half of her job share and newly pregnant Zoe one of the nurses. All in all, life was sweet and when she kept Vince out of the equation, she was happy. In fact, the only cloud on her horizon was the concert in December that was fast approaching and the reunion with him that she had a horrible niggling sensation wasn't going to end well.

Vince looked at the open spread in the glossy magazine and pulled a face. He knew Delilah read this shit and she wasn't going to like what she saw; hell neither did he. The pictures of the album wrap party on the beach on Antigua were all blue skies, white sand and a perfect azure sea, which lapped serenely on the shore around the feet of the beautiful people posturing there. There was Teddy with the always perfect Loris wrapped around him with the title "Our favourite couple looking forward to their wedding next summer", it was so sickly sweet that it made Vince feel like sticking his fingers down his throat.

Lou was cavorting in the surf with a woman Vince didn't recognise or remember and Seb was surrounded by a gaggle of laughing dusky beauties, a smug expression on his face. Then there were the others of him. He sighed, Lou said they looked innocuous, but would they to Lola? It wasn't his expression in the pictures that bothered him, it was bloody Lucee's look of total puppy dog adoration as she clung to his arm.

She was Loris's best friend so he'd met her before and if he was brutally honest he hadn't liked her that much. There had been something odd about her that he couldn't quite put his finger on, yes she was stunning, although a little skinny for his own personal taste, but she left him cold. She'd homed in on him like a magnet at the party and despite all his best efforts, he'd been unable to shake her. So out of politeness he'd talked to her and posed for the pictures. In the end it had been Lou who had saved him by dragging him off to swim out to a rock just off the beach and thankfully that had been the last he'd seen of her. Looking at the pictures now he felt a certain amount of dread.

He'd found the address book under the trunk when he'd got back to the French house, having meant to give it to Lola on that last night, had put it down meaning to retrieve it after they'd had supper and then forgotten all about it when they had given in to all that pent up emotion. He'd been out in the Caribbean for a month when the reality hit him and he realised that he hadn't. He'd tried calling without success and when he asked the reception staff at the exclusive hotel had told him they'd had no messages from her. He'd assumed then that she'd probably found herself a job and was busy, so he'd decided to try again when he got back. That's when the trepidation set in because all he got was an answerphone and his messages weren't answered. Eventually a very pleasant lady phoned him back and told him that she had only recently moved into the house and she didn't know who Delilah was. She'd wished him good luck and Vince had put the phone down with the uncertainty of their situation gripping his heart like a vice.

He rolled the ring in his hand down his fingers and dropped it onto a fingertip holding it up to the fading light so that the diamonds glinted. So much life in such an inanimate object he thought and so much trouble. When he'd agreed to go to that auction for Cesca there hadn't been a problem with that Saturday and anyway he'd seen the "Delilah" ring and just knew that fate had drawn him to it. The history even matched, the youngest son of a Marquis sheltering from the rain in a Paris doorway with a young woman called Delilah from a travelling troupe of players. Normally the two of them would never have met, but they were drawn to each other from the first glance and against all odds fell in love. The inscription inside the ring read "Me marier, Delilah, ma lune et étoiles" "Marry me Delilah, my moon and stars." Perfection. So what the hell was fate playing at now, he wondered?

Delilah sighed as she dressed for the evening ahead, it had been a busy day at work and she'd rather be in her Pyjamas in front of the TV than rushing around like a lunatic getting ready. Lord knows she was dreading tonight, a scenario completely at odds to her excitement back in May when she had bought her ticket. It wasn't that she didn't want to see Vince again because she desperately did, she just had an inkling that her fairy tale relationship was about to turn back into a pumpkin come midnight. On top of that she was meeting up with the others before the show and knew there would be awkward questions.

Mia, Lena and Nicki all knew what had happened in the summer, but Delilah had not said anything about the disturbing lack of contact since to anyone except Mia. So how much did she let on, those cosy pictures in the glossies of Vince and that stunning model Lucee at the wrap party were distressing, had he fallen for someone else? Mia had told her confidently that Vince had his fan face on, but she wasn't so sure. Somewhere in the last few months she had slipped into self-preservation mode and she was terrified that a man was going to make a fool of her for the second time in the same year.

With no time to faff about she quickly settled on a simple pair of jeans that seemed a little snugger than the last time she'd worn them teamed with a white cotton shirt and brightened the outfit up with red pumps and a chunky red necklace she'd bought the previous weekend on a visit to Camden Market. Pleased with her choice she threw a coat on and with a farewell wave to her parents rushed out into the cold to meet her fate. The girls had arranged to meet in a small bar just around the corner from the theatre where Scarecrow were holding their charity concert and Delilah was despite her best efforts fashionably late. There was as expected much air kissing and the odd surprisingly warm hug. She had sent Mia a text to let her know she'd been caught up and had asked her to order for her so that she didn't hold them up.

'I ordered you this, ok I hope?' Mia pushed a bottle of sparkling apple juice and a glass over to her and Delilah smiled at her friend. They might not have known each other long, but they were already able to second guess each other.

'Babe you look stunning as always. I'd kill for those shoes, they're so cute, Camden?' Lena held out a perfectly manicured hand in the direction of her feet letting the harsh lighting make the single diamond solitaire on her ring finger sparkle. Delilah took the hint and held out her hand admiring the simple, nonetheless ultimately perfect ring.

'Congratulations Lena, I'm so pleased. I bet Neil's beside himself isn't he?'

'I couldn't believe it when he asked, it came completely out of the blue. He's just got a job in Australia and we're going to live there, isn't that amazing? We're going to get married on the beach in Bali later next year and I can't wait to be his wife.' Delilah looked at Lena's happy flushed face and hoped that she seemed to have finally got real and left behind her ambitions with Teddy.

'Well it's about time, hi Delilah.' Nicki had a sympathetic smile as she hugged her and Delilah guessed she'd seen the pictures with their accompanying insinuations. Well at least Nicki understood she thought having been in the same predicament herself although that hadn't turned out too well, had it as after all these years Nicki was still alone. Briefly Delilah wondered just what power the Scarecrow boys had to keep all their previous lovers mooning over them years later.

They talked over each other a lot of the time. They all wanted to know every last detail of Lena's plans and she was happy to tell them, so why did

Delilah get the feeling that she was trying to talk herself into believing what she was saying. There was an edge of resignation in her voice and her eyes were devoid of any emotion, hmm not overflowing with love she thought. Well it was her choice, she could have said no and who was she to interfere as she could be wrong. Nicki was just off to do some volunteer nursing work out in Africa for a year and Delilah realised that she had never even known that Nicki was a nurse. They'd talked a lot on the tour, but they had never discussed work and Delilah wondered whether that was because Nicki knew she was newly unemployed and hadn't wanted to upset her. Although Delilah knew about it Mia told the others about getting her permanent Job with the designer Barney, it had been a dream come true for her and she was so pleased for her friend. As they had headed out to the theatre Nicki had put a gentle hand on her arm and held her back.

'Are you ok Delilah? You look a little pale.'

'I'm fine, I've had a long busy day at work and could have done without this.' She replied ruefully with a faint smile. 'Who am I kidding Nicki, I'm terrified. I really need to know whether we're still an item or whether I was just his summer groupie.'

'That's a bit harsh, is that what you think?'

'Wouldn't you. You've been there. Do you remember what you told me, that there is always another you, another me?' She nodded sadly. 'Well I'm just being practical. Let's face it even if there is still an "us", he's back on tour on the opposite side of the world for half of next year. So what happens then?' Nicki couldn't quite meet her eyes and Delilah had her answer.

The show would have been amazing had Delilah been able to control the cramping in her insides as her stress levels grew. There was the usual mix of the old and the new and as always it was lapped up by the theatre full of adoring fans, but for Delilah it seemed to go on forever. She couldn't concentrate on the music until an up tempo dance number called "The next girl" about moving on and the lyrics were so pertinent that they settled in her brain cancelling out everything else that followed. It was no good, she needed to know where she stood so that she could at least attempt to move forward with her life. With leaden legs she had met up with the others after the show in the bar where Nicki announced that she'd had enough of the whole backstage business and had waved farewell to Mia and Lena before Hugging Delilah and whispering softly "it'll be fine, keep in touch."

It wasn't fine. In the depths of the theatre Delilah spent what felt like an intolerably long amount of time looking totally out of place waiting for the group to turn up and she wondered if this was how it had been on the trip and she just hadn't noticed. Security had already been sniffing around, although so far Lena's backstage passes were holding up, but she'd already confided that in the past she'd been chucked out regardless. Great start thought Delilah panicking that she might not even get to see Vince. Although the room was a reasonable size the ceiling was low and she felt claustrophobic and as it had so often recently a nauseous sensation gripped her stomach. That of course was the moment at which Vince had suddenly appeared at her side. She couldn't read his face, unable to work out whether he was worried or angry and the firm grip on her arm that encouraged her off to one side of the room didn't help.

'God you look awful Lola.'

'It's nice to see you too.' Over his shoulder she could see both Tash and Lucee and although in different parts of the room, both were staring intently at them. 'I've had a stressful couple of months…' Nope that went over his head, obviously having to up sticks and move somewhere completely new as well as starting a new job, while not hearing anything from your boyfriend is not stressful.

'Are you sure you don't need some air or a seat?' Yes, her legs were wobbly, but all she really wanted him to do was hold her close and kiss her. He ran a nervous hand back through his hair, which had been cut much shorter than she remembered. 'I've so much to tell you. Trouble is, Roscoe has organised this bloody interview and it seems I'm the only one Teddy wants with him. I've told them they need to keep it short. Are you sure you're alright?' She nodded dumbly and then with a guilty half smile he was gone, after what five minutes, no I've missed you, no hug, no passionate kiss, just gone.

She had just staggered blindly across the room narrowly missing Lou who had started after her before being blocked by Loris, although she didn't see this. Shaking uncontrollably, she sat beside Mia and Lena and she was still reeling from the non-event that had just occurred when the two burly security boys appeared again. 'The boys have their partners here so they don't need your sort hanging around. So off you go quietly like good girls, eh?'. There was no doubting what was about to happen, Lena's face said it all. With deafening laughter ringing in her ears and the room suddenly airless Delilah didn't need to be told, she needed to get out of there fast before she suffocated or threw up. It was perfectly likely that the laughter had just been people having fun and had not been aimed at her, but she felt violated anyway.

Bitter tears prickled at the edges of her eyes again and blurred her vision as she rubbed angrily at them. Her cheeks were hot and flushed with embarrassment and the nausea returned, when was this nightmare ever going to end. Through the din she had heard someone calling her name, but her momentum had carried her out onto the busy pavement. She couldn't stomach anyone's pity and so she was halfway onto the bus home when the other two almost caught her up. Through the rear window she could see Mia and Lena, their faces fixed in exasperation and watched as they faded into the distance and disappeared from view. When she could no longer see them she buried her head in her hands and allowed the tears to fall.

The large Caribbean lady with a heavy looking shopping bag plonked herself on the seat next to her with a contented sigh. 'Ah that's better my feet have had enough.' She turned and offered Delilah a friendly smile. 'Are you alright child?' Delilah nodded. 'Man troubles eh? Bastards all of them.' Delilah forced a smile from somewhere. 'A pretty girl like you shouldn't be having problems like that.' A couple of boys sat opposite with a tub of fried chicken and the smell brought on the nauseous sensation again. 'Ah I see. He doesn't want it, God bless you. When's the babe due?'

'I'm not pregnant.' Delilah said hesitantly her numb mind jolted rudely back to the present.

'Well, I've got four girls and six grandchildren and I knew when every one of them was due before they did.' She laid a warm fleshy hand on her arm. 'But it's none of my business child. Ah my stop.' With a final reassuring pat on the arm she pulled herself up and left Delilah with a horrible niggling suspicion that occupied her mind enough that she missed her own stop and had to walk back.

As the hands on the clock in the kitchen moved past midnight Delilah now in pumpkin mode and dressed in a pair of sloppy comfortable pyjamas was making tea and toast, after all who doesn't find tea and toast comforting? A jar of crunchy peanut butter sat on the side waiting to be slathered on to the crisp white bread when it was removed from under the grill. Delilah herself was humming that bloody new Scarecrow number as she worked and so engrossed was she in her endeavours that she didn't notice her mum slipping into the room behind her. Alice watched her daughter for a moment feeling a tad confused as it had been Delilah's sobs as her heavy feet had carried her up the stairs that had woken her. Not that she ever slept properly until her baby was safely back in the house, even if she was a grown woman now. So why the sudden change in demeanour she wondered?

Alice felt a stab of guilt as she realised how little time she'd spent with Delilah since her return from France. She had been so busy, what with her own mother's poor health, all the hassle connected to their move and supporting Bryn as he made the difficult transition into a new job that he already despised. Delilah had clearly been unwell when she'd arrived home, but whatever it was that she'd been nursing she'd got through it by herself. Alice had barely acknowledged how skinny her baby had become before she had regained her appetite with a vengeance and put the weight back on. Then there had been the whole Antigua photo business, but Alice had quite cruelly she realised now, passed the buck to Bryn who had ended up listening to most of his Lola's tearful outpourings. I'm a bad mother she thought sadly.

'Do you want tea mum?' Delilah scrutinised her mother's face reading the guilt written there.

'That would be nice dear. I'm not intruding am I?'

'Nope.' She fumbled with the kettle and poured out a second mug. 'You were right you know.' She added a splash of milk and passed it across the table.

'It didn't go well then?' Her mother sighed wishing that she hadn't been.

'I had barely five minutes with Vince before he went off to do an interview and we were slung out on the streets like yesterday's rubbish. "The boys all have their partners with them they don't need your sort tonight." She imitated the bouncers gruff voice, that's what security said. "Our sort", groupies that's what they meant. Obviously that photo of Vince and that Lucee woman wasn't just "one of Vince's typical fan photo's" or else why would she be there backstage and the comment about partners.' She spread peanut butter onto her toast and took a bite. 'God, why am I so hungry at the moment? Do you know what mum? I'll love that man until the day I die, yet right now I just feel relieved. It's as if this huge weight has been lifted, do you think that's odd?'

'Not really. You've been under so much pressure this year one way or another and this was really the final burden, wasn't it? I mean there was Nick and Livy, then the redundancy and you had barely time to get past all that when along came

Vince. Don't get me wrong love we both liked him, but you've never been sure where you stood and your father and I struggled to see where you stood in his life. He gave you no contact details and didn't reply to your messages, so what were you supposed to think. You had to deal with moving right away from everything and everyone you knew to start a new life and a new job, which my darling you coped with marvellously. So I can understand why finding out how Vince felt was a mixed blessing and ultimately a huge relief. It means my dear that you can move on.'

'Hence the celebrative supper.' She stared into her mug and wrinkled her nose. 'Have you changed the brand of teabags recently, only this tea has a horrible metallic back taste to it?' Alice stared at Delilah her mug of tea paused halfway to her mouth and a horrible sinking feeling in the pit of her stomach. Why hadn't she noticed?

'No, same as always.' She glanced at her daughters face as she thought about it. 'I went right off tea when I was carrying you...' Alice waited for the penny to drop whilst fervently praying she was wrong.

It took a few moments, but then she remembered the comment made by the woman on the bus and sudden realisation hit Delilah. It was if someone had reached inside her head and given her brain a good hard shake and her hand flew to her mouth to mask the primal wail of despair suddenly building inside. 'Shit, I'm pregnant. What the hell am I going to do mum?' Her mother pulled out a chair and Delilah crumpled into it unable to breathe.

'First stop panicking. Breathe into this.' Alice passed her daughter a brown paper bag from a drawer and watched as her hyperventilating settled and she began to breath normally. 'Nothing is certain until you've taken a test and even then…We'll get one tomorrow. What we won't do is tell your dad until, well until I can find a way of telling him gently.' She rested a gentle hand on Delilah's head and leant down and planted a kiss on her forehead just like she had done all her daughter's life. 'It will be fine.'

'How could I have been so stupid though mum? You've always gone on and on about being careful, about the effects of antibiotics and illness on the pill. We'd always been so careful, but that last night I ignored everything.'

'It was your last night together and it's easy to get carried away in the heat of the moment. I would have done the same in your shoes.' Alice held her daughter tightly wishing that she could make everything right and knowing she was powerless to do anything.

'I thought it was over and I just wanted him to remember me. But mum it is now and... Oh God how will I cope?' Bawling like a toddler as the tears of self-pity fell, Delilah didn't think they would ever stop. How could fate be so twisted, how could she find what she'd always been looking for only to lose it so dramatically. She'd meant what she'd told her mum, she had been relieved, but her heart had still felt like it had been crushed into a thousand tiny fragments and would never be whole again. And Vince? Well she'd meant that too, she'd never given herself the luxury of admitting how much she loved him before and yet she knew that her last thought in this life would be of him. This wasn't how life was meant to be, Cinderella wasn't left struggling to bring up a child by herself, she was swept away by her prince to a world of happy ever after.

~

FOURTEEN

~

The next few weeks passed in some sort of a blur, literally as she didn't seem to be able to stop crying most of the time. The blue line on the pregnancy test had made it all pretty certain and the scan that her GP hurriedly arranged confirmed her situation beyond all doubt. The sonographer had confirmed her dates, which made her twelve weeks pregnant, which made that last night in France the likely culprit. She laid on the couch and watched the swirly black and white baby shaped image come into view, heard the strong steady heartbeat and yet she felt nothing.

Back in school most of her friends were dreaming of meeting Mr Right, buying a house and having babies and their talk had always left Delilah cold. She hadn't felt maternal, she'd never fussed over babies and she'd never felt the jealousy that some of her other friends felt when they were beaten to that particular achievement. She had wanted to travel, to see the world and have some sort of career before she'd had a child. She'd seen Nick and Livy's baby daughter and apart from thinking that they'd produced a pretty baby, she'd felt nothing more.

But this blob on the screen wriggling inside her belly meant one thing and one thing only, her life was going to change beyond all recognition. It meant that in a few months' time her precious freedom would be nothing but a fleeting memory and instead she would be responsible for another living being. Her dreams of her own place were dashed, as although her job paid well it would be doubtful that she would still be able to work full time. Indeed, she'd only been in the job for a couple of months so would she still even have a job and once more the panic crept back into her mind.

She looked back at the screen, the sonographer was rattling on and she'd not heard anything she'd said until now. She'd asked if Delilah wanted a copy of the photo for her partner and that's when reality hit her like a sledge hammer, she was alone and was going to have to do all this by herself. The one thought that surprisingly never crossed her mind was to get rid of the child.

Once everything was confirmed Delilah set about trying to get in touch with Vince, because at the very least he needed to know he was going to be a father. Where to start? She had very little information to go on. She had tried the number in France, which as she suspected had been disconnected and having come home without the little book of contacts that Vince had said he would put together, she was a bit stuffed on any other front. Anyway Amelie and Henri were in Paris and she'd never even had a number for Jeanne and Eustache other than that piece of paper that Jeanne had given her, which was long since lost. She had looked through the Andover telephone directories for Vivienne Angel without success, although she hadn't expected the mother of someone so well known to be anything other than ex-directory. She had never asked what Cesca's surname or company name were, so that was a blank as well.

That left R J Management and the record company. Both had been incredibly unhelpful although the boy at the record company had at least been sympathetic. The girl at Scarecrow's management had laughed her socks off and put the phone down muttering the word tart under her breath, so she wasn't going to be passing any messages on. Her parents and Mia both tried with no more success, although her father had been treated with a little more respect. They said they'd pass it on, Bryn had told her, but he had shaken his head sadly and said that he didn't expect them to actually do it.

Leo her boss had been immensely supportive and had made it clear that she didn't have to worry on the job front. When the baby arrived they would sit down and work out the best hours for her to work. She could have hugged him. Knowing her story Leo had tried a few of his old legal tricks, which was very sweet and just as futile. Fate it seemed had erected a bloody great big impenetrable wall between her and Vince and try as she might she was stuck behind it. She had sat down and talked the legal stuff through with Leo as her dad wanted her to drop a paternity suit on Vince. Up until that moment she hadn't known why after years as a high flying barrister Leo had left the profession, but now trying to talk her out of going down that route, he'd told her.

His last case had been on the defence team of Jimi Verna, an aging pervert scumbag rock star who was denying paternity of a child. There had been a great number of dirty tricks involved and the child's mother and her parents were ripped to shreds in the media before the case even got to court. He'd looked sternly at Delilah and warned her, Vince knew so much about her and her family and he had the money and the connections to destroy her long before the truth came into view. If that was the route she wanted to take, then she would have to live with the consequences. So Delilah had decided that it was back to doing it alone then.

After one particularly bad day in March she crossed the line and disgraced herself. She had been told that her blood pressure was too high and that she should rest more, this had coincided with a sudden realisation that she finally actually looked pregnant and she had consoled herself with half a jar of strong pickled onions. The resulting heartburn had brought on a tidal wave of anger and she had phoned R J Management. She hadn't a clue who the girl was that she was bellowing at other than she had a really irritating voice that grated on her nerves and she really didn't care. It had developed into an unpleasant slanging match ending only when the girl slammed the phone down. Delilah spent a further five minutes shouting obscenities down the dead line before her frustration was spent.

She wasn't then surprised when the letter from barristers Messrs Pinkly and Perkins arrived through the door telling her politely. "We request that you desist in these scurrilous accusations against our client" or else. Delilah folded the expensive piece of vellum up and tucked it away in her important papers file to be removed and read whenever she felt like exploding again.

Her son arrived in the world two weeks early after a short labour in the early hours of the sixth of June 1996 weighing three kilos, just over six pounds.

He had a healthy pair of lungs and used them to maximum effect to demonstrate his feelings about his birth, his mother felt like doing much the same. As he was born on the anniversary of D-Day Delilah decided to name him for her Welsh Grandfather Rhodri who had fought on the beaches on that momentous day, although he'd been Rori from the start. He had a shock of dark hair and his father's intense cinnamon eyes and it was love at first sight. So Delilah, who had never had a maternal bone in her body was immediately filled with the desire to protect her little son, which amazed her as there had been times when any love for the child growing inside had been in short supply.

The reaction of friends and family had overwhelmed her, leaving her tearful and happy all at the same time. After Alice and Bryn, Mia and her brother Tom had brought blue balloons and an assortment of teddies, although it had been Tom who had been the keenest to hold the baby. Hazel her Grandmother had sat with her great grandson against her ample bosom and had wept tears of delight as she'd stroked his downy head. Her dad sung him welsh lullabies and her mother had fussed over Delilah worried that she was being ignored.

Lena sent a package from Perth with a selection of baby clothes and a card gushing love from her and Neil. Inside of the package there was a hastily scribbled note on pretty pink paper that smelt of Lena's favoured perfume. It read simply "I wish I'd known sooner perhaps I could have done something to help. I'm sorry I've not been a terribly good friend and I want to make it up so I've written to Teddy. I can't promise anything and Neil would kill me if he knew as I'm not supposed to have any contact with him." She'd written a thank you letter back with a coded postscript with thanks of another kind that she hoped Lena would understand and Neil wouldn't.

Unfortunately, just five days after giving birth Delilah found herself in the back of an ambulance being rushed to the nearest hospital. The infection that had crept up stealthily had taken possession of a large proportion of her body before she realised there was anything seriously wrong. Three days in intensive care and a further two weeks in hospital followed and a totally depleted and despondent Delilah had struggled to care enough to fight.

In the end Rori had been her saving grace, he was her reason for living and she knew that she couldn't leave him alone. The day she was discharged her consultant, a nice man with kind features and prematurely greying hair came to see her. Sitting down beside her on the bed, much to the consternation of the ward sister he brought unwelcome news, he feared that the infection may have caused permanent scarring and had possibly left her unable to have any more children. It wasn't in any way a definitive answer and they wouldn't know for sure until her system settled down. He left her with the knowledge that when she felt the time was right they could look into it. She'd thanked him for his care, but inside she felt numb.

Mia was a star in the weeks following her return from hospital when weak as a kitten a lot of the time she had struggled to manage anything. Surprisingly she had taken charge of Rori when Delilah had needed to rest and despite having never had a child soon became adept at just about everything in his routine. Delilah reluctantly found some sort of peace with the knowledge that Rori possibly wouldn't have any siblings in the future, she'd deal with that problem when it arose.

With the love and support of family and friends her health soon returned to its normal robust state and she threw herself into motherhood with gusto. Her father continued to push her to file a paternity suit against Vince and she continued to resist, always concerned about a possible media circus and the certain knowledge that Vince would hate her. There were times though when her resolve weakened and only her deepest fears that Rori would be taken away from her stopped her from giving in. They'd manage, when her maternity leave ended work wasn't going to be an issue, which meant that she'd have enough money to survive. Alice was happy to help with childcare and her grandmother had insisted on starting an education fund for the newest addition to the family, so things weren't so dire that she needed to chase Vince for money. So no paternity.

Life continued to pile misfortune on the Scarecrow exes and that September Lena arrived back in the UK alone and a shadow of her former self. Out of the blue Delilah had got a weepy phone call from her mother who'd told her the whole sad story behind her daughters return. Lena had gone out to Australia just after Christmas to join Neil, she'd managed to get herself a little job at a magazine, they had a nice little harbour front flat and everything had been rosy. Although Neil continued to talk about them getting married he always seemed to have had a hundred and one reasons for putting it off.

    Lena had come back from work one day at the end of august to an empty home. Everything that Neil had possessed was gone and there had been a letter on the kitchen counter from the rental agents confirming the termination of his lease on the 31st, just a couple of days away. There was no note from him and when she checked their joint bank account she discovered that he'd emptied it the day after her wages had gone in. Effectively she had been alone, homeless and completely broke in a strange country with a temporary visa. After phoning her parents in a desperate panic they had told her to come home and sent her the money for her airfare.

Delilah and Mia had gone to visit their friend and had been shocked at how fragile she'd seemed and by the time they'd got over to Suffolk, she had finally heard something from Neil. There had been a brief contradictory letter, in which he had told Lena that he'd met someone else just before she'd arrived in Oz and fallen in love with her. Then he had berated Lena for keeping him hanging on all those years while she "whored around" with Teddy, before in the next sentence apologising for being such a coward and for the hurt he'd caused. Even worse the letter had a UK postmark, so it looked like Neil was back in the country.

Her voice had wavered as she told her friends that she had never really loved him and didn't blame him for hating her. Her hands they noticed had been trembling in her lap as she explained that she should have declined his proposal as it had just been an easy way out. It had been a depressing get together and nothing Delilah or Mia said seemed to make things any better. As they hesitantly left, she had grasped Delilah's hand tightly and in a tear filled whisper had apologised for not finding Vince for her. She had wrapped her arms around her friend not really knowing what to say and hoping that the hug said it was okay. Neither were surprised when Lena's mother had rung again a few days later to tell them that she thought her daughter needed space to recover. Whether they agreed with her or not, they had accepted the request and Lena slipped out of Delilah's life in much the same way as she had done so many years before.

~

VINCE
EARLY 98

~

FIFTEEN

~

'I'm afraid my hunch was correct Delilah; the infection has left a great deal of scarring.' Her consultant Mr Storey's normally kind face was serious as he sat on the edge of the bed. 'I won't dash your hopes completely as the body can always surprise us, but in my professional opinion I think it doubtful that you'll be able to conceive again naturally. Obviously, with the continuous progress of medicine you will probably have other options, but there's no guarantee. I'm sorry.' He laid a soft hand on her arm. 'But on a more positive note I may have made life a bit more comfortable for you, it's not a great comfort I know, but better than nothing.'

'Thank you Mr Storey.' Delilah tried to rustle up a smile, but inside her heart was breaking. After months of discomfort and a nagging worry at the back of her mind, she had made the decision to have this exploratory operation. Her consultant had made it very clear that she may not like what he found, but she'd signed her consent anyway. Now she was going to have to knuckle down and accept his findings, wasn't she?

Bitterness is such a useless emotion, or so Delilah had thought in her early teens. Of course in hindsight, it was easy for a child to make such a sweeping statement when life hadn't yet touched her with its cold hands. Now sitting staring blindly out the window at the rain sodden lawn waves of the useless stuff were washing over her and a torrent of self-pity threatened to drag her under. She was angry, angry at herself for being careless enough to get pregnant and angry at being so stupid that she hadn't recognised the signs.

The resentment was directed at Vince for deserting her and leaving her to bring his son into the world alone and lurking underneath it all was the terrible pain that in producing her fatherless son, she would probably never have another. She knew that in future she would have to tell any man who got close to her that she was unlikely to give him any children. If she was lucky she might find someone who would be ok with that, but would any man in that position still be happy to bring up another man's child?

In a fit of pique during one of her darker moments since the diagnosis, she had discussed hitting Vince with that wavering paternity suit, but Leo had been able to talk her out of it for the umpteenth time. No, that ship had sailed long before her little boys first birthday and if she tried to put it back in the water it was going to hit the rocks and they would be drowned. Life had to move on and she needed to find some way to accept the fact that Vince hadn't wanted her and didn't want anything to do with his beautiful son. Trying to elicit money out of him, because that would have been the only reason to go for paternity, would have been like admitting failure and she didn't need that on top of everything else. No, she had survived this far down the line so there was no reason why she couldn't carry on as she was. She just wished that her current all-consuming emotional state of mind was easier to work through.

The glossy magazine laying on the coffee table where it had been thrown in disgust was like the flickering light of the flame calling to the moth, Delilah couldn't help herself. Lucee's new home it shouted with a picture of the model lounging elegantly on an expensive looking sofa. "The top model invites us into her stunning newly furnished home for a chat". She wondered whether Mia had meant to leave it out for her to see or if she'd done it accidently. The thick silky paper fell open easily to the article suggesting that Mia had read it more than once and Delilah's eyes flicked through the carefully lit pictures looking for any of Vince, there was only one. Lucee dressed in some floaty number was standing in front of a large wall mounted photo of her posing arm in arm for the camera with a poker faced Vince. He had what Lena had always classed as his "photo with a fan face" fixed in place and it exhibited no intimacy at all, weird she thought. In the piece of writing accompanying it Lucee playfully suggested that there would soon be a happy announcement and that she was looking forward to marriage and babies. Mia shouted that she was finally ready and Delilah closed the magazine and put it back carefully where she'd found it as she didn't want Mia to know she'd read it.

That had been a waste of time as Mia had wanted to ease the blow that she was about to deliver, which she admitted over dinner and had left the magazine out deliberately. Mia had explained that her boss the eccentric designer Barney had embraced Lucee as his current muse as apparently the whole "frightened deer" thing, appealed to Barney's sense of the theatrical. So it had seemed only natural that when Lucee wanted a wedding dress she'd have asked Barney. Mia had worked on it, describing the piece in excruciatingly minute detail and told Delilah she would have been very proud of it had it been for anyone else. Leaning over the table she had whispered that she had seriously considered leaving a couple of seams loose to embarrass the woman when she wore it. Delilah had smiled and said, 'but you didn't, did you?' Mia had shaken her head sadly, too much pride in her work and Delilah had told her that was how it should be. Delilah herself felt nothing, her heart had long since become a huge empty void uninhabited by emotion.

Mia knew that she'd had far too much, the champagne had been flowing and she'd been drinking, never had much capacity for booze, always quickly intoxicated, which was why she rarely touched the stuff. The odd glass of champagne though was ok and up until this afternoon she had worked in an industry where there was always a bottle of champers on offer somewhere. That had come to an end at six o'clock when she had officially left her prestigious job to branch out on her own and at the beginning March a new Mia would be born with the spring.

Tonight was her leaving do and her boss Barney had insisted on the team visiting this club and so here she was sitting in the VIP area surrounded by celebrities and getting slowly ever more inebriated. She had been ok until the Scarecrow mob had arrived, but then sitting there watching Vince playing happy couples with Lucee had all been too much. All she could think of was Delilah's recent diagnosis and how she was juggling life with Rori all by herself, without any help from his father and the red mist descended. Yes, Delilah managed brilliantly and had yet again had decided not to pursue Vince for money, but that wasn't the point was it?

Lucee had been hanging on to Vince like a shipwreck survivor to a life raft and any woman who'd come within a few feet had been stared down and dared to come closer. This left Mia with a bit of a problem because the more she drank, the more she wanted to give Vince a piece of her mind and the bloody woman was in the way. How long can she go without needing the loo she thought glaring at the glamourous model. Shortly after that piece in the magazine, when Lucee had hinted about happy news she'd let slip to Delilah that Lucee had told Barney that she and Vince would be married soon.

That thought made her furious, Lucee with her scrawny boy's body and permanently frightened eyes walking down the aisle in Barney's stunningly beautiful dress that she'd made, with a happy and smiling Vince, while Delilah had to work long hours to support his child. She knocked back another glass, oh dear the world was starting to move, bloody hell Lucee why can't you just fuck off for five minutes she thought.

Then her chance came as her nemesis sashayed off to talk to a woman who Mia recognised as another one of Barney's regular models. She watched as they air kissed each other's cheeks mwah, and made her move. Unsteadily admittedly, she weaved across to where Vince stood lost in thought, drink in hand and stood swaying in front of him. Lucee was still distracted, good. He looked at her blankly, she doubted that he recognised her with the now short punky red hair and without the Goth makeup. Oh well, who cares she thought.

She steadied herself and glared at him, Lucee had seen her, not much time...'You...You're a fucking bastard. How could you desert her when she desperately needed you, how could you leave her to go through all that by herself. What kind of man would just abandon her to cope alone?' She screamed at him, probably a lot louder than she had intended as everyone was looking at them in spite of the volume of the music. 'Bastard!' She turned, tears falling down her cheeks and ran, out of the club into the cold air and vomited behind a rubbish bin.

She didn't know how she managed it, but with trembling hands she phoned Delilah. 'Oh God Lola, I've done something really stupid, I'm so sorry. I am so, so sorry.' She slurred, wiping traces of vomit away with a tissue.

'What have you done, are you ok?'
'I'm really pissed.'

'I guessed that, but what have you done?' Delilah spoke to her pretty much how she would have spoken to Rori. 'Do you need picking up, I can come out...'

'No, no I'll walk. I've just seen Vince.'

'That's nice. What did you do?' There was a touch of exasperation in Delilah's voice now.

'I shouted at him, gave him a piece of my mind.'

'Did he know who you were?'

'No.' She began to cry, huge racking sobs. 'She, Lucee wouldn't bugger off and I'm really pissed.'

'No harm done then. He probably thought you were some lunatic recently escaped from the local asylum. Are you sure you don't want me to pick you up?'

'No, I need some air.'

'Phone me when you get home then, yes...'

'Yes mum.' Mia retreated back behind the bins and retched what remnants were left in her stomach.

Delilah put the phone down and sighed. It had been a good job that she had been up with Rori or else Mia would have woken her up and she would have been considerably less charitable. Her heart was in the right place, but after a few drinks Mia was a proper loose cannon. She blew on her freshly made tea and took a sip, she was going to struggle to get back to sleep now. So Mia had been close enough to talk to Vince and nothing had changed, not that she would have expected it to. Vince was hardly going to come running, was he, not when he had Lucee. When she'd seen that offending article and Mia had first told her about the wedding dress she had slipped into a period of melancholy. She was the one who would live her life with Vince, her children would play in the garden in France and not Rori. As always she'd picked herself up and carried on and after all that she'd suffered recently, Delilah was a survivor.

'Are you alright sweetheart?' Bryn walked into the kitchen tying a knot in the belt of his plaid dressing gown. 'I thought I heard the phone.'

'I'm fine dad, and the phone was Mia...'

'Too much to drink eh?'

'Totally wrecked.' Delilah shook her head 'I asked if she needed help getting home, but she decided to walk, clear her head.' She chuckled softly. 'She ran into Vince and gave him a piece of her mind. I doubt that he even understood what she was saying let alone knew who she was.' She took another sip of tea as her dad re-boiled the kettle. 'It's just going to be me and Rori, isn't it?'

'No, look at you, you're a beauty. Some lucky man is going to come along and you and Rori will live happily ever after. But then I am biased.' He yawned reluctantly, 'you'll be fine Lola, you're a good mother. Vincent Angel doesn't know what he's missing.' He kissed her fondly in passing, 'go back to bed love and get some sleep.' Delilah watched as his familiar form merged with the darkness and finished her tea.

Totally bemused, Vince watched the departing back of the attractive girl as she ran out of the club, he hadn't any idea who she was or why she had yelled at him. Life in the public eye could be strange sometimes, it attracted the weird and the wonderful and this incident definitely fell into the weird bracket. Lucee was livid, that much he knew, could see it in her body language and the sour expression on her face. He was so fed up of the jealousy and her ever shifting moods.

The relationship had been on and off now for what, nearly two years? Even now Vince wasn't entirely sure why they kept ending up together, laziness he guessed. Well not for much longer, Vince wanted out. He'd never been one for all this posturing and posing in the right places, at the right time and life with Lucee demanded that he did just that. They seemed to do nothing but argue, she seemed to be permanently angry at him for something he had or hadn't done and he didn't have a clue what it was. Lack of commitment Teddy had told him, she probably wants some sort of assurance, which was all fine and dandy coming from a man who had just divorced her best friend after little more than a year of marriage.

In the taxi on the way back to Lucee's flat they sat stony faced, some distance apart and the chatty cabbie having picked up on the icy atmosphere had finally kept his silence. When they arrived Lucee had stalked off leaving Vince to pay and thank the driver.

'High maintenance that one, I don't know how all you famous fella's cope with it. Give me my nice normal missus and her home baking rather than little miss angry.'

'Do you know what? I'd rather have your missus too.' He tipped the guy. 'Thanks a lot mate, but I'd rather this stayed between us...?' He said with a thin smile.

'Hear no evil, see no evil that's me. I doubt that you'll want the advice, but you two don't seem to be playing on the same field, I'd get out while you can...'

'That my friend, is my intention.' He started to walk away. 'Oh if they find me in the Thames tomorrow, please feel free to shout about this exchange from the rooftops.' The taxi driver roared with laughter as he drove away.

Lucee was already in her flat by the time Vince got up there and for a few moments he hesitated at the threshold as if uncertain of whether to go in. He hated this place, the flat was too modern and her décor was too sterile for his taste. He especially disliked the endless photos of her from her modelling assignments that graced the walls as you walked in, sheer vanity he thought. She was waiting in the lounge, her face like a thundercloud, hands set on her narrow hips and her eyes fixed on him.

'So who was the tart?'

'Oh for the love of Christ Lucee, how the hell do I know?' Wrong move, should have turned and left. 'She was drunk. I don't know, perhaps I once screwed her sister, her friend, her bloody mother for all I know and she felt slighted. Perhaps she got the wrong person. What is your problem? All you've done lately is blame me for something and I don't even know what I've done.' He was beyond caring really. 'Look Lucee, I've had enough, I don't bloody love you and to be totally honest I'm not entirely sure we even like each other. So I think we should bring the whole sorry affair to an end for both our sakes.'

'But, I've bought my wedding dress.' She whined pitifully.

'Why on earth would you do that?' He couldn't keep the loathing from his voice.

'Don't you know why? I found the ring, in your safe and I thought at last, at last he's going to propose. But you didn't and actually I do love you.' Her voice was getting shrill and angry tears were forming in her eyes.

'The ring...' Vince replied dumbly forgetting that she had stayed at his place while this monstrosity was being finished and that she would have used his safe for all her borrowed jewellery.

'Oh God, it was for her wasn't it.' Realisation hit Lucee hard and he flinched at the hand that whipped out suddenly, her long nails missing his face by inches. 'You were going to ask that fucking little whore to marry you, what the hell is wrong with you? Why would you? Hell Vince she didn't exactly come running after you, did she? Just another bloody name to add to her list, I mean you barely knew each other, what a few weeks on tour, a few quick shags...'

'You know perfectly well that we had longer than that.' His voice was ice cold now, his eyes dark and she shrunk away from him, fear replacing the anger on her face. 'Her name was Delilah and she was worth a thousand of you. I've spent all this time with you not knowing at night whether I'm facing some depraved succubus or crawling into a grave to sleep with a fucking corpse...' He knew he was being a total bastard, but he couldn't stop, he wanted to hurt her badly.

'You know what happened to me...'

'Oh yes, you remind me of it all the time. But you see Lucee, I know the truth and know just about everything in your life, how you wanted to be famous and you didn't bloody care how. So you offered sex in exchange for your portfolio and afterwards when you'd made it and the poor bastard wanted some recognition you tried to make out he'd assaulted you. Ha, what a joke. How much did he lose Lucee, to save your face? You need to see a bloody shrink, spend all your teenage years shagging anything and now use sex as a bargaining chip. What are you going to do to me, go to the press and tell them what a callous pig I am? Go ahead, it doesn't matter. As you're so fond of reminding me I'm nobody now.'

He turned to walk away, desperate to get out the door, glad it was over, wondering how it had gone on so long and wishing that he didn't keep making the same mistakes with the same sort of women. She screamed at his retreating back her voice laced with venom. 'It was me you know? I had her thrown out that night, your whore and I'm glad…'

'Fucking bitch…' He muttered darkly under his breath as he slammed the door behind him, the sound echoing along the empty hall.

In the early hours, standing at the window of his London base with its view across Hyde Park, Vince contemplated the beautiful ring that he'd retrieved from his safe. He'd cocked up well and truly by obsessively chasing this glorious piece for Delilah and in the process had left her feeling abandoned. You've caused some trouble, he thought and with a gloomy smile ran a calloused finger over the welsh gold. Why had he become so infatuated he wondered? Because it had been exactly what he'd wanted and at the time the story attached to it could have been written for them.

Was it cursed as Francesca had suggested, the ring didn't have the happiest history did it? And now as time marched on the ring's sad history had become a self-fulfilling prophecy, hadn't it? He held it up to the light and the prisms in the beautifully cut stones sent sparks of brilliant light flying into the night. Gently he let it slip back into the safety of his fist and closing his eyes silently willed Delilah's face into the forefront of his memory. The image was dimming; like Delilah it was disappearing like a ship into the mist. Oh Lola he thought despondently, where the hell did you go?

He'd looked for her for months, but all he'd found were dead ends. She hadn't been in contact with the record label or Roscoe's management company, so perhaps Charles Snelling the P I he'd hired had been right, she didn't want to be found. Trouble was he didn't blame her, how could he? He'd promised her all of his contact numbers and hadn't given them to her and then he'd decided to go to that bloody auction instead of seeing her off at the airport.

That awful December night after the show, she'd been dumped out the door like unwanted garbage and if that had happened to him he would have taken it as a sign that their affair was over. Perhaps it was time that he seriously tried to move on, perhaps it was time that he sold the ring, let someone else carry its burden. Not yet though. Reluctantly he laid the ring tenderly back onto its cushion of silk, closed the ornate box and locked it back into the darkness of the safe.

There was a message from Louis on the phone telling him that he had finished his last round of chemo and would be on his way back to the UK at the end of the week. He'd asked Vince to give him a shout if he was able to pick him up from the airport. Thinking about Louis brought back memories of the last days of the group back in the summer of 96 and he really wished it hadn't. If reminiscing about Delilah was painful then allowing memories of the death throes of Scarecrow to surface brought him sleepless nights. He still didn't totally understand why that incredibly negative report from his private investigator had started that bloody awful chain of events, but it had.

Roscoe, Teddy and Seb who had all had quite enough of his moping about over Delilah had told him to get a grip, grow some balls and move on. Roscoe and Teddy in particular had seemed hell bent on him getting together with Lucee, despite the ten-year age gap and the fact that they had nothing in common. Of course he'd found her attractive, she wasn't a top model for nothing and he wasn't a monk. The trouble was, well she was troubled, challenging and there was something he just didn't like about her. Nevertheless, lonely, totally fed up with everyone's constant pushing and despite his misgivings he had drifted into a relationship with her, big mistake. Louis had stopped talking to him dismayed that he could just give up on Delilah and start up with someone "so 'orrible". He himself had ended up so distracted by Lucee's constantly changing moods, that he'd failed to notice the signs that Louis was beginning to self-destruct and even now that was something he felt uncomfortable about.

As his friendship with Lou fell apart and Lucee caused him endless heartache he'd buried himself in the bottle once more, which caused even more friction in the group. The final straw was Roscoe desperate to cash in on their success insisting that they add more dates to the end of the US tour and Teddy who already saw the group unravelling agreeing, as he wanted to make sure his solo career took off. Teddy's wedding to Loris had taken place with a half dozen dates still to play and the band in total disarray.

A week later Seb pushed Lou over the brink and he took off for his monastery retreat in the French Alps leaving the group without its keyboard player. Vince had stopped talking to Seb, because of his behaviour and because he was feeling guilty for not seeing the state his friend was in. He had stood his ground and told the others that he was not doing anything more than his contracted gigs and by the time they played their last concert in Los Angeles at the beginning of July Scarecrow had blown itself to bits.

His rift with Lou had lasted almost a year, until his beloved old friend had phoned him with the distressing news that he had just been diagnosed with cancer. Vince had dropped everything and rushed to his side. This hadn't gone down well with Lucee who loathed Lou and she had no reason to like him any better when Vince had told her he'd rather be with his friend than her.

Teddy, his relationship with Loris dying at a rate of knots had likewise been keen to heal the lift between them, but Seb was still smarting that his livelihood and fame had gone down the toilet with the demise of the group. No sad loss in Vince's books and they were still estranged even now with Vince neither knowing nor caring where Seb was. Lou's cancer had bought the other three old friends back together, but Scarecrow was dead and buried.

He'd never really intended his relationship with Lucee to go on, she though had persisted and Vince too tired of arguing to finish with her completely had taken it on a whenever, whatever basis, spending time with her when more important commitments allowed. He'd been a prize prat and really should have known better where she was concerned, she wasn't Delilah. Sighing he flopped down in an old cracked leather chair and picked up the bottle of scotch from the table beside it. Then just like he always did when Delilah slipped into his mind he began to drink himself into oblivion.

~

FATE
SUMMER 2000

~

SIXTEEN

~

Delilah had celebrated the coming of the new millennium with a dose of flu and by the time everyone else was having a wonderful time she had taken enough cold remedy to bring down an elephant and was dead to the world. She'd had no more expectations of the year 2000 than any of the years preceding it and once the gremlin sticking red hot needles in her eyes and rubbing gorse up and down her throat had finished, she just carried on as before. Rori grew taller at an alarming rate and became ever more precocious creating a certain amount of financial stress for his mother. Like most parents of growing children, a great deal of her income seemed to disappear on shoes and even buying with growing room hadn't worked.

Her only life saver had been the education fund that her grandmother Hazel had set up for Rori before her death, which currently meant that she could afford to send him to a much recommended nursery attached to an excellent prep school. Work was just that, a way to make money, any ambition had been blown out of the water when her beloved son had arrived in her life and so she was still in the same job that she'd taken when she'd first moved up to town, but even so life wasn't so bad.

Since Rori's arrival she had learnt that she didn't need a man to be happy, although there were times when she missed having someone holding her close in the middle of the night. Her recent relationships hadn't been resounding successes and more than once over the last few years she envisaged herself becoming the ultimate old maid. Fair enough she had not exactly been a shining leader of the dating scene and the only men she seemed to meet were the dull, the ever so nice and the downright sleaze bags with over active hands, so more frogs then. Most didn't get past the first date and ran a mile when she started prattling on about Rori, which she had a tendency to do when she'd had a couple of glasses of wine. Delilah now joked to anyone who would listen that she attracted frogs and not a prince among them. Then she'd casually throw in the "I'm over him, I'm moving on" speech, which everyone knew was total bollocks as whether she admitted it or not, she was still obsessed with Vince.

Sitting outside a cafe beside the Serpentine in Hyde Park on a blissfully warm May lunchtime Delilah watched distractedly as a giggling Rori fed the ducks and geese. She worked a half day on a Wednesday and loved her free afternoon with her small son. Today though despite the glorious sunshine she felt like she was enclosed in a cloak of melancholy. They'd just come back from a family holiday on a campsite down in the Dordogne and on the long drive back up through France she'd made a stupid error of judgement. Ever since she'd made the decision not to chase after Vince she'd made a point of staying well clear of his corner of France, even when they'd been passing on the way to somewhere else. Why this time she'd chosen to ask her father to drive through St Clair she still wasn't sure? Well now that was a bit of a lie, because she knew perfectly well why.

She'd been sitting in the dentists a few weeks before the holiday waiting for her appointment when she'd picked up a random celebrity magazine to pass the time. It was, as they often are months out of date, going back to the middle of January. She had flicked through it doing no more really than looking at the pictures of beautiful people posing in hideously expensive designer numbers in the stunningly decorated rooms of their beautiful houses. The piece that had started everything had been right in the middle. A big double page picture of a group of pregnant first time mums from across the celebrity spectrum, who had decided to start a charitable foundation to help impoverished children around the world. Standing on the periphery of the group stood a very heavily pregnant Lucee, her fingers laced protectively under her burgeoning bump and a huge smile on her glowing face. Delilah's heart had sunk. She'd not looked at anything like that since the magazine where the woman had rattled on about getting married and Mia had told her about the wedding dress she'd made for her.

For some unfathomable reason she had then felt the need to go back to St Clair and take a last look at the house. Stupid move. Her parents had parked in the shade of a lime tree filled with the humming of contented bees and had taken Rori to the adjacent playground to play on the swings while she satisfied her curiosity. Psyching herself up at the carpark exit Delilah had taken in her surroundings and had noticed with great sadness that the bakery looked like it had been long gone and the village bar was in the process of being changed back into a house.

Nothing had changed much on the walk up the hill though, the run down house overlooking the valley was still unloved and the local buzzard was still hunting over the sunflower fields. She had decided against the direct assault and had crossed the road onto the footpath through the cow's field, which she knew came out just before the start of the woods. The cows were long gone, nothing had grazed the field for a while and the insect filled grass had been long enough to trail her hands through as she passed. Climbing the gate at the end she walked down the track and onto the road past Amelie's once beautifully cared for home.

The lawn there hadn't been cut for some time, there'd been weeds in the gravel and her beautiful flower beds were overgrown with weeds. It had been obvious that the house was in deep hibernation and had been empty for a while. Vince's place was just as she remembered it, but looking at it she'd felt nothing one way or another. She remembered the gut feeling she'd had standing under the oak tree before she'd left, that this was never going to be her home and she'd felt the same sensation again.

The wrought iron gates were shut so she'd had to peer surreptitiously through them to see inside. Someone had taken the time to give the shutters a fresh coat of blue paint and the rosemary Vince had planted along the front of the house that summer had been in bloom. But the sight that had driven her away and back down the road had been the line of baby clothes in the garden and the fashionable pram outside the open door. Vince she had concluded, had been obviously only too happy to be a husband to Lucee and father to their child. As she'd walked morosely back to the camper and her worried parents Vince's memory had started to croak. By the time she reached the village he'd turned warty and green and she'd quietly accepted that he had turned out to be just another frog.

So why the melancholy today if that was how she felt? In reality she didn't know, she just felt low. No that was a lie, she knew perfectly well why she was so depressed and it had nothing to do with Vince did it? She missed Mia and her loss was beginning to weigh heavily on her shoulders. Shortly after the nightclub incident Mia had started up her little bespoke Wedding dress business. Barney had promised to push some clients her way, "a little help for your business", he'd purred and she'd accepted gratefully, but they had never materialised. Then a few months later an exclusive wedding shop selling designer gowns had opened just a few hundred yards from her little flat. Mia had been devastated. Delilah had tried to support her friend as much as she was able, but Mia had run away to her two brothers in the States to lick her wounds.

There she had met Mark. He ran a chain of upmarket bridal boutiques across the US and had been a widower for a number of years having lost his young wife to cancer. Oblivious to the twenty-year age gap Mia had fallen in love and by the time 1998 had rolled into 99 they were married and had produced the cutest pair of twin girls in the autumn. Mia was now living in California and Delilah was delighted for her friend and although she had understood that their friendship would be different with thousands of miles separating them, she hadn't envisaged them drifting apart.

Mia living in comfort with her husband and babies had everything she could have wished for and even had a nanny. This allowed her the time to design gowns for her husband's shops and to relax and spend time on herself. Delilah never seemed to have much time at all, which was why she made the most of these Wednesdays. They did try to keep in touch, but their lives were very different and their contact, like their friendship had been sketchy of late.

She sipped her strong black coffee and watched the world as it milled around her totally oblivious, Rori was feeding his last morsel of bread to a rather imposing male swan who took it incredibly gently from his tiny hand. Delilah jolting herself back to reality nearly had forty fits that he was that close to something so big and called him back. He toddled over a sad look on his face 'No more', he said miserably as his mother smothered him in her arms. Another boy with blond curls appeared beside them a big smile on his cherubic face and the lack of food for the birds was soon forgotten. Delilah smiled at the harassed red headed woman chasing after the small boy. She was flushed from running and her hair, which Delilah knew was normally tucked up into a neat bun was now sticking out all over the place. She signalled the waiter for another coffee as Zoe collapsed onto a chair.

'How can something so small move so damn fast?' She held a hand up to gain the waiters attention. 'And cake...bring cake, preferably chocolate.'

'You're asking the wrong person. I'm reasonably fit, but I have trouble keeping up with Rori sometimes.' She chuckled at her friend who still looked harassed. 'But look, a comic saves the day.' She said pointing to the two small boys sitting quietly at the next door table their heads together over a brightly coloured magazine.

'Hmm, thank God for Thomas the tank engine I say.' Delilah smiled, Zoe was a good friend. She was a nurse on the unit where she worked and as a single mother like her they'd bonded over their pregnancies. It wouldn't be that way for much longer as Zoe had met a Surgeon on a course the previous year and wedding bells would be ringing in August. Delilah had felt the briefest stab of jealousy when she'd told her, much like she had when Mia had cautiously shared her news, but it was quickly ignored at her friend's happiness. Ben, Zoe's cherubic son called for his mother to look at something and Zoe scraped herself dutifully off the chair to see.

A woman pushing a baby in a pram briefly took Delilah's attention, they say that everyone has a twin somewhere and this woman looked just like Tash, what are the odds on that she wondered. The gold band on her finger glinted in the sun and she was walking arm in arm with a good looking man who also seemed vaguely familiar to Delilah, although she couldn't work out why. As he put two cups and some chocolate cake on the table she thanked the waiter with a smile, good job he was used to the pair of them she thought.

Her eyes returned to the young woman, who had taken a tiny baby out of the pram and was holding it up to see the birds, as new mothers do. The man stood beside her with a mixture of pride and love on his face until he saw Delilah, when he did something very odd, he whispered something to the woman and she turned around and looked straight at her.

This was a very different Tash who she greeted today and Delilah thought how very pretty she was. Her hair cut into a tidy bob shone with health in the bright sun and had reverted to what was probably her own natural mouse. Her pretty features free of any makeup glowed with health and her body shape even after a baby suggested someone who liked the gym. Delilah greeted her warmly, because at the end of the day neither had ended up with Vince so what argument could they possibly have now? Tash returned the warmth, although had looked like she'd seen a ghost.

'Wow, congratulations.' Delilah said pointing over at the pram still trying to work out who the man was. 'Husband and baby, lucky you. And don't you look good too.'

'Thank you, you're being very sweet. I wouldn't have blamed you for telling me to f-off, I wasn't very nice to you was I?'

'I was a big girl Tash, water off a ducks back.' She smiled remembering that wasn't how she'd felt at the time. 'What did you have, did I see a flash of pink?'

'A little girl, we called her Lottie. You remember Harry?'

'I'd like to say yes, but...' Tash laughed softly.

'He was Scarecrow's road manager.'

'That's the one. I knew he was familiar, but I couldn't work out why. You look happy.'

'Gosh yes. I was such a fool Delilah.' She glanced affectionately at her husband. 'He says that he fancied me for years, thought that he was being really obvious, men eh?'

'You were kind of fixated on Vince...'

'Just a bit, totally oblivious to what was under my nose. So how are you, is life going well, do you have someone?'

'I have a man in my life who keeps me on my toes.' Delilah pointed fondly at Rori who had cottoned on that his mother was talking to someone new and was watching with fascinated eyes. All the colour seemed to drain out of Tash's face as she looked at Rori and it took Delilah a couple of minutes to work out why. Most people who didn't know who his father was said that he looked like her, but those who knew were only too aware of what a carbon copy of Vince he was. Tash caught herself quickly, Delilah thought as the young mum regained her composure again.

'What a handsome young man, I bet you're really proud of him. Is he like his father?' Her voice gave her away, she recognised Vince in her son.

'Totally, I don't think I had anything to do with him at all, but then neither did his dad.' That was rather harsh, but it just slipped out and judging from Tash's expression it wasn't lost on her either. Zoe, who had just sat back down was watching the conversation with interest and Tash took this as her cue to leave.

'It's so nice to see you again Delilah, would you like to meet up for lunch one day and have a proper catch up?' It was a genuine request asked in an affectionate tone, almost as if they were old friends.

'Umm, yes that would be great, I'd like that very much.' Hell why not, thought Delilah? After all she hadn't liked Nicki much at first, had she? They swopped phone numbers and with a shy smile Tash returned to her waiting husband who raised a hand to wave, which Delilah returned.

'Spill...' Zoe's tone was accusing.

'Long story and stranger than any fiction, another day perhaps.'

'She recognised Rori, I'm assuming she knows his father.'

'Uh huh. Cakes nice, try it.' Delilah changed the subject. She wouldn't get away with it for long and perhaps it was time she told Zoe the whole story, but not now, because that was something that needed a bottle of wine or two.

Standing by the Serpentine gazing blankly out over the water Vince felt like he was wearing a sign proclaiming loudly "man about to be stood up" or worse still "lurking pervert". For the fourth or fifth time in the last ten minutes he glanced at the expensive watch on his wrist, his irritation palpable. He had no idea why he'd agreed to come here today and right up to an hour ago he'd still been having second thoughts. He'd had virtually no contact with Tash since her wedding to Harry, other than to send them a card when they'd had the little girl, which he'd put a decent sized cheque in for her piggy bank, so what now? She'd rung him out of the blue the previous week and although her tone had been chatty there had been an edge of desperation in it.

She really needed to talk to him, please would he have a drink with her the following week, it was vitally important. God knows what was so damn urgent, perhaps there was something wrong with Harry? He'd looked after the band from the very beginning, he'd offered to be their roadie as he'd had a van and when fame had beckoned they'd employed him as a trusted Road manager. First and foremost, he was a friend, so if there was anything wrong…He looked at his watch again, if she was late she'd find him long gone. The text tone on his mobile drew his attention, it said simply "I'm so sorry Vince, please forgive me.'

~

SEVENTEEN

~

Delilah looked at the text from Tash with confusion in her eyes, it was very cryptic, did it mean she wasn't coming? She was just about to reply when she heard men's voices from inside the cafe courtyard, a loud discussion about music and one of the voices was unmistakable, Vincent Angel. She ran a hand through the still very new short elfin haircut to separate the strands of chestnut, which had flattened in the warmth. Licking her lips out of nervous habit and taking a deep breath to settle the butterflies trying to escape from her stomach she walked towards her fate whatever it may be.

Nonchalantly she arranged herself into a casual pose a few feet away from Vince and waited for him to notice her. He stood chatting to one of the waiters, unbuttoned shirt exposing a well-defined chest and his hands tucked into the pockets of a pair of cargo shorts. His bare feet were slipped into a pair of flip flops and he was mindlessly tracing a pattern in the gravel with his toes as he talked. She was just considering announcing her presence when he turned almost in slow motion and for a fleeting moment his face was creased in confusion. Then a huge smile spread across his handsome face and he walked towards her, although still with some uncertainty in his eyes.

'Hello Lola.'

'Hi Vinnie.' She smiled and the uncertainty vanished. He reached out and caught her hand as if nothing had ever happened, but Delilah could feel the elephant between them its huge unspoken bulk keeping them apart. Obviously Tash had engineered this.

'I was going to grab myself a cold beer, join me?' Vince asked in a matey tone, although his eyes pleaded.

'Well it is warm and I think a cold beer would go down nicely, thank you.' His whole face lit up as he disappeared into the cafe almost at a run. Delilah smiled although she was more than a little confused. Vince had genuinely greeted her like a long lost friend who he was desperate not to let out of his sight. That didn't sit happily alongside the man who'd callously had her thrown out of the backstage party, who hadn't returned any of her messages and who had got a firm of barristers to send a threatening letter telling her to bugger off. She was beginning to think that something very odd had occurred....

'It's Italian hope that's ok?' He said as he walked back over to where she'd found a table in the shade of a large tree. He had done up his shirt and carried two bottles of beer in one hand and a bowl of crisps in the other.

'You needn't have dressed on my account.' She chuckled raising an amused eyebrow.

'My mother always taught me to be dressed in polite company.' He offered her a bottle.

'Didn't teach you to offer a lady a glass then...' He screwed his face up and took in a long admiring glance.

'Since when did you require...a glass?' She laughed, he joined in and any ice melted away. For a few minutes he gazed into the distance seemingly lost in his thoughts as he took a couple of large gulps from his bottle and Delilah watched him intently across the rim of her own. The ice cold crisp amber liquid was refreshing and brought back fond memories of sitting like this that other summer, which seemed so far away now. Ok it was now or never...

'Went past the house in France a couple of weeks ago, always said it would be a great place to raise a family...'

'Family?' A perplexed expression crossed his face.

'Baby clothes on the line and the last photo I saw of Lucee she looked very pregnant.' He roared with laughter, which was not the reaction she expected.

'Oh Delilah, I assume from that comment that you still don't read any of the celeb rags do you? So you went up there and added up two and two and came to five. Sold the house the summer of 96, I couldn't stomach living there anymore so saw no point in keeping it and the couple who'd been renting it were keen to buy.' He came and sat next to Delilah an indulgent look on his face. 'We split up beginning of 98. I don't think she was too keen to start boasting about being dumped so there was only a very minimal piece in a couple of the magazines. Anyway it took her all of ten seconds to take up with Benjamin Martin, Roscoe's druggie prat of a son.'

'Well you can't blame me, the last I heard from Mia about the woman was that she had a wedding dress put by at Barney's and had been wittering on in the press about planning her wedding and having babies.'

'Yes, so she told me the night I told her it was over. God knows what gave her the idea I wanted to marry her. The relationship had been a disaster from the start and I think in the time we were together we spent no more than a fortnight in each other's company without wanting to kill each other. I thought she saw it in the same context I did, but obviously not.' Then the penny dropped and he exclaimed. 'Jesus Mia, that's who it was, God I'm stupid.'

'You remember then; she didn't think you did at the time.'

'She was so pissed she was almost incoherent. If I'd known, I wouldn't have let her just go off like that, in reflection perhaps I shouldn't have anyway. She was ranting on about deserting people, which makes perfect sense now.' He took another pull on his beer. 'What made you go back to the house?' Delilah shrugged by way of an answer and he let the subject drop. 'Do you have anyone in your life who makes you happy Lola?'

'Yes.' Blunt, but it wasn't entirely a lie, Rori made her happy and he hadn't specified. She half expected him to ask, "how the child was", but his face had crumpled and she felt guilty. Hmm she thought...

'I'm pleased; you deserve...' That soft gravelly voice caught slightly and he put the bottle down. 'This is all my fault you know.' He flashed her a wry smile. 'I had everything written down for you in that pretty little address book I'd bought. It had everything in it, my home phone number, address, mums and Lou's. I left it on the chest in the hall, meant to give it to you, but I forgot all about it because it wasn't there when I looked. It wasn't until I was cleaning the place up for the tenants before that last gig that I found it under dad's old chest, must have fallen down there when you got the blanket out that Friday night.'

'I'll admit I was a bit surprised that you hadn't given it to me, because you'd promised, but at the same time I wasn't sure where we stood...'

'My fault again, I knew exactly where I wanted us to be.' He looked distraught.

'It all went a bit tits up didn't it? I mean had my parents told me they'd sold the house when I first got home, I could have told you when you called from Antigua and could have at least given you Grannies number and address. However, I did call the hotel and asked them to pass on the message, several times...'

'That was bloody Roscoe, he told the hotel staff we were not to be disturbed under any circumstances...They did that to my mum, but she had Roscoe's mobile number and she rang him and screamed at him down the phone, called him a lot of very unsavoury things in French. Sorry, his number was in there too, you could have done the same.' He chuckled at the thought. 'Then Roscoe insisted that I do that damn interview after the show in London, I didn't want to. When I saw you and you looked so pale I tried to persuade Seb to go in my place and he told me to fuck off...' He grabbed a fistful of crisps and crunched them absently, not tasting, lost in the memory. 'When I came back you were nowhere in sight, I waited a few minutes as I thought you might have popped to the loo, you did look sick Hun. When you still didn't appear I sent Cherry to look for you but she said you weren't there and the attendant hadn't seen you. That was when I panicked. Lou said he'd seen you with Mia and Lena, said that he'd seen a couple of the security guards with you as well. He thought they were being aggressive so had started to go and intervene, but Loris cornered him and when he looked again you'd gone.'

He ran a hand back through his hair and gazed fixedly at the ground a frown etched on his face. 'We tracked down the guards and they said that Teddy had wanted you gone before we came back from the interview. Caused ructions within the group for months and had we not been committed to the US tour we would have split there and then...' There was that wry smile again. 'Teddy owned up and I didn't talk to him for months, I made his life hell, poor old Teddy.

'It was Teddy. I don't understand why would he do that...?'

Ah, but he didn't, that was Lucee's final triumphant comment she spat at me as I left her…She had you thrown out, told Loris and she asked Teddy to take the blame so I wouldn't hate her, fucking bitch…' He shook his head sadly his mouth set. 'We did look Lola, Louis took the stations and Cherry and Stevie trudged into just about all the cafes and bars in a mile radius, I went to the two hotels you told me you stayed in up there…but nothing. I'd already found out you'd moved, so in the end I assumed that you probably just went home…'

Delilah sighed, it hadn't been him. Well that was something she thought gloomily.

'I kept trying, I turned into a proper detective. But all I got were dead ends until I spoke to someone at your stables, do you have any idea how many stables there are where you used to live? Anyhow once I found the right one a girl called Liz told me you'd moved up to London. She said that if I'd caught…Bunty was it, she could have given me the exact details, but apparently she was off on a world cruise and wouldn't be back until February. We were just off to start the Australian leg of our world tour so I put it in the hands of a very well respected Private investigator. His report reached me as we landed in the states at the end of March saying that he'd reached a dead end and had been unable to locate you. The report stated that he'd spoken to Bunty and she had told him politely where to go and refused to tell him...' He looked crestfallen, it was as if he was reliving the moment his heart had broken all over again.

Very interesting she thought, because Bunty had told her that she had spoken to a man who had been trying to trace her. "Because she had won a major prize in a charity raffle and her old address was on the ticket." Bunty had given him the details as she had seen no reason not to. "He seemed really respectable Delilah, very charming, head to toe Saville Row." So she wondered, why had his report specified that he couldn't find her, when he most certainly had. The whole tale just got stranger and stranger.

'Here's something really odd would Lena have tried to contact Teddy about us?' Delilah nodded, poor Lena she still thought about what happened to her back then and it still made her sad. Not that it mattered now as Lena had started writing as part of her therapy and now had two chic lit novels in publication. 'Ah, she wrote to Teddy from Australia in June, he didn't get the letter until a couple of months later. It arrived at his hideaway in Battersea and was really cryptic, just said she needed to talk to him urgently. Eventually he wrote back after he and Loris came back from honeymoon, but never heard a dicky bird, assumed it wasn't important.'

'You don't know then.'

'What about?' He looked confused.

'Lena. By the time Teddy wrote back in what would that be...September?'

'Thereabouts.'

'Lena was back in England at the beginning of September and a total mess. I knew she'd written bless her, but there wasn't going to be any reply.' He raised an eyebrow. 'She came home from work one day to find that Neil had emptied their bank account, and a letter from the rental agency confirming the end of the lease. She hadn't even enough money left to get a flight home. It was the final straw and she had a breakdown, it was heart breaking. She's well again now, but she's different, quieter'

For some reason Vince always felt a certain amount of responsibility towards Lena and he felt sad for her. 'God that's awful, sorry Lola I really didn't have a clue. I still imagined her living life to the full out in the sunshine with a man who genuinely loved her.' Delilah shot him a quizzical look.

'I've got eyes; I saw the way he looked at her. Fate dumps some shit on us all doesn't it?' He sipped his beer his mind elsewhere for a moment digesting the information about Lena. 'I've never really given up. You'd laugh, late last year I saw a girl who looked like you pushing a pushchair through Hyde Park. I was jogging and she was a couple of paths over going the other way, by the time it had registered and I'd changed direction she was gone...funny huh?' No not really thought Delilah as that had probably been the day she thought she'd seen him and the reason he couldn't find her was because she had also changed direction in the hope of bumping in to him, but he hadn't come the way she'd thought and that was why. Funny, no, tragic, yes.

She stuffed a handful of crisps in her mouth and choking on their dryness took another swig of beer and coughed. She was trying to think how best to tell him, because for whatever reason he obviously didn't know about Rori, well either that or he'd got to be a bloody good actor. Her mind slipped back to that accidental meeting with Tash and the shock on her old adversary's face when she saw the small boy at Delilah's side. Then the tears and the endless apologising, now what she wondered had Tash done. Vince who'd sat heavily down beside her had lapsed into silence and his face was unfathomable. She took a final mouthful of beer and a deep breath to calm the panic.

'That night, straight after, I didn't know what to feel. I'd had my doubts you see.' He looked surprised. 'Well you didn't take me to the airport.' She put her hand up to stop him as he was about to interrupt. 'I know the auction. Then there were no contact numbers, no reply to the messages I left at the hotel in Antigua and that bloody photo. To be honest I half expected to hear that there were no passes waiting for Lena. So when we were booted out with the lovely comment "The boys have their partners here and they don't need any hassle from a bunch of girls like you". I just thought, well I thought that I'd been right.'

She offered him a guilty glance. 'I'm not saying I wasn't upset, because I was devastated but I also felt relieved, strange eh? But then something came up and I needed to speak to you really urgently, so I contacted the record company and the management company, both told me where to go. The guy at the record company was really pleasant and very apologetic though, the girl at R W management just put the phone down. I'm afraid I became a crazed stalker and the final call I made was perhaps just a tiny bit unhinged. So I wasn't completely surprised when I got a letter from a lardy-da firm of barristers telling me very firmly to go away, just disappointed that you had deserted me so completely without a word...' A bit of an understatement she thought uncharitably.

'But I didn't send any letter and they knew, both knew I was looking so I don't understand.'

'Well I don't understand what planet your PI was on because Bunty gave him all the details and some and he even came to see me and gave me a cheque, perhaps someone nobbled him.' Now that was a likelihood. 'Anyhow at the time I was having a few problems with my blood pressure...' Now that was a hint. 'And my GP had told me to avoid too much stress, so I did as I was told in the letter. "We request that you desist in these scurrilous accusations against our client," and desisted.'

She took a moment to take stock in her mind, at which point Rori and Ben appeared from around the corner with Zoe charging along behind. The two small boys squealing with pleasure were chasing a squirrel, which dived into an imposing looking bush to escape. Delilah saw Vince's eyes dart towards the commotion an amused smile on his face as he watched their antics. She held her breath pretty certain what would happen next and she wasn't disappointed. Rori saw his mother and forgetting the squirrel charged through the tables to her and threw his arms around her knees with a triumphant squeal of 'Mummy' and out of habit she picked him up and plonked him down heavily on her lap. He sat there for a few moments evaluating his mother's new companion through curious cinnamon eyes and quite out of the blue said. 'You've got the same colour eyes as me.' Out of the mouths of babes thought Delilah trying not to laugh at the irony of her precocious son's random comment.

'Yes, so I see, all the best people have eyes this colour.' Vince leaned over to his unknown son and Delilah's hand slipped to her mouth in shock at seeing just how alike they were with their heads almost touching. Rori grinned at his new friend enjoying the attention.

At this point Zoe trotted over and Delilah could see the confusion on her face giving way to complete understanding and her eyebrows shot up as she glanced at her friend for confirmation of what she was seeing. Delilah nodded gloomily, she would cop it in the ear for this one as she still hadn't told Zoe the long story.

'He's a handsome boy, he looks like his mother. How old?' Delilah looked at him daggers drawn, what game was he playing?

'No, actually he looks like his father and he'll be four in June' she was shocked at just how shrill her voice had become and Vince looked completely baffled. 'Come on Vince, you do the maths.' Zoe decided this was a good time to be leaving and lifting Rori off his mother's lap encouraged him away with the promise of ice cream. With Rori gone Delilah flashed Vince a sideways glance in annoyance at how dim he was being. 'Rori came into my life on the sixth of June 1996 and nothing was ever going to be the same again.' She waited. 'The girl in the park, well that was me. I knew it was you because you have a very distinctive running style and so I tried to intercept you without success. Life's a bitch sometimes.'

'Ah that explains the pushchair?' Nope he's definitely not on the same song sheet she thought. She looked at the confusion on his face and knew she couldn't be cruel any more, he really didn't know and he wasn't being very bright either.

'You're being awfully dense Vince, Rori answered your question without realising. Do the maths.' Comprehension started to dawn on his face as his eyes shot suddenly in the direction that Rori had disappeared.

'Did you know that night?' His voice was breaking, his eyes a little wild, a hundred questions flying through his mind.

'No, well yes later. The penny finally dropped when I got home and quite randomly my mother guessed. I'd not felt well since coming home from

France, then it all got a bit manic what with Nana being ill, the moving and the new job so although all the signs were there...' She sighed, still mortified by her own foolishness after all this time. 'I put it all down to stress messing with my system. It was a woman on the bus home that night that started me thinking, just a random stranger who asked me when my baby was due. I couldn't believe that I hadn't considered pregnancy, I mean I knew that the pill stops being effective after illness, so... A scan confirmed that I was three months along and with more than a little panic I started trying to contact you.'

'I know this is a stupid question, but did you...?'

'Did I tell them I was pregnant? Oh yes. One girl accused me of entrapment, called me despicable. After that letter came I knew I was going to have to get on with it. From the moment he was put into my arms, all six kilos of wailing, hungry wonder I loved him with a passion. It was the night after his birth when the enormity of our situation hit me that I cried for the first and I might add the last time.'

'But you shouldn't have been alone...' His voice cracked slightly as he reached out and clasped her hand firmly. Delilah felt the old familiar tingle run through her at his touch and fought the urge to wrench her hand away.

'Well, fate had other plans.' It came out harsher than she intended. 'Sorry. He's a mini version of his dad, so forgetting you has been one hell of a problem. He's a smashing lad though, he's bright and funny and Dad's been trying to get him interested in football, Chelsea, I guess you'll be pleased with that.'

'Good for Bryn.' And the smile was back.

'You wouldn't have said that back then. He was determined that I sue for paternity...'

'Why didn't you?'

'My boss. He'd been a rising star in the legal world before his last case. He worked on the Charlotte Jones case, do you remember it?'

'Vaguely, wasn't that the failed paternity against old Verna. She said that he was the father of her daughter.' Delilah nodded and raised an eyebrow. 'Ah, I see, didn't turn out too good, did it?'

'Nope, so you can understand my reluctance, you knew enough about me to tear me to shreds and I couldn't risk that. Then there was that bloody photo of you and Lucee at Teddy's wedding and I worried that you might have taken him away from me. So I pulled myself together and got on with it. We've done ok.' He still had his hand firmly clasped over hers. 'It was the right thing Vince; I've never doubted that.' She turned her hand over so that their fingers intertwined and smiled as he squeezed it affectionately. 'No more apologies though, I'm really tired of everyone telling me they're sorry...'

'I understand. We all used to wonder about whether there were any mini versions of us out there. Girls who'd shared our beds, who'd found themselves pregnant and either not known who the father was or who perhaps didn't have the finance to pursue things. I wasn't always that careful and I know I wasn't alone in that.'

'Didn't Hilly end up with a little girl?'

'Two actually, Trudy the second one was born disabled and the strain eventually sent him over the edge, but he paid out for them both without question.'

'I don't want anything Vince...' She pulled her hand away, but he caught it again.

'Don't worry about it. Hilly didn't, hell when Trudy became sick he spent so much time with Marianne her mother that he ended up marrying her.'

'Sorry I shouldn't...' Vince sat quietly watching her as she composed herself. This Delilah was a totally different animal than the one he'd said goodbye to in France, she'd grown up, had to he guessed. He took a deep breath, this had to be done whatever the outcome and he intended to fight for what he wanted.

'No apology needed. Anyway you have no say in it, he's my boy and I'll be there for you both. Whether you like it or not Delilah Grace. If I'd known, I would have been there holding your hand when Rori came into the world and I'd have done my turn in the middle of the night...' His face suddenly darkened. 'I'd have been there, he wouldn't, surely...'

'What, who, Vince?'

'Oh God, I think it's all making sense. I'd have been right in the middle of the US tour and I would have wanted to be back in the UK with you. That was a sell-out and the last album was flying high in the US charts. We'd never had that kind of popularity in the States, we were always a fringe group before with a small loyal fan base and for once Roscoe was going to make a mint...'

'Roscoe, but Vince he's your friend.' Delilah was catching on fast. Roscoe had the most to lose and the most to gain from Vince not knowing about her and Rori. She wondered how much Roscoe had to do with Vince getting together with Lucee. Teddy loved up and about to marry Loris who was well on her way to being a worldwide success, what could have been better than the groups popular lead guitar and chief songwriter dating "The face of 96". Publicity breeds publicity and she and Rori wouldn't have fitted into the great scheme of things, would they? 'Do you think he paid your private eye off?'

'He had the means and the motive. It's a bit of a surprise if that's the case though, as the bloke didn't seem the sort to be easily bought. But then they say that everyone has their price.' Delilah watched him as he started to pace, his mind trying to digest the information racing through it. 'I'm going to have to look into this.' He stopped. 'This is an awful lot to take in. I came here today a man without a tie in the world and I'm leaving a father. I'm sorry, that sounds whiney.'

'Don't be silly, no more apologies remember.'

'Ok.' He pulled her up from the seat and encircled her into what he hoped was a friendly nonspecific hug and planted a brief kiss on her forehead. For a moment he looked like he wasn't sure what to do next, but with a smile he held out his hand, 'phone?' Delilah pulled her mobile out and handed it to him watching as he saved all his contact numbers and sent a text to himself so that he had hers. 'Not making that mistake again. Speak to you later, hopefully I'll be able to contact Snelling and will have a few answers. Oh and I love the hair.' He waved as she walked away, watching intently until she became a speck in the distance.

The metallic jingle of her mobile phone in her bag signalled a text, it was from Vince and was short and to the point "What did we do to deserve this?" Delilah who was sitting on the mossy grass beneath a shady tree in the park by the Serpentine having just grabbed a big mac from the nearby MacDonald's had no answer to that, so she just sent back "☹". For the last few years she had imagined this reunion and now it had happened she was struggling to make sense of her emotions. When Vince had turned and smiled her heart had filled with a sudden exhilaration, did she still love him? Of course she did, but there were darker emotions lurking at the edges of her mind, doubt, mistrust, and fear. She shared his grievances, only now she was quite confident that the truth was going to be far worse than either of them imagined.

If Vince was going to be part of Rori's life, then she had to find out how that was going to work. It wasn't just about him though, was it? She had spent his short life having the final say on how her son was brought up and sharing those decisions was going to be a challenge. When he'd been born her parents had made it very clear that they would always support her, but he was her son and although they never came out and said it, she'd made her bed! So what to do? The evening sun was warm and Delilah rested her head back against the rough bark and closed her eyes. Above her the breeze whispered secrets to the leaves on the trees and the water sang joyfully as it lapped against the shore and just like that she made up her mind. It probably wasn't a sensible decision, but just like in Venice she needed to make a choice, take a chance and she needed to do it now, so she sent him another text telling him where she was, there were matters to discuss.

For a few moments they sat together in amiable silence their thoughts hidden from each other. Vince was still trying to come to terms with it all, the woman he'd lost and had been searching for was sitting beside him having just sauntered back into his life and told him he had a child. He cast a quick glance at her as she read the copy of Snelling's report, her expression unfathomable, he knew she wasn't going to like it very much, hell he didn't like it very much either. He'd faxed it to Vince after his phone call, Charles Snelling had been livid and had been threatening all sorts once he found out who the protagonists were. It had taken Vince half an hour to calm the man down. Once thinking clearly, the PI had been only too happy to investigate. What's more he'd offered to do it for expenses only, an offer that Vince had turned down as he wanted it done correctly and so was only too happy to pay the fees at the current rate. Vince had been horrified by the extent of the report once he held it in his hands compared to the two pages of cheap paper that he'd been given.

Every detail had been on there with comments in relation to expenses in the margins. From his thoughts on how best to draw out Delilah's friend Bunty, "women of her breeding will be more likely to trust a man dressed in a Savile Row suit and an Eton tie than someone in off the peg clothes". To how he fabricated the raffle ticket stubs for the local hospice with Delilah's name on and an ID badge, which he noted, "I offered the lady the opportunity to call the hospice, but they never do". Finding Delilah then had been easy, he had even charged Vince for the non-existent £100.00 prize that he had delivered to Delilah and got her to sign for. Delilah chuckled briefly at that particular piece telling Vince that she knew that the money didn't belong to her and not wanting to get anyone in trouble had anonymously re-donated the money to the hospice. The report had contained just about everything, where she worked, what she did and most importantly the fact that she was pregnant and when the baby was due. None of this had reached Vince and he wanted to know why.

'Vince before this goes any further I need to tell you something.' And here it came.

'You're not really Delilah Grace, just an alien imposter.' He grinned to make it easier and she smiled back.

'I feel like one.' She turned to look at him her eyes serious under a deepening frown. 'I think you should have a DNA test.'

'Ah well, mmm.' He screwed his nose up. 'I've got a confession, while we're on the subject.' She looked at him waiting for the bombshell. 'After I phoned Snelling I contacted my brief. I wanted to sort a few things out so that if anything sudden were to happen to me then you and Rori would be ok.' He took a deep breath, how was he going to tell her? 'Anyway he told me I would be a fool to do anything without the DNA …' Was that annoyance written on her face now?

'Well of course. Think about it Vince. From a legal point of view if nothing else, I've just walked back into your life and told you that you've a child, he could be anybody's.'

'But it's obvious...'

'He has your eyes, he looks like you, "so what" a judge would say, "proves nothing". If you want to be part of his life Vince I want there to be no doubt, not even the faintest whisper. Not in your mind and not in anyone else's. Because they will try to sow the seed and part of you will listen and that little seed will grow bigger until it destroys things completely.' He looked perplexed, he'd not harboured any doubts at all and now he could see exactly where she was coming from. 'Rori was done by the hospital when he was born as they were told paternity might be contested. I'll get my doctor to send yours the results.' There was no way he was going to argue with her when she had that look on her face. 'Oh and you're not to tell your mother until you have the results, I certainly don't want any doubt there.'

'I didn't want you to think I didn't trust you.'

'I would have been surprised if you had.' He was shocked at that, but she just shrugged as if she was surprised he hadn't thought about it. 'I've had a lot of time to think...' Hadn't they both.

~

EIGHTEEN

~

Roscoe Martin was flying high. These days his management lists carried some of the biggest names in the business, not bad for a man whose fortunes had been rock bottom in the years following Scarecrow's first split. Putting them back on the map had changed everything as not only had they managed two top ten albums in the short time before imploding, but other artists had jumped at the chance to indulge in their success by signing with him. Loris had been more successful than he could have imagined and her latest album had been sitting in the number one slot for several weeks.

Unfortunately, it had been written and produced by Vince and Louis from Scarecrow and he didn't figure too highly on either of their Christmas card lists after that American tour fiasco. Still, even with their royalties taken out he was making plenty of cash. Teddy had stayed loyal to his management company and so Roscoe had been pleasantly surprised when his burgeoning solo career had taken off in the wake of his divorce from Loris. Any publicity it seemed was good publicity.

Life outside of work was comfortable too. His daughter had just produced a gorgeous little girl to go along with her two sons and his slacker of a son Benjamin had finally got a good job and settled into married life. This had been especially gratifying as Roscoe had more or less given up on him with his playboy lifestyle. When Vincent Angel had dumped his supermodel girlfriend Lucee it had been Ben to whom she had turned and now they were married, perhaps a little hastily, but where's the harm in that? The sound of carnival music blaring out of a loud speaker caught his attention and he wandered over to the window to see what was going on. Down below his window a flatbed truck advertising some charity event was crawling up the road with a group of scantily dressed youngsters dancing on it and Roscoe for a few moments enjoyed the spectacle. Yes, everything was going swimmingly he thought.

This was why the private investigator sitting outside his office was causing him so much apprehension, he had a previous bad experiences with them and so he was naturally wary. Returning to his neat and tidy desk he asked his new PA to send him in. The man who walked through the door had a military bearing, a sombre expression and was dressed in Saville Row suiting with a pair of very expensive Italian shoes on his feet. Not what he was expecting at all as the last one he'd had dealings with had been more than a little shifty. He stood with his hand outstretched in greeting.

'Mr Snelling I believe, Roscoe Martin. Please take a seat.' Charles Snelling had a firm handshake and a pleasant smile, although Roscoe imagined that it was used sparingly.

'Please just Charles, thank you for giving me some of your valuable time.'

'Roscoe and I'm intrigued.'

'I come to you with a matter of some delicacy I'm afraid.'

'Can I offer you some coffee?'

'Please.' He leant down and pulled a manila file from an expensive leather briefcase and laid it on the desk. 'May I tell you the story?' Roscoe gestured for him to continue and the PI told him his well contrived pack of lies. 'A couple of weeks ago I had a call from the most delightful gentleman who wanted to take advantage of my services. He wanted me to find the father of his grandson who deserted his mother before the child was born. Apparently when his daughter found out that she was expecting she had tried to inform the father, but was frustrated at every turn and eventually she received a letter threatening her with an injunction if she didn't stop harassing him. This frightened her enough to back off, afraid for the health of both herself and her unborn child.' The PA came in and put two mugs of coffee on the desk. 'Thank you. Anyway the child arrived and he was at that time keen that she sued her young man for paternity, but still hopelessly in love, she refused. All very tragic'

'I'm sorry I don't mean to interrupt, but why come to me?' Roscoe took a warming sip of his coffee, hopefully trying to distract from a mounting feeling of panic.

'Well The gentleman I'm looking for is Vincent Angel, I believe your management look after him.'

'Vince, used to. But why come to me? Surely that's his business.' Stay calm Roscoe, he thought.

'Because four years ago Mr Angel came to me and asked me to find a young lady called Delilah Grace. He told me that there had been a terrible misunderstanding and due to a series of unfortunate mistakes of his making, he'd lost contact with her. I found her extremely easily, she had moved up to London and at the time I was lucky enough to find some contacts who were only too happy to help. Mr Angel had informed me that his group were heading off on an overseas tour and that I was to hand my findings into your office and you would inform him of my progress.' He passed the file across the desk. 'This is a copy of my original report, which I gave to the woman who told me she was your PA...' He checked his notebook, 'a Natasha Wood, unusual looking girl with a very unfortunate appearance, shame as she could have been pretty. Anyway at the time she seemed incredibly stressed about the whole thing and I noticed that her hands were shaking when she took the report. Although I found this very strange I assumed all was well as I was paid in full a couple of weeks later.'

'Jesus Christ.' He knew it, knew that bloody affair would come back and bite him.

'Hmm, so you can understand my confusion when I realised that this gentleman's daughter was the same Delilah Grace that I had found for Mr Angel. I found him to be a very pleasant man and I couldn't for one minute understand why he would have paid my extremely high fees only to ignore my findings. And he certainly didn't strike me as the sort of man who would leave a woman he clearly loved to go through such an ordeal alone. So I have come to you. I know how to contact Mr Angel, but I felt I should run this past you before I do so, as I feel there has been some sort of impropriety within your office.'

'First of all thank you for coming to see me. I remember Vince looking for this lass and I also remember that the report he was given, said that you had been unable to locate her. Christ what a mess.' He stood up and walked back to the window glancing out but without really looking his shaking hands planted firmly on the sill. 'Charles I was wondering if I could ask a favour. Would you let me do some investigating of my own before you talk to your client?' The thought briefly crossed his mind that he could offer this man a bribe to go away and forget about it, but he doubted he would take it, not dishonest like the other one.

'I can give you a week, no more. I have a reputation to uphold and after that I'm afraid I shall have to not only report to my client, but I feel I will need to explain the whole business to Mr Angel as well.'

'I understand. I'll see what I can find out.'

'Very well. Thank you for your time Mr Martin. I shall await your phone call, one week though, that is all.' He stood and shook his hand leaving Roscoe with a pensive expression on his face, his life no longer as straightforward as it had been just half an hour ago.

Charles Snelling walked out of the smart modern office building with a smug smile on his face. This had to have been one of the most unpleasant pieces of business he'd ever been a part of and he was glad it was reaching its natural conclusion. He still wasn't sure that he was prepared to just let it slide as Vince Angel had asked, he'd just have to see how it finished. When Vince had phoned him to ask about the investigation he'd carried out for him, Charles had been intrigued. As far as he had been concerned he had found the young lady as requested and had been able to furnish Vince with a great deal of extra information as well. So why was he contacting him now to ask for his results? Hearing Vince out he had felt his annoyance rising, he was an honest man running a highly respected practice. He didn't take bribes to change reports, but he could understand why his client would have thought that he would.

Charles had wanted to sue RW Management, because in his eyes his character and integrity had been defamed. Perhaps this hadn't been made public, but how many people had Vincent Angel quietly told that Charles Snelling couldn't find a grain of rice in a bloody risotto and how many times might he have been given favourable references had the correct report been given. Yes, Charles wanted blood.

Having sent a copy of his original report to Vince, the two of them had come up with a plan to flush out the perpetrators and make them pay. He was pleased that despite everything it seemed that two pleasant young people had found each other again and perhaps might make a go of things, he wished them success, he wished they'd had it sooner. If that had happened to one of his children he would have wanted heads stuck on pikes on Tower Bridge. Names and addresses had been given to him and he had told Vince that he would investigate. The truth had been shocking and he wasn't sure he would have believed it had he not exposed it himself. The previous sunshine had been enveloped by a thick black cloud and the first spots of rain were starting to fall as he put up his elegant black umbrella and walked just a little quicker to the tube station.

Firstly, he'd tried to speak to the model Lucee, but he couldn't get past her people. This wasn't exactly a major blow as according to Vince she had done nothing more than evict Miss Grace and her friends from the backstage party. He had explained that he'd had been a little drunk at a party and had told the woman all about his lack of contact with his girlfriend and for whatever reason Lucee became obsessed with seizing him for herself. Lucee's friend Loris was marrying Scarecrow's vocalist Teddy and the two women had thought that it would be a brilliant idea if Lucee got together with Teddy's friend and band mate Vince so that they would still see each other regularly. As it turned out neither woman's relationship had lasted very long and now that both of them were at the top of their professions they were no longer friends either. Charles had been horrified that two very beautiful women would feel the need to be so devious.

He'd then spoken with several people at Scarecrow's previous record company finally ending up chatting to a young man, who although now further up the corporate ladder was then one of those who would have taken Delilah's phone calls. He remembered the whole incident very well as he had been unsure of what to do at first and had phoned RW Management for advice. He had spoken to a woman who said she was Roscoe Martin's PA and she had explained that Delilah Grace was a fantasist who was making Vincent Angel's life a misery.

Thinking back now he remembered that he had thought it strange that she had appeared to need to think about her answer. He then admitted that on investigating further it seemed that Vince was actually looking for this lady and he had been torn between admitting that she'd phoned and staying quiet that he'd stuffed up. He'd looked after number one and stayed quiet. He had been most apologetic and Vince had since told him that the young man had been big enough to actually contact him and personally apologise.

That left one Natasha Wood as was. She was now married with a new baby and when he had turned up on her doorstep had cordially invited him in, happy to unburden herself. She had told a story of jealousy and revenge as old as time. Vince had never noticed her, yet she had been in love with him and would have done anything for him, but there was always another woman in her way.

First there had been a woman called Julie whom she had befriended to get closer to the object of her obsession. Then there had been Delilah, a young woman who turned up on tour and immediately caught Vince's attention. Natasha caught up in her own seething jealousy and spurred on by a friend had tried to scare her off but all to no avail, but she'd had the consolation of knowing their affair would be history when the tour ended. Then standing backstage after the London show she saw her dreaded rival and assumed that she had come back to try and reunite with Vince, not knowing that their relationship had carried on through the summer.

She had watched as he had pulled Delilah off to one side and it had seemed from her vantage point that he wasn't too pleased to see her. She had barely taken this all in before seeing security throw her out and content in the knowledge that she'd been dealt with, had gone home herself. A few weeks later she had received a phone call from someone at the record company saying that for some reason Delilah was trying to contact Vince. Natasha had been given a chance to get revenge on her rival and she took it. There had been endless tears and apologies, but what on earth was wrong with these vile women he had thought.

When he had taken in his report and she had signed for it Charles had found her demeanour worrying, he'd seen enough guilty people over the years to recognise the look and the shaking hands. It seems that she had realised then that she had gone too far and had owned up to her boss Roscoe Martin, offering to resign. He on the other hand had been very kind and had told her he would deal with it. She knew nothing more.

About this time the man who she was now married to had told her how he felt and she had realised that actually she felt the same, so Vincent Angel had been forgotten. Then she had met Delilah out with her son, who was so obviously Vince's and the enormity of what she'd done had hit her. Having brought the young couple back together she had explained and apologised to both injured parties and

Charles felt that the intense guilt this new mother still felt was probably punishment enough. Walking down the steps to the tube station Charles pressed the telescopic button on his umbrella and it snapped itself closed with a satisfying click. That had left Roscoe Martin...

Vince squeezed past a couple of women as they weaved out of the door of the Soho pub. One of them made a crude drunken pass at him as she stumbled giggling after her friend and he waved her off with a polite shake of the head. The last time Roscoe had invited Vince out for a friendly drink had been just a month after he'd split with Lucee and he'd felt the need to explain about her and his son. Bloody quick that had been and Roscoe had wanted Vince to be happy for them, for his sake. This time although Vince was prepared for what was coming, it still bothered him.

    Charles Snelling had laid the groundwork, but neither of them knew the full extent of his former manager's deceit. He glanced across the crowded room and picked out Roscoe on the far side, a half empty pint glass in his hand. Vince gestured "do you want another" with one hand and Roscoe shook his head. Fighting his way through to the bar he bought himself a bottled beer.

'Hi Roscoe, long time no see.' He embraced his old friend with forced affection. 'So what are you after this time, huh?' As if he didn't know.

'Can't I just invite an old pal out for a friendly drink?' Vince took in the slurred voice and the distinct tremor in his manager's hands and guessed that he'd had a few already. He started to hear the alarm bells ringing, this was going to be worse than he thought.

'Well last time I had to play nice with my ex, who I'm sure you remember still hated my guts at the time. So can you blame me for thinking the worst? How are Ben and Lucee, still playing happy families?'

'They're fine, best thing you ever did was to dump her.' He relaxed briefly and they both slumped casually into the comfy leather chairs. 'Are you ok Vinnie, you look tired?'

'Yeah, it's just been really busy. I've been renovating the new place and I've had all the promotional stuff for Frenchie's new album and you know how much I hate all that.'

'Hmm, Vince...' There was that tremor again as he clutched his glass even tighter. 'I'm going to make this quick, I have a massive apology to make and I have a feeling that afterwards you're not going to be speaking to me for quite some time.' Vince stared at him waiting. 'Do you remember the private investigator you hired to find that lass of yours?'

'Charles Snelling, I remember. "If I can't find them they don't want to be found." He couldn't find her and everyone told me I needed to move on. No, you and Lucee told me I needed to move on and I now know that she started the whole damn wheel turning in the first place, scheming cow.' It still made him angry so he took a deep breath and glowered at Roscoe's guilty expression.

'Well, he found her and there's worse...' And here it came. 'It was a stitch up mate, I'm sorry' Vince raised an eyebrow and stared at him with an evil expression.

'What?' Vince feigned shock and not for the first time he realised just how good an actor he could be.

'Delilah, that was her name wasn't it? Well, she was on the phone a week after the charity concert wanting to get in contact with you. I know you told everyone you were hunting for her, but it appears that Tash took it as a great opportunity to get her own back. She told the others a pack of lies and insisted that under no circumstances should any of them let you know that she'd been in contact...' Vince said nothing just stared at his former friend, he'd told Roscoe to pass it on to his staff about

Delilah and he hadn't. 'Anyway I didn't know about any of this until the day after your PI delivered his report. Tash read it and realised that the game was up. He had found where she was living and working...' He stopped trying to sort out in his mind what he was going to say, 'and that she was pregnant.' He looked at Vince, but he just stared back. 'Damn it Vince I had no choice. Tash was in the shit if I handed that over, because the minute you were in touch with the girl she'd tell you how often she'd called and you'd have blown a fuse. Anyway I know you and I knew that you'd not have left her by herself and that was going to leave me with a massive headache. So Tash and I doctored the report, made it as believable as possible and then got onto the company briefs and asked them to scare the girl, told them she was a nuisance, a stalker.' He shrugged his shoulders. 'The girl was collateral damage, a casualty of war.'

Vince clenched his fists involuntarily, felt his chest tightening. 'She was pregnant and you call her collateral damage!' He hissed as he tried to contain his anger. Yes, he already knew the story from Charles Snelling's report on the whole sorry affair, but that didn't stop him wanting to deck Roscoe. 'My child Roscoe...'

'You don't know that Vince. The little tart could have been with anyone and claimed it was yours, think on that.' Roscoe was desperately trying to justify himself. 'Girls like that, they're ten a penny and you know that. If you'd only been sensible you could have had the world with Lucee and any babies that came, well at least you'd know.'

'But you see, Rori is mine, I've had the results of the DNA test, which Delilah insisted on. Because of bloody Lucee, Tash and you I've missed the first four years of my son's life. I didn't see the first smile, his first steps and that magic moment when he called me daddy, does that make him collateral damage? I have very nearly lost the love of my life and my boy for what Roscoe? For you to save face, for bloody Tash, a few quid in your pocket?' He was going to have to leave or else he was going to do something he'd regret. 'Collateral damage, Unbelievable Mate.' Roscoe briefly attempted to rise, but Vince was already halfway out the door and there was little point, they were done.

Delilah poured brandy into a glass and knocked it back in one go, wincing as the rough liquid slid down her throat. She glanced nervously at her watch, Vince would soon be on his way to meet her. She felt totally wretched and there was a gnawing sensation in her stomach as she waited for yet another disappointment, which she was certain was coming. Wrinkling her nose, she poured another glass wishing she knew where Vince hid the good stuff. The unforgiving reflection in the glass showed an exhausted woman who would have liked to have come home from work, slung on an old pair of PJ's and slobbed out in front of the television with a pizza. Instead she'd fallen into a bubble bath, dressed in something pretty and struggled through a bowl of cardboard tasting cornflakes and all for what?

She glanced about taking in her surroundings. She'd been here several times during the last few months, but mostly just to pick up Rori on her way home from work. She'd usually been knackered and so had made a bit of small talk, grabbed her son and left, subsequently being alone in Vince's territory felt strange. Things had been weird between them, although that in itself didn't surprise her considering the circumstances. Before they had been reunited Vince had been living the single life, no responsibilities, no problems and now he was a father to a precocious four-year-old who he hadn't known even existed, or so he said. God, why did she still think that when she knew the facts? The flat was masculine, all leather, chrome and gadgets with a high tech cook's kitchen, which she was seriously envious of. Wandering along the hall she found the room that Vince had set aside for his son, neutrally decorated with the kind of accessories that could be changed with a child's whims. At the moment it was Thomas the tank engine bed covers and curtains with seaside pictures on the wall.

The room next door had been turned into a play room and Delilah felt her hand slip to her mouth in astonishment. A huge train set dominated the floor and she assumed it was not dissimilar to the one Vince had told her he'd loved as a boy. There was a box of sports gear, footballs, tennis racquets and a pair of skates. Against the wall sat a guitar, well of course there would be one of those she thought. Don't spoil him she'd told him, some chance.

The original plan had been to just introduce him as a friend of mummies, but ever since he was big enough to understand she had been drilling the "don't talk to strangers" message into him and so in the end they'd told him the truth. With the innocence of a small child he'd been wild eyed and excited that he finally had a daddy, perhaps if he'd been older it would have been harder for him to accept. The plan to not tell Vivienne until the DNA results were back also went completely pear shaped.

Vince had just started having Rori for longer periods by himself when his mother just turned up uninvited one day. Vince told Delilah that he'd tried to make up a story about Rori being the son of a mate who had needed a last minute babysitter and that he'd offered. Unfortunately, from the first moment Vivienne had set eyes on the miniature version of her own son she'd known the truth beyond any cock and bull story Vince told her. He'd had no option then other than to tell her the whole story, which had earnt him a clip around the ear for his troubles.

To compound matters, he'd given Delilah his mother's phone number as she wanted to meet up and have a talk. Delilah knew she couldn't get out of it, so had braced herself for the onslaught that never came. The Vivienne that she met for lunch had remarried to a man she'd met on a cruise and was nothing like the controlling matriarch who she'd met previously. She had been nothing but apologetic and hoped that Delilah wouldn't hold her past behaviour against her where Rori was concerned. Her charm offensive had worked and Nanna Vien as Rori called her became part of his fast extending family.

Delilah closed the door. With Rori revelling in his new found family, where did that leave the two of them? Ever since they had found each other again they had been pussy footing around each other, not exactly the romantic reunion she had dreamed of, but then she hadn't factored in the possibility that Vince was involved with someone else. Why she didn't know? He had ditched Lucee a couple of years ago and the man was hardly a monk, so why didn't she ask him if he was attached, after all he'd asked her.

According to the glossy's, which Delilah had rustled up from various waiting area's at work, the woman concerned was an up and coming young soap actress with long ash blonde hair that fell perfectly around a pretty face and the inevitable gym honed body. They'd been an item for about three months and the photos suggested well established lovers who were easy in each other's company. Having taken in everything she'd needed to Delilah backed off, she had her answer, they, were nowhere.

She would have felt much more comfortable at home, so why had she agreed to come here tonight? Rori was away at the seaside with his grandparents for a week and she could at least have felt relaxed, but Vince had been insistent and so here she was drinking his crappy brandy and mentally beating herself into a bloody pulp in his man-den. His key in the lock made her jump, so deeply was she lost in her own misery that the brandy slopped over her hands and down the front of her dress. She must have looked extremely guilty as Vince took in the scene before him with eyebrows raised in amusement.

'Brandy, I assume it's still your poison of choice?' she offered gaily.

'Yeah, but I prefer the decent stuff.' He grinned as he reached inside an elegant walnut cabinet just inside the door. 'Funny, just felt a touch of déjà vu then, someone else said that to me years ago. Do you remember Hilly's old girlfriend Nicki? She was on that tour with you. Cornered me that night in Amsterdam, threatened me if I didn't treat you better than we treated Lena.' He chuckled fondly at the memory.

'Nicki was a surprise' She held out her glass for him to top up. 'She came across as though she was above us all, but it was just an act. She's nursing with some charity out in the middle of Africa somewhere at the moment. We keep in touch, not as much as we ought to I guess.'

'Well there's a thing I never knew she was a nurse. To be honest it took me a few minutes back then before I remembered who she was. Hilly should have stayed put, Marianne was a queer fish.'

'Was?'

'Their daughter died a couple of years ago and she didn't want him anymore. I sometimes wondered if she ever loved him at all or whether in her eyes it was just a means to an end and when the lass passed on he was of no further use to her. Perhaps the world's made me a cynic, take no notice.'

His shoulders were drooping as if the sorrows of the world rested on them and his eyes were distant as he leant against the open balcony doors sipping his brandy. They stood there on opposite sides of the room in a silence that hung between them as solid as any wall. She didn't know what to say, it was blatantly obvious that the meeting with Roscoe hadn't gone well and having known a lot of men like Roscoe she was quite certain that she didn't want to know the details.

'What am I doing here Vince?' She needed to know. 'I've been at work all day, I'm tired and really tonight was between you and him. I know what he thought of me and I can guess his motives.' He looked up as if suddenly realising she was still there. 'During the tour it was fine, I kept you happy, but in his eyes I was nothing more than a groupie, as Seb sweetly put it "a bed warmer". He wasn't happy that you took me to France, thought I was going to cause trouble and let's face it in the end I did although not the way he thought. Am I right?' He nodded sadly and she mirrored him with a quiet nod, pleased that she was right. 'So what's this about? The mystery's solved, Rori is yours no matter what, you've got a girlfriend, great, introduce her to Rori, no problem, you don't need me. So why am I here?' She sounded exasperated without meaning to, but she just didn't understand.

'There's no girlfriend, Ginny and I were never going to be a long term partnership, it was fun, a comfortable interlude with no pressure and no expectations. I knew that Hollywood was her ultimate goal and I wasn't part of the plan, so it was always a case of when we split up rather than if. I told her it was over less than an hour after I met you in the park, told her the whole story and that was the end of it.'

'Oh...' Had she blown it she wondered as the panic rose inside.

'I didn't expect you to throw yourself at me and I didn't blame you for not trusting me, so I wasn't surprised that you were distant. Then there was Rori and I was really grateful that you allowed me space to get to know him without complicating matters by wanting to rekindle our relationship.' He offered her a soft smile. 'Then I started to panic because you didn't want to and I wondered whether any chance for us had passed. You never gave us any time to talk, so that's why you're here tonight because we need to talk.' Anxiety filled his eyes and Delilah realised that this is what had happened over those last few days in France. They hadn't told each other how they felt and just like back then they were on the brink of disappearing into the cold light of day and feeling like they were saying goodbye.

She couldn't bear it a moment longer and knew that this was her one and only opportunity to take control of the situation. He'd offered her an opening and she was going to take it and to hell with the consequences. Afterwards she didn't remember crossing the space between them before launching herself at him wrapping her arms around him and kissing him with a desperation she couldn't remember feeling before. She needn't have worried as his arms encircled her in seconds and it didn't really matter who was kissing who or whether anyone was watching from the road below as clothes were discarded and bodies entwined. There were no soft whispers of seduction, no coyness because as far as they were concerned it was a case of need, want, have and for Delilah for as long as she could still breathe she wasn't letting him get away again.

How many hours later it was that they lay exhausted wrapped in each other's arms she couldn't quite tell and nor really did she care, the only thing that mattered was that she was here and he still wanted her. She lay against his chest listening to the steady beat of his heart as his fingertips traced the curve of her neck until he drew her lips to his again.

'Well, I guess that answers that question.' He grinned a naughty twinkle in his eyes. 'You still make me feel the same as that night you fell over that bloody sword.'

'Even now with all the imperfections.'

'Women, always worried by a few lines, like we ever notice. You my dear one are still utterly delicious. In fact, I'd go so far as to say becoming a mother has brought an assurance that you never had before, a glow as if now you know what your body is capable of.' This was the moment she'd dreaded, but he'd opened the dialogue and what she had to tell him might bring it all crashing down around her.

'You know that hoard of children you were hoping for?' He looked puzzled. 'Unfortunately if you stay with me the likelihood of that is a bit remote. I had a few problems after Rori was born and I've been told that I may not be able to...'

'Do you think that matters, nothing matters if I have you and anyway we have Rori. Fate has brought us back together, let's not worry too much about whatever whims it might have in store. Might be dead next week.' He shrugged.

'That's cheery Vince.'

'True though. Let's take it as it comes, it's all we can do. Funny though what goes through the mind changing the subject.' He sighed as she snuggled down into the pillow her eyes fixed on his. 'I wonder... Would we have felt the same if everything had gone to plan?'

'You mean would you have felt trapped?' She smiled knowing exactly what he meant, the question had crossed her mind quite often over the years.

'Mm, I'd like to think it wouldn't have made a difference, I have always thought of myself as a halfway decent bloke. I'll be honest though I really don't know how I'd have reacted.'

'What if, is meaningless. The only thing I know for sure is that you'd have hated me if I'd pushed for paternity.'

'I...'

'Be honest, you'd have thought that I was "that sort" of girl, just after the notoriety, the fame and the money. You'd have thought I'd done it deliberately and I didn't. I wasn't ready to settle down and be a mother, I wanted to live a little and see the world I told you that. Trouble is we don't always get what we want. Do we?'

'Bloody sure I'm going to get it now. You'd have to run away to the ends of the earth to escape me now.'

'You think, huh?'

'Oh yes.'

'You've recovered haven't you?'

'Oh yes.' His eyes were like open books and she sighed in pleasurable expectation any more talking could wait until the morning.

On her thirtieth birthday in October Vince took her back to Venice and on a bougainvillea covered balcony in the moonlight he gave her the ring that could never have belonged to anyone else. She picked up the little Japanese lacquered box that she had so admired in the auction catalogue all those years before, her face filled with delight. To her it was the most enchanting birthday gift in all the world and one she would always cherish.

'You bought it for me?' She asked despite knowing the answer.

'It was meant as a birthday present, I was going to give it to you that last week in France. I had it all planned, we were going to go to the zoo where I'd organised for you to feed the otters and the penguins. Then we were going to go on a hot air balloon ride down the Loire with a champagne picnic and I was going to give you your present then.' He sighed. 'Regrettably it all went a bit wrong and I couldn't work out how to make it right. So instead I cocked it up completely didn't I?'

'A bit.' She smiled running her fingers over the delicate artwork. The Samurai was still kneeling awkwardly in front of the Geisha a twig of cherry blossom in his upstretched hand and her face was still glowing with love. 'It's so beautiful, just perfect' she sighed with pleasure.

'You're supposed to open it.'

'Oh, there's more.' She slipped the catch and stared in awe at the ring where it lay nestled in the boxes velvet lining. 'Oh God Vince, it's beautiful, but too much...' Not that she'd give it back.

'Don't be silly, look on the inside it still has the original engraving.' She looked at him wondering what he was up to and then held the ring towards the candlelight. Her breath caught in her chest as she translated the French, "Marry me Delilah, my moon and stars".

'Are you...were you?'

'That had been my intention, still is. Will you Lola, or have I missed my chance?' His face was earnest and the cinnamon coloured eyes that she loved filled with concern. She held the ring up and handed it to him.

'I'd say you'd better do it properly.' His smile must have lit up the entire canal as he dropped on to one knee at her side ring in hand.

'Delilah Grace, my moon, my stars and the only woman I'll ever love will you marry me?'

'Well as you've got the ring...' She grinned wickedly before bending down to kiss him fiercely. 'Yes and it would have been yes. You're my soulmate and I've never stopped loving you, will never.' He slipped the ring onto the ring finger of her left hand, it was a perfect fit as if it had always belonged there and she hoped that somewhere out in the ether the original Delilah would be pleased that it had found a happy home.

~

FRANCE SUMMER 2005

~

NINETEEN

~

A benevolent early summer sun adorned a perfect blue sky and the natural world rejoiced as the earth below was enveloped in warmth. Birdsong echoed in the crisp air and the garden flowers were filled with butterflies and bees invigorated by the glorious day. The view across the wildflower strewn meadows of the Alpine valley was so spectacular it almost made you want to stretch out your arms and run singing towards the majestic mountains like Maria in the Sound of Music.

Delilah knew that the view was deceptive. The land rose steadily before its twisting accent to the mountain pass in the distance and so running up it singing was not really an option. As she looked out across the meadows a herd of red and white cows their udders heavy with milk came into view with one of the brothers from the nearby monastery following behind them, his habit swinging jauntily as he walked. The ringing of their brass bells echoed across the valley as they came in to the monastery farm for milking and the sight made her smile.

Ten years ago she had reluctantly gone on a trip organised by a friend she'd not seen for years and kissed a stranger, which had changed her life forever. How does that happen? How can one kiss become so entrenched in the memory that it eclipses all others? Today was the anniversary of that day when she'd got lost backstage at a concert, taken a wrong turn and fallen quite literally into the arms of Vincent Angel. Lost in whatever madness had possessed them she had agreed to spend the summer with him hidden away from reality in the middle of France and fallen in love. They had been blind and hadn't seen the adversaries lurking in the background waiting for them to make a mistake, waiting for the opportunity to pounce. Their error had been a simple lack of communication and the resulting catastrophe couldn't have come at a worse time.

Rhodri their son, the consequence of that summer affair had just turned nine, but to his mother it seemed only yesterday that her serious son had been placed in her arms for the first time. Had she really ever been that young and naive she wondered, well bringing a child up alone had soon changed all that. Sometimes it seemed extraordinary to her that after carelessly misplacing each other for five years she and Vince had found each other again, but after the heartbreak time and fate had been kind and despite everything they still loved each other. There had only been one hovering grey cloud on the horizon and despite making no attempt to prevent it, there had unfortunately been no sibling for Rori and Delilah guessed that her doctor had been right in his assessment. They knew that there were always other options if they wanted to go ahead with them and the two of them had talked about the possibilities, but both had concluded that they were happy as they were.

She closed her eyes and thought back over the years. Despite Vince's wonderfully romantic proposal in Venice when he had slipped the moon and stars ring on her finger, they hadn't found the time to get married. He had been caught up between supporting Teddy on his solo excursions and touring with Scarecrow who had reformed again briefly for a couple of years. That had been quite like old times as they had gone back to the original line up with Hilly on the drums, like he'd never been gone. Despite his protestations about doing it, Vince had loved being back in the studio and on stage with the boys, which suggested to Delilah that the problem had always been Seb. They had parted amicably the previous year, but the world probably hadn't seen the last of them. All this had meant that the wedding kept getting postponed, although Vince was always quick to reassure her that it would happen at some time. Delilah hadn't minded though as all that mattered was that the man she had loved for so long was back in her life and had become a great dad to the son he very nearly didn't get to see grow up

It had been dearest Louis who had made it happen. He had lost Cesca to another man and after finally getting a test done had discovered that the girl who called him daddy really wasn't his. So after years of procrastinating he decided to take his vows and make his sanctuary, the peaceful Abbey tucked in the Alpine foothills, his final escape from the world. Before he retreated to his own personal forever he had wanted to see them married and so they had made the effort. So four hours ago after five years of waiting she had walked down the aisle of the Abbey church and with Louis beaming proudly at his side Vince had slipped a simple wedding band on her finger to join the lonely moon and stars ring.

There had been nothing starry about their wedding, just Rhodri, their parents, a few close friends and well, most of the village. There had been no photographer from a glossy magazine and no fanfares and it had so far been a blissfully happy day. Mia had designed and made the stunning dress of buttermilk silk that she still wore with the fake-fur trimmed cape copied from her mother's wedding outfit around her shoulders. Nana Hazel's pearls hung around her neck and her great-grandmother's welsh gold earrings dangled below the chestnut curls that Lena had lovingly piled up on top of her head. After the service they had retreated back to the barn where they were toasted in champagne by their loved ones and tucked into a delicious buffet. Perfection.

Her friends here today were still the same group she had held dear for so many years, although they were spread to the four winds these days. Married for the second time with a second pair of twins, Mia was living in the US close by her brothers. Lena had adopted a hippy lifestyle in a country cottage with an ever growing hoard of dogs, cats and chickens, writing Chick lit and growing her own veg. Still happily single was Nicki who was nursing for a charity in Africa and she said, loving every minute. Delilah though wasn't blind and had seen both Hilly and Teddy flirting with their blushing exes, neither of whom had ever quite got over the two alluring men. What was it about the Scarecrow boys that elicited such devotion, she wondered with a smile? Zoe with her Surgeon husband lived in London and her son Ben was still and probably would always be Rori's best friend. Delilah kept in touch with all of them as often as possible and they had all agreed that at least once a year they would all make the effort to meet up somewhere for a girly weekend, which was working so far.

Notable absences were Vince's old friends from St Clair. Amelie and Henri had disappeared off the grid after moving to Paris and even Vince had lost contact. After the death of her mother Jeanne and Eustache had sold up and emigrated to Australia where Eustache had got a job in the wine industry and Jeanne had gone back to teaching, so contact with them was understandably sporadic. With almost everyone he'd known having left St Clair, they'd never felt any need to return and anyway Vince preferred to remember things as they were. They had been content to stay in London until a visit to Louis the previous spring, when they had fallen in love with this Alpine village and bought a house. It wasn't home yet as Rori hadn't wanted to leave his friends. He was keen to join Ben as a boarder when they went up to Senior school in a couple of years and so they would make the permanent move here then, well that was the plan. In the meantime, they came as often as they were able and were already established as "locals".

She knew Vince was there behind her long before he slid his arms around her shoulders and dropped a gentle kiss against the nape of her neck.

'Thought you'd done a runner, changed your mind?' He whispered huskily into her hair.

'Crossed my mind, but then so do a lot of things.' She replied playfully. 'Although I did make myself pretty especially, so that would have been a terrible waste of time.' Wriggling out of his embrace, she got up and carefully smoothed out the pretty silk dress. Rolling his eyes dramatically, he pulled her to him, holding her close enough that she could feel the steady rise and fall of his chest and the beating of his heart.

'Ha, ha you're funny. No regrets?'

'None.'

'Do you love me?'

'Yes of course I do.'

'Forever?'

'Well I promised, didn't I?' She smiled up at her husband. 'And where else would I want to spend eternity other than here in your arms.'

'Just checking.' He kissed her then and filled with euphoria Delilah knew that this was the moment that would be firmly locked in her memory for the rest of her life no matter how long forever lasted...

~

Author's Note
~

This tale was born on a miserable wet and windy afternoon, when I had no excuse not to finish a job I'd started several months earlier. I was sorting through my large collection of old photographs and found an album I hadn't looked at for probably twenty years.

On a whim in 1981 aged 21 I signed up for an overnight trip to see my favourite group in Brussels. I thought it would be fun to combine seeing the group with a bunch of like-minded people and maybe make some new friends. My fellow travellers were an eclectic bunch of various ages and I found myself sharing a room with another girl who shared the same name. Looking back at the pictures the memories flooded back and I remembered how much fun we had.

Amongst our number we had a music journalist who got the whole bunch in backstage after the show. I'd been going to gigs for years and had never had that opportunity before, so I was looking forward to the experience. I don't know what I was expecting, but it wasn't what I found. My room share had met the band before, so she introduced me (well to the lead singer anyway).

Still I digress. I was looking for the loo, but instead found a cloakroom where one of the band was hiding, he did that apparently. The group's manager was there as well and having relieved me of my camera insisted on photos. All very innocent stuff, but seeing those photographs made me think...What if? And Girlfriend or Groupie was born, now re-christened "I Guess that's Love".

So Denise if you're out there, thanks for all the fun times, (even getting thrown out of the backdoor of the London Coliseum after drinking too much champagne). I wouldn't have had any of those adventures without your friendship and this wouldn't have been written.

~

Acknowledgements

~

I'd like to thank my friend Penny, who stuck with the book all the way through and kept me on the right track. Thanks also to Deb and Christine who read my stumbling beginnings.

Special thanks to my baby Patrick who came up with the original cover for Girlfriend or Groupie, Paddy you never fail to surprise me. Sorry that in the end I found my perfect picture by
Nataliia Moroz. "Girl looking at a star filled sky."

As always my grateful thanks and love to my long suffering husband Bill who puts up with my frustrations when I'm writing and to Tom my oldest for moral and technical support.

~

About the Author

~

Deni Rogers lives in Eastbourne on the south coast of England. When she's not writing she works as a clerical minion on a busy surgical ward in the local NHS hospital. She and husband Bill have 2 grown up sons and share their lives with their completely loopy chocolate Labradors Purdey and Myka.

~

Made in the USA
Charleston, SC
19 October 2016